THE LADY AND THE HUSSITES

THE LADY OF BOHEMIA, BOOK 2

SARA R. TURNQUIST

Copyright © 2017 SARA TURNQUIST

© 2020 Cora Graphics

© Shutterstock.com

ISBN ebook: 978-1-956410-20-4

ISBN paperback: 978-1-956410-30-3

All rights reserved.

This is a work of fiction. Names, places, characters, and events are fictitious in every regard. Any similarities to actual events and persons, living or dead, are purely coincidental. Any trademarks, service marks, product names, or named features are assumed to be the property of their respective owners, and are used only for reference.

No part of this book may be reproduced in any form or by any electronic or mechanical means, including information storage and retrieval systems, without written permission from the author, except for the use of brief quotations in a book review.

If you would like to stay up-to-date on this and all other series from Sara:

https://saraturnquist.com/list

For my sister, who is such an inspiration.

PROLOGUE

The year is 1419, three years after the martyrdom of Jan Hus and the start of the Hussite Wars. The tensions between those loyal to Hus and those loyal to the Catholic Church are intensifying. There has been a breakout of fighting in the Czech lands. King Wenceslaus has died, and many blame the conflict for his untimely end. His widow, Sophia of Bavaria, acts as regent and has raised a band of mercenaries to try and stop the Hussites in Prague.

Pavel Krejik and his new wife, Lady Karin Krejikova, have found one another after much struggle and strife. Having revealed their loyalty to Hus and his teachings, they now travel to Hussite controlled lands, hoping to avoid capture on the way.

They have left behind Karin's father, who is torn between his loyalties, and their friends. Although Pavel's closest friend, Stepan Dvorak, has firmly sided with the Catholic Royalists, his previous attempt to strike down Karin upon discovering her beliefs was stopped just short of a killing blow. This ended his tenuous betrothal to Karin, freeing her to wed her true love, Pavel.

But Stepan's father may not be so ready to release her family from the marriage contract. The Viscount Dvorak's wife has been imprisoned for plotting to end Karin's life, and he is prepared to attack in any way he can by any means available to him.

Their friends, Zdenek Ambroz and Radek Miklas, are uncertain where their own futures lie in this conflict. In a country torn, amidst friendships likewise ripped apart, they are trying to find their way.

And now, the continuation...

THE KINGDOM OF BOHEMIA DURING THE HUSSITE WARS

CHAPTER 1

STIRRINGS

Karin Krejikova awoke as the rocking came to an abrupt halt, shaking her from a gentle slumber. Eyes now open, she tried to remember where she was. The interior of a fine carriage came into focus and realization cut through the fog of sleepiness. She was traveling to the safety of her now in-laws' home well in Hussite-controlled territory with her new husband. Even then her eyes sought him out—Pavel. Next to her on the narrow bench, his attention was drawn out the small window.

A yawn overcame her and she stretched her arms, relishing the feel of her muscles being re-energized. As she resettled herself and smoothed over her dress, it occurred to her how strange it was they should pause. Had they reached their destination?

The sun sat high in the sky. Hadn't Pavel said it would be night-fall when they arrived?

"Why have we stopped?" Karin placed a hand on Pavel's strong arm. Those arms had brought her protection and comfort each in its own time.

He held a hand up in her direction, but his eyes didn't waver. Something beyond the thin walls of the small, enclosed vehicle had his attention. Her chest tightened. What could it be? Shifting, she maneuvered to glance out her own window, straining to hear what may be outside her visual range.

Men and horses moved about just beyond the reach of the carriage. One of the riders approached. The red of the royal military garb flashed in the sunlight.

Her breath caught and she jerked back into the car, pressing her back against the seat. Closing her eyes, she forced herself to breathe. When she opened her eyes, the blue orbs of her beloved husband were in front of her. He reached for her hand. She slipped it easily into his.

"You can do this," he said, his words measured.

She nodded, drawing in a long breath.

He lifted a hand to touch her red locks, but only lightly. "You are stronger than you know, Karin."

Allowing herself to get lost in his eyes for a moment, she knew he spoke the truth. Karin had been through much in these last months. *They* had been through much. Was there anything they couldn't face together?

She returned his assuring smile.

Moments later, the door to the carriage jerked open. The menacing face of one of the king's men glared in. He eyed them from top to bottom before speaking.

"My lord," the soldier said, all but spitting out the word.

Had the coachman shared that this carriage bore someone of noble title? What else had he shared?

"Would you mind stepping outside?"

"Is this necessary?" Pavel challenged him. His voice remained flat as if he were bored by the irritation of being detained. "My wife is recovering from a foot injury."

The guard shifted his gaze to Karin. She glanced at her fingers, trying to appear nonchalant.

"I apologize, my lord, but I must insist upon it. By order of the king." The man's mouth curled into a slight snarl. Scrapes from above the carriage startled Karin. She gripped Pavel's arm. Were their belongings being unloaded?

"Very well." Pavel moved toward the opening.

The guard took a step back.

Karin froze. How could she follow Pavel? Would these guards find out the truth? That she and Pavel were Hussites? That she bore the names of other prominent Hussites on a paper rolled and braided into her hair?

"But," Pavel continued.

The guard spun, his attention on Pavel.

"I can assure you the king will hear of this."

"Noted," the man said, his brow furrowed and his eyes narrowed.

Once Pavel exited the carriage, he reached in for Karin.

Leaning on his strength, she managed to step out and onto the soggy earth.

Their trunks lay opened and sifted through. The coachman, having been relieved of his seat, stood near the front of the carriage. Another guard questioned him. His gaze landed on Karin. She searched his face. Could they trust him? Or would he give them away to save his own skin?

Prodded forward, Karin lost eye contact with the coachman. She tightened her grip on Pavel's arm. He drew her closer, as if preparing to protect her somehow. But was there anything he could do against these armed men? What could he do should the guards identify them as enemies of the crown?

"I am eager to hear the reason you have relieved my wife of her comfort." Pavel's eyes flashed as he turned to the man who had ushered them out of their seats.

"As you see." The man waved his hand. "This is an inspection. You may be aware that Hussites have infiltrated our peaceful lands. We are only trying to isolate and eliminate their presence and influence. I'm certain you understand. Since you are nothing but loyal to the king."

Pavel did not speak. His eyes hardened and his jaw clenched.

"And so, it is my job to search you . . . and your wife."

What did he mean by that? What was he intending to do?

Pavel pulled her closer.

"You may search me, if you must. But my wife will not be part of your games." Pavel's voice was firm.

"I will determine what will be." A sneer crossed the man's features.

The guard rifling through one of her trunks nearby looked over and stood, walking toward them. Pointing at her, the lead guard spoke to the second. "Let's search her first."

Pavel pulled Karin behind himself, but it was no use. Yet another guard joined the first two and helped extricate Karin from Pavel. Then rough hands pulled her to the first guard, uncaring as she tripped over her injured foot with pained cries.

Then she stood in front of the sneering guard, vulnerable and afraid. Not only for herself but also for Pavel. For them both. For what this guard might find. Her back to Pavel, she could not take comfort or strength from him.

The man made small circles around her, his gaze intense. She closed her eyes against the harshness of his stare, praying it would be over soon. With each round, he moved closer and closer until his breath grazed her neck.

Without warning, his hands were on her shoulders and moving down her arms. She wished Pavel wasn't looking. The hands continued down her back. Jeers sounded from the other men.

Lord, help me!

"What are you doing?" An approaching voice shattered what concentration she had left.

Her eyes shot open to see yet another man in royal garb—the guard who had been questioning the coachman.

"My job," the searching guard replied. His words were edged with a roughness she had come to associate with the man.

The questioning guard's disapproving look gave Karin hope. Was the approaching guard in command?

"Get these trunks loaded and help the lord and lady into the carriage before I decide this merits a letter to the general."

Relief washed over her. The guard in front of her did not seem as pleased. His face twitched, but he did not move. He remained mere inches from Karin.

"Now," the head guard said with more force.

The guard with the sneer took a step back from Karin. Her knees weakened. She gritted her teeth and forced herself to remain upright.

Pavel rushed to her side, steadying her with an arm around her waist. He hurried her back to the carriage. Settling her inside, however, he did not join her. Standing just outside the doorway, he watched through narrowed eyes as the men reloaded the trunks.

The coachman returned to his seat before long and the guards mounted their horses.

"We apologize, my lord, for any inconvenience," the head guard said. "Safe journey."

With that, the men moved away and trotted off into the distance.

Pavel nodded at the coachman before sliding into the seat next to Karin. He gathered her into his arms, holding her securely.

Was it she who was shaking or the carriage?

"I'm sorry," Pavel said over and over. "Karin, I'm sorry. I'm so sorry. I should have been able to protect you."

There were whispers. Everywhere. What was all this gossip? Could people not find anything better to talk about? As much as Radek burned with frustration, he knew these whispers were not about him. Not after something so life-altering had happened. With the breakout of violence within the borders of their country, people were bound to talk. In all truthfulness, it was all Radek could think about, too.

Though Radek usually kept his thoughts to himself, he struggled with his musings and found he had to voice them. But should he disclose his opinions on this, of all things?

He and Zdenek made every effort to not become a part of the hostilities in their homeland. Yet it became more and more apparent this would not remain possible for long. War was overtaking their country and the events of this last week proved monumental. For everyone.

Radek took a long swig of his beer and set the tankard down with a solid thud. "I should think people would have more respect for the king's memory and stop all this fighting." His eyes met Zdenek's.

In the midst of draining his own pint, Zdenek pulled his cup back from his mouth and swallowed hard.

Even in the dimness of the pub's atmosphere, Radek saw his friend's wide eyes and raised brows. They didn't talk of such things. Maybe because of what had happened between their friends, Stepan and Pavel. Or maybe because they were avoiding the reality of what they would eventually have to do—pick a side.

Zdenek ran his hand along the rough wood of the tabletop. "I think the people are inflamed by their cause. And while the king's death should bring a country to mourn, they are caught up in their movement."

Radek nodded. "I thought this Hussite nonsense would have run its course."

Zdenek blinked several times and shifted in his seat. "I don't know."

"Do you not think these radicals and their violence are not what brought our king to an early grave? His heart broken over the fighting within our borders?" Radek continued, surprised by his own impassioned speech.

Zdenek continued to fidget. "I don't know." He lowered his voice. "But I do know that Prague is not a safe place to say such things."

As if he could spot Hussites by sight, Radek glanced around.

No one listened to them. The men in the pub were caught up in their own merriment. All was as it should be. At least within the walls of this establishment. But they couldn't stay here forever.

Prague remained in the hands of the Hussites. A number of Hussites had left the city and held rallies all over Bohemia, stirring the people. There was even word of Catholics still faithful to the Pope being driven out of their hometowns. Disgraceful!

Zdenek watched Radek with curiosity. An eyebrow drawn upward and his mouth quirked, he made quite the picture.

"Let us talk of more pleasant things," Radek said, raising his pint in the air before taking another long sip.

Zdenek's shoulders relaxed.

"Whatever happened with your brunette from Hradek Kralove?" Radek lowered his glass but for a moment. Another swig followed shortly.

Zdenek's face colored. He opened his mouth, but nothing came forth.

Radek smiled. His friend had been caught.

The door to the pub burst open, slamming into the wall. A rather large man stood in the doorway, a spear in his hand. He was heaving.

Glaring about the pub as if he, too, could name Hussite from loyalist on sight, he bellowed, "Arm yourselves, men. The Royalists are marching on Prague."

Radek rose and exchanged looks with Zdenek. Their time to pick a side had just come.

Lenka Bornekova sat in silence as her husband worked. Hunched over the small desk, he wrote the necessary letters to inform the leaders of the Hussite movement in Prague he would come soon. What a change these last couple of months had brought! Not only was he communicating with these Hussites, he intended to aide them. Karin *had* changed him. It almost brought a smile to her face. Almost.

But Lenka could not smile after the happenings of these last weeks. The king's death, the fighting in Prague . . . It brought on more reason to worry after her *katka*. Where was she? Was she safe? They had not heard anything since sending them off the day after their wedding. That had been two weeks ago.

Instead of dying down, the hostilities escalated. Was it just last week that Wenceslaus's widow sent a force of mercenaries into Prague in an attempt to regain control? They had thought the fighting had been bad before, but the country discovered a new depth to the violence. From all reports, there were many portions of the city that were completely destroyed, some with severe damage.

Had it been so long since Lenka had walked the streets of Prague or visited the grand castles there? Still her heart ached at the thought of the beautiful city in ruins. And all for naught.

Petr found himself in a unique position. Foremost, he was a member of the nobility, a voice that carried weight. And, because of Karin, it was now known in some Hussite circles that he was sympathetic to their cause. Not only that, he remained supportive of the regency. He was in a much sought-after position—to negotiate with Wenceslaus's brother, Sigismund, who now inherited a claim on the Czech crown.

And so Petr would do what he could to pick up the pieces and bring peace to their fractured country. That's what Lenka wanted— to see hostilities end. Imagine, this might mean they could travel to see Karin and Pavel soon. If they could bring this conflict to a swift end.

"What are you thinking?" Petr's voice interrupted her musings.

Lenka met his eyes, already on her. They were bright, as was his smile. "How it will be when this fighting is over." She continued working her fingers on her sewing, turning her attention back to it.

"You're thinking about Karin," he said, the lilt of his voice betraying his laughter.

And why shouldn't they be light-hearted? The willingness of the two sides to negotiate was a good sign.

"Perhaps." She wiggled her head, not fighting the smile that graced her features.

He stood and moved to where she sat. Pressing a kiss atop her head, he allowed his hand to linger on the side of her face.

"It may take time, dear wife, to find compromise," he warned. "But if the others feel what I do, there will be great determination to see it through. I can't imagine anyone on either side wants to see this war continue."

She nodded, gazing up at him. "Be safe."

"As God wills." His hand moved to touch her hair.

Her eyes pleaded as they peered into his. "Write me?"

His mouth turned up at that as he leaned down to press a kiss to her lips. "Of course."

Pavel shifted in his sleep. How long had he lain here, restless? How many nights had found him in the same situation? Opening his eyes, he gazed across the pillow to where Karin slept. It didn't matter how often he awoke next to her, he would never cease to be grateful.

The hardships of the last year came rushing back. He almost lost her. Twice. Once to his best friend in marriage and a second time to his best friend's sword. If he'd been only a few seconds later . . . He dare not think what might have been. And he didn't have to. God had sustained her. And helped him. Now they were together. Safely within Hussite territory at his parent's home near Tabor.

Shifting his gaze back toward his wife, he was thankful she lay in peaceful slumber, her features relaxed and her red-blond hair splayed across the pillow. He resisted the urge to lift those tresses to his face and feel the silken locks between his fingers. As much as he would like to, he didn't want to risk disrupting her rest.

Overcome with an urge to protect her, he ached to hold her. His throat became dry and pained. So much had happened to her. They had overcome many obstacles. And with the state of affairs in

Bohemia, there would be much yet to endure. He must shield her from whatever might come their way better than he had during their brief detainment on their travels.

Running a hand across his face, he rolled onto his back, guilt welling within him. The pressure of it settling on his chest. She relied on him. Yet in that moment when she needed him to stand for her, he had not been able to.

What was he going to do? How could he protect her in the face of raging war if he could not even protect her from a patrol guard?

A hand on his shoulder drew him from his thoughts with a start. He jerked his head toward the intrusion, arms raised in defense. But it was only Karin reaching for him.

"Are you well?" came her soft, sleep-drugged voice. Her eyes were wider than he would have expected having been roused from a dead slumber. The pupils were large, seeking to draw in any and all light in the room. It seemed as if he could dive into those green-rimmed orbs.

"Yes," he assured her, taking her hand and drawing her into his arms. "I am quite well. Just having a hard time sleeping." His hand traced the line of her spine, caressing her back through her nightdress.

"Something bothers you?" She nudged her head until her face settled in the space where his shoulder met his neck.

He closed his eyes and took a deep breath. How could he tell her without causing worry? So he remained silent.

"Please tell me." Her hand resting on his chest grabbed at his nightshirt.

Letting out the breath he held, he let go his reservations. He did not want to start their marriage keeping things from her. Yes, it would be best to be honest about his concerns. And trust her to handle them.

"It's just that I worry," he said, placing his free hand on hers. He played with her fingers. "What will happen to our people?"

"You mean the Czech people? Or the Hussites?" Her breath was warm against the skin of his neck. It intoxicated him.

He paused his ministrations on her hand. "I suppose I mean both." Then he resumed his movements, rubbing each finger in turn. "What will become of the Czech nation? Will the Hussite movement survive to see another month? And what of us? Do I join the fighting? What about you? I need to protect you. But then . . . " His voice trailed off. He hadn't meant to say so much.

"Then what?" She prompted. "Tell me what's on your heart."

He sighed and closed his eyes. "I didn't do so when we were stopped by that patrol."

She leaned up on one elbow so she could look at him. "Pavel Krejik! I will not hear you say such things. You did everything you could and you know that. Some things are out of your power."

Looking into her eyes, he searched for some relief from the weight of guilt he felt. There was love there for him, not judgment. And it was a balm to his soul.

"I only ever want to keep you from harm." He intertwined their fingers. "You are precious to me."

She leaned over to press her lips to his. And no more words were necessary.

The darkness was thick. But the lone rider pushed his horse on through the uneven terrain of the Krokonose Mountains. His path was illuminated only by the moon and stars, which created a blanket of glittering dots above him. Nothing, it seemed, lay between him and those twinkling orbs. Surely, he could reach up and touch them if he cared to. But he dare not stop, not even for such lofty goal. No, his mission was much too important. It drove him to press his steed further into the night without rest.

The plans of Wenceslas's widow had fallen short, but not all had been lost. No, there had been enough distraction for this individual to gather information, and he would carry this information to the crown. These heretics, these Hussites had to be stopped. They could not be allowed to garner support across any of the borders. This man, who'd trekked the mountains alone, discovered that this was exactly what had happened.

Why had he volunteered for such an assignment? Someone of his station was far above such tasks. Yet he had yearned for the solitude. The ache in his heart called for his withdrawal from genteel society. And now, he saw that it had served them all well. For he had found what he had suspected to be true. These traitors to the crown were currying favor with Poland and this would be dangerous indeed.

He dug his heels into the flank of his horse, urging even more speed out of the animal. He would stop and rest the horse in due time. As for now, he would press on. His destination was just beyond the horizon.

As soon as he delivered the pertinent information, his mission would be complete and burden relieved. Stepan Dvorak and his horse continued, disappearing into the night.

CHAPTER 2

NEGOTIATIONS

"No!" Jan Zizka declared, slamming his hand on the table. His voice rang out, piercing every corner of the room. His form loomed in front of a long wooden table facing several seated nobles.

Petr worked to retain a neutral expression. Talks with the Hussites had not been going well. The man in front of them now, Jan Zizka, was a commander and prominent leader of the Hussite movement. He was not satisfied with the compromise they proposed. A chill ran through Petr. Was it the cavernous nature of the room, empty but for the table, chairs, and occupants, or was he truly that concerned about the massive man in front of them?

"You have to be willing to yield something," the duke to Petr's right tried to reason with Zizka. As the highest ranking of the nobles there, the duke's voice represented them all. "The castle of Vysehrad has always belonged to the royal family. The people of Prague had no right to occupy it during hostilities. What do you want with a castle?"

Zizka muttered something indiscernible while glaring at the duke.

"Pardon?" The nobleman rose to his feet.

Was the tension of the meeting driving a duke to display his emotions? It was more important than ever they keep those in check.

"As if you would understand," Zizka repeated in a loud voice. "You leave the fighting to your military men. Always have. You wouldn't understand the strategic advantage of a fortified castle. I must think this, or else consider you may be daft."

The duke's fists clenched at his side and the muscles in his jaw twitched.

"Our goal," Petr spoke, "is to see an end to the fighting. For the sake of our people. *All* of our people."

Zizka's eye landed on Petr. It made Petr squirm a little in his seat. The man's gaze, half disguised by a patch, was as strong as his military presence. There was a boldness to his stature Petr could only dream to exude. Petr doubted the man ever entered a physical confrontation that he didn't come out the victor.

"Like it or not," the duke challenged Zizka, "we have the endorsement of the Hussites to negotiate on their behalf. And this is our decision. This is not a discussion, but a chance to inform you of what we intend to do."

Petr didn't think it possible, but Zizka's eye hardened even more. His own hands clenched into fists. Was he preparing to charge the group of them like an enraged bull? He relaxed ever so slightly, perhaps thinking better of it.

"You will regret this. Sigismund," he spat the word out, "will not keep his word. He is not the rightful heir, and we will not stand for a kingdom in which he is on the throne."

Before any of them could respond, Zizka spun and exited the room.

No one moved until the clomping of his boots on the floors had dissipated into the distance. Even then, all they could do was exchange harried looks.

Karin gazed out the window of the study. A dusting of snow covered the earth. How she missed the beautiful gardens of the chateau! Despite how she had hated being sent to Hradek Kralove at the time, she reflected quite fondly on times spent there. With Pavel. After all, had it not been for her time there, they may never have crossed paths. She breathed a prayer of thanks for the Lord's provision. Yes, He knew the plans He had for her, even when her world had seemed as if it was falling apart.

Movement in the doorway off to her right caught her attention. Karin turned toward the intrusion.

"My apologies," Pavel's mother, the Baroness Marketa, said as she paused at the threshold to the room. "I didn't realize anyone was in here."

"You aren't disturbing me." Turning her whole body to face her mother-in-law, Karin put a smile on her face. Her interactions with the baroness had been few, and regardless of her efforts, they had been filled with politeness. Nothing amiss about that. But would they ever move past these pleasantries to something deeper?

Marketa stepped into the room, returning Karin's smile. "I came in search of a favorite book."

Karin nodded. They were in the library after all. Moving her already tightly crossed arms up and down, Karin looked toward the floor. What was there to say?

"My dear, are you cold?" Marketa asked, brows furrowed. "I will have the fire started . . ." The older woman stepped toward the door once more. Would she summon a servant?

"No, I assure you I am well." Karin put a hand out to stop her.

Marketa paused and eyed Karin. Did the baroness not believe her?

"That is, I am a little cold, but only because I am standing by the window."

"I see." Marketa shifted, appearing rather uncomfortable in the space. She didn't go after her book, nor did she engage Karin.

After some moments of awkward silence, Marketa stepped

forward and nodded in the direction of the wall behind Karin. "In the summer, I have a magnificent garden just below that window."

"Oh?" Karin shifted her gaze out the window again but kept her body facing Marketa.

The baroness took a few more steps forward, close enough to point downward and to the left. "Just there."

"Ah, yes," Karin said, as she glimpsed the outline of what must be the garden's spot on the property. "I am eager to see it."

Marketa nodded. "I enjoy nothing more than working the garden."

"You work it yourself?" Karin's eyes were on Marketa then. She couldn't have been more shocked if the baroness said she grew stones out of her soil. Karin tried to picture the woman in front of her, all prim and proper, with her hands deep in the dirt, skirts soiled from kneeling in the earth. It wasn't possible.

"Yes. I find it quite soothing." Marketa, eyes fixed on the land below, seemed oblivious to Karin's reaction.

Karin refocused on the spot where the garden lay covered in snow. It was unimaginable now that life would spring forth from the earth in a few months. But perhaps she could bond with her mother-in-law in that garden. She so wanted to have something in common with this woman.

Marketa opened her mouth, but a sound in the hallway drew their attention.

A figure passed by and then paused, backtracking a few steps. Did someone wish to speak with her? With Marketa? As the passerby came closer to the opening, Karin made out the face of her husband.

"The two women I adore most in all of Bohemia," Pavel said, smiling, as he walked into the room.

Karin's mouth turned up and she glanced at Marketa. This was something they had in common.

"I am not intruding I hope." His gaze flickered from one woman to the other.

"No," Karin assured him. "Your mother was showing me where her garden will be."

"I am sure you will love it." Pavel beamed. He knew her well. Crossing in front of his mother, Pavel approached Karin and pressed a kiss to the side of her face.

"I fear Karin has long since desired my absence." Marketa stepped to the shelves by the door.

"I would not say . . ." Karin's brows furrowed.

"It is all right, dear." The baroness reached for a book on a shelf above her head. "I have what I came for." She glanced from Pavel to Karin. "I enjoyed our conversation."

Karin nodded.

And then, with the graceful air with which the woman moved about any space, she quit the room.

Karin sighed, letting all the air out of her lungs. Had she been holding her breath?

"Are you well?" Pavel's eyes sparkled as they narrowed but slightly. Was he so concerned?

"Oh, yes," Karin placed her hands on his arms, turning toward him. "I only wish your mother and I could leave these simple pleasantries behind. How do I develop a more meaningful relationship with her?"

A smile tugged at Pavel's perfect mouth as he pulled her closer. "It will happen. These things cannot be forced. My mother is kind, but she keeps to herself. Give it time."

Karin nodded, letting her hands slide up his arms to join behind his neck. She lifted onto her toes, preparing to draw his face to her own, but something gave her pause.

His eyes were inviting, yet something was amiss. Something in him held back, distracted.

"What is it?" She attempted to keep her voice light but feared it betrayed her as it shook.

"There is something I need to speak with you about." His smile fell. Something deeper overtook his features. There was a seriousness in his eyes.

Swallowing against her trepidation, she released her hold and let her hands rest on his upper arms.

"Would you prefer to sit?" he asked.

She blinked. Did he need to speak at length? If so, she would prefer to be farther away from the cold of the outside seeping in through the window. "Please."

Taking her hand, he led her into the hall and down to their bedchambers. The barely contained storm within her raged. Did they need this level of privacy? For what purpose?

The room was warm with gold and red tones. Mahogany furniture covered with fine red linens created a seating area near the fireplace. Pavel drew her to one of the large chairs. And, moving his chair nearer, he sat closer than he needed to. Not that she minded. His presence soothed her even as the hair on the back of her neck pinched at her skin.

Resisting the urge to smooth her hands over her dress, she kept her eyes focused on her husband. He was her rock. And whatever he had to share, they would face it together. Was it the warring of their people that made her so nervous? If not for this fighting, would her heart be tripping over itself?

As she met his eyes, she found him looking deeply into hers. She almost twisted away. But Pavel took her hands. Though his eyes were almost too intense, she felt warmed from within by his touch. His gaze softened and she relaxed. How could she not adore him when he looked at her like this—as if she was the only thing in his world that mattered?

"What is it?" Her voice was but a whisper.

"You are just so . . . " his voice caught. He drew in a ragged breath. "You take my breath away, still."

Karin's face warmed. She wanted to turn away in modest denial of his compliment but found she could not pull back. As they always did, his eyes drew her further in, called her to a deeper connection with him. Was there anything deeper than what they already shared? Leaning in, she pressed her lips to his.

Would she ever tire of this feeling? Of the tingling heat that rushed through her? She hungered for more, but he drew back, breaking their contact.

"Karin, I fear I must say this now or I will be lost to you."

Her eyes opened just enough to look at him.

There was sadness in his gaze again. She drew farther away, giving him space to gather his thoughts.

"Tell me," came her soft words, after a few moments had passed in silence.

"Commander Zizka has gone to Plzen." His eyes cleared from the darkened haze caused by their kiss. They were once more the same striking blue she knew and loved. "I have received word that he intends to march to Southern Bohemia and face down an army gathered by the Catholics."

Karin's eyes widened. If this came to fruition, this would be the first time the Hussites would take the offensive. As it was, they had only acted in defense of life and freedom.

"And my presence has been requested."

His words slammed into her. Struck by this thing out of her control, she was stunned into silence. He could not go—it would be too dangerous. But how could she open her mouth and insist he do as she bid? That was not who she was and that was not the man she married.

"Karin?" He rubbed her arms.

She waved a hand in front of herself as if that would wave off his concern. "What do you think you should do?" It took all she had in her to force out those words and remain calm.

"I think I should go. We believe in the cause. And we want to see the Hussite movement prosper, do we not?"

Karin chose her words carefully. "Yes." She allowed the silence to return. But in her spirit, she knew she must speak more. "I understand that I know nothing of military tactic, but is it wise to be on the attack?"

Pavel's lips made a thin line. Had she upset him? Still, she did nothing to take the words back.

At length, he spoke. "Commander Zizka has become a prominent leader among the Hussite forces." He slid a hand down to hers and rubbed it with his thumb. "At some point, we have to accept that we are at war. We must look to our leaders to make the best decisions. This is a point of trust."

Nodding, Karin attempted to swallow past the lump in her throat, but her mouth was dry all of a sudden. She wanted, once again, to look away, but could not. Wanting for a deep breath that eluded her, she found words for him. "Then you must do what God is calling you to do."

Drawing her into his embrace, Pavel held her firmly. "I prayed you would understand, my love. You have no idea how I struggled. I did not wish to bring you hardship. I had all but decided to stay."

Karin frowned against his shoulder, closing her eyes against tears threatening to fall. How she wished he would stay! But that was not who he was. In the midst of her uncertainty, she clung to him and prayed God would watch over him.

What was that sound? Zdenek maneuvered his long fingers to clasp the hilt of his sword. He had been admittedly more jumpy since the attack on Prague. It was the first time he had been dragged into a real fight with swords drawing blood and bringing death. Had it affected Radek? It changed Zdenek. There would never be a moment's peace as long as these ghosts haunted him. The faces of the men in battle were before his eyes when he closed them at night. Would he ever shake them?

Jerking toward the disturbance, he was relieved it was only Radek shifting in his sleep. Lying back down, he rested his sword where it stayed—regardless of whether he was asleep or awake—next to him.

Neither he nor Radek had planned to join the Hussites. They had not even wanted to take a side. So much for that.

They had been thrust into this movement when they joined the Hussites to defend Prague from Wenceslas's widowed queen's mercenaries. Why would the queen send mercenaries to attack her own people? It was unimaginable.

Angered by the atrocities he had seen, Zdenek had become an all too willing volunteer to defend his countrymen from those that would oppress them. Radek had come along with him, but there had been reluctance in him. And so they found themselves with Commander Zizka's group in Plzen.

Closing his eyes again, images from the earlier battle flashed before him. Opening his eyes, he hoped to erase them. They were replaced by the dim traces of the camp surrounding him. Turning and wrapping his body around the sheathed sword, he tried to gain some comfort from the protection it offered. But what refuge was there for his mind? Was there anywhere safe to turn his thoughts?

An image of the girl from the ball at the viscount's chateau appeared—Eva. Her deep brown eyes called to him. His whole being sighed and relaxed into the joy those eyes offered. He pictured Eva as she had been when he called on her after the ball. Why? It had been a difficult visit.

Zdenek found her only to discover she was the daughter of one of the merchants in Hradek Kralove. Not a poor merchant, but not well off enough to be an enticing offer to his family. Though saddened, Zdenek would not be discouraged. This girl had captured his attentions.

Perhaps there would be something he could say, some way to convince his father. Wartime affected people. It made things that were impossible possible. Maybe there was a way for he and Eva.

He allowed his thoughts to dwell on her face and the smile that had graced her lips when he came to her home. The glittering of those dark eyes still made him sigh. Only then did he find peaceful rest.

Stepan steered his horse into the chateau's stables. But there was no one to greet him upon arrival. The stables were empty save the other horses. There was not even a stable boy in sight to take his reins. Where were all the stable hands? What could be so important they were not prepared to wait on incoming travelers? Even one of the masters of the house?

At last a lone man appeared from the direction of the house. Spotting Stepan, he rushed forward, grabbing for the reins as Stepan shifted his weight.

"Sorry, my lord," the man said. The young man opened his mouth again. Was he preparing to continue with his excuse?

Stepan dismounted and grunted, glaring at the man through slitted eyes.

The stableman closed his mouth, dropped his head, and led the horse in the direction of the stalls.

Looking after him, Stepan shook his head. At least the man did not add insubordination to his transgressions. Stepan took off his gloves and headed toward the chateau.

The distance to the large home was not lengthy, but it was sufficient for Stepan's anger to grow. Was no one to receive his return? Would he simply walk into the house as if he were a common servant?

Moving farther into the chateau, confusion clouding his anger, he sought any sign of life. And soon found it.

Trunks surrounded him. Maidservants and manservants moved about this way and that, carrying and crating things.

Stepan spotted a young man barreling toward him with an armful of books. Shoving his arms forth, Stepan stopped the servant from knocking him over. It did, however, cause the man to lose his balance.

Books littered the floor and in the center sat the young servant, eyes wide, staring up at Stepan. "Sorry, my lord!"

Stepan raised a hand and the young man flinched. Did he fear Stepan would strike him? "I would have you tell me what all this is." He waved an arm over the scene.

"I know naught but that we have been told to gather anything of value and prepare it for removal."

Stepan released the man, who then gathered the strewn books and scurried off down the hall.

Why would his father have the servants do this? And without a word to Stepan? Brows furrowed, he stormed off toward his father's study.

When at last he neared the massive chamber, he was rewarded with the sound of his father's booming voice from within. Even with the door closed, his father's robust vocalizations carried down the hall.

"I want to be ready to depart in two days' time. I don't care how long it takes. Keep them working through the night if need be."

Stepan did not bother knocking. Work through the night? What could be the reason for all this haste? He reached for the latch and swung the door open.

The viscount and a manservant eyed Stepan as he entered.

Vlastik's stone-faced stare soon broke into a smile. "My boy, you are here at last. And not a moment too soon." He shuffled papers on his desk, waving the manservant off.

The servant nodded to Stepan as he passed out of the study.

Stepan watched as the man pulled the door closed. Not that it was necessary—anyone who wanted to know what they were talking about need only stand within ten feet.

"What has happened, Father?" Stepan's words rushed out once they were alone.

Vlastik did not bother to look up. "We are quitting the chateau. It is time for us to remove ourselves from Bohemia."

"Leave Bohemia? We cannot abandon our people. Not now. And what about Mother?" Would they not stay and fight?

The viscount peered up from his papers, and Stepan realized his folly all too late.

Vlastik's stony eyes met his son's. "There is nothing we can do for her. She has chosen her path. Now she must walk it."

Abandon Mother? Stepan had never heard his father speak this way. Certainly not about Mother. Not even since the happenings of the last few months. While it was true his mother was a murderess, and that she was imprisoned for her crimes, his father had never spoken such.

Vlastik came around the desk and put a meaty hand on Stepan's shoulder. "Listen, Stepan, it is not safe for us to remain in Hradek Kralove. This country . . . it has gone mad."

"All the more reason we should stay and try to talk reason to the people. They are swept up in a radical movement. And they need some reality."

"I could not agree more." Vlastik's eyes were serious, but there was sadness there too. "But we must fight from a position of safety, not vulnerability. Come now, we will depart in two days." The viscount went back to his desk and sat, picking up some papers and studying them.

Stepan sighed. There was no convincing his father. Still, he vowed he would return and fight. But he needed to see his father to safety first. "What do you require of me?"

"I am glad you asked." Vlastik's eyes lit up. "There is a small matter we need to see to before we depart." He held out the papers in Stepan's direction.

Stepping forward, Stepan took them in hand. As he glanced over them, the breath rushed from his body. It was his and Karin's wedding contract. "What farce is this?" Stepan burned as he sought his father's eyes.

"It is no game. We have a binding contract, and I intend to exercise it to the full extent of the law." Vlastik's eyes gleamed.

He was angry. But Stepan knew that. Not to say Stepan was not angry, he was; there was a great deal of hurt in him, too. But he wanted to move past it, not dwell on it. Looking at his father, he saw what was akin to a dog hanging onto a bone—vicious, intent on keeping what ground he could.

"What can we do? Karin has married Pavel. She cannot undo that." Would his father not see reason?

"Nor can she simply undo this contract. You will see. This is not over." The viscount's eyes narrowed into slits and his mouth slid into a crooked grin.

Stepan did not see his father like this often, but when he did, he knew it was time to move out of the way and anticipate damage.

Countess Lenka Bornekova worried after her daughter. She worried after her husband. To put it simply, she filled her days with concentrated concern. It was not like her and it did not suit her. But in a war-torn country, was this what life was to look like?

Even now, she awaited her husband's return. He had been away for far too long on his errand of peace. She had reason to fear something would happen to the party of negotiators in the midst of this war mongering. When had she become such the worrier?

Sitting by the fire, she awaited her handmaiden's coming to warn her of the coach's appearance on the horizon. She had long since given up her sewing. Her nerves had rendered her hands too unsteady. So she read. Or attempted to read. How many times had she read this paragraph? A half dozen?

A sound in the hall broke her concentration. Lenka glanced up. Would it be good news? Her faithful maidservant, Sharka, stepped into view.

"What news do you bring?" Lenka put her book to the side.

"None, my lady, I wondered if you would care for something to drink." Sharka remained at the doorway, not advancing into the space.

She appreciated this about Sharka. Unlike the servant girl, Mary, who took it upon herself to be a busybody in every room she entered, Sharka was a calming presence. Lenka didn't care to watch a servant move about the room, rushing here and there, cleaning this and that, fluffing pillows and cushions. It made Lenka all the more nervous.

Wasn't that kind of thing more appropriate when the mistress of the house wasn't in the room? But Mary was loyal. Perhaps they should have sent her with Karin. But it would not have been safe. So Lenka was stuck with her.

"Thank you, no." Lenka reached for her book, sighing. "Just let me know when Lord Bornekov has been spotted."

Sharka curtsied and turned to leave. She almost bumped into another servant entering. Lenka watched as Mary stepped around Sharka.

Here we go. Opening her mouth, Lenka wanted to dismiss both women for the sake of her privacy, but Mary interrupted her.

"My lady, Lord Bornekov's coach approaches."

Lenka was on her feet in a heartbeat. "How soon?"

"Perhaps twenty minutes." Mary seemed uncertain.

Lenka would have to be ready to meet him in fifteen. "Thank you, Mary. That will be all. Sharka, if you will remain."

Mary nodded, curtsied, and exited.

Sharka shut the door behind Mary and stepped toward her. Without direction, she re-pinned a section of Lenka's hair and read-justed her headdress. Then she took a step back and nodded.

Lenka smiled at her handmaiden. Yes, Sharka was invaluable to her. Standing, Lenka moved away from the warmth of the fire, making her way toward the main entrance of the grand house. There she waited as the minutes passed slowly.

How long had she waited until the large door creaked? She did not know. But her eyes were on the split between the wood and stone, her heart thundering in her ears. And then her husband appeared.

Her gaze flew to his face. Was he just as relieved as she? As his eyes caught hers he opened his arms to welcome her into his embrace.

"Let us away to your cabinet," he whispered.

This did not surprise her. He had come to enjoy their time spent in her private drawing room. Those times had become frequent of late, as things between them became more relaxed.

As they parted, he signaled the manservant as he shrugged off his warm outer coverings. They would be having tea then.

The man nodded, relieving his master of his extra layers.

Then Petr directed his wife upstairs toward the room she had just vacated. Her skin tingled where his hand grasped her arm. Would there be a more intimate reunion to come? Once inside the confines of the small drawing room with the door securely closed, Petr pulled her into his arms.

She went to him.

He pressed a kiss to the side of her face before his lips met hers. It was a quick kiss, but meaningful all the same. It was not so long ago their greetings were all politeness. Nothing more.

Petr drew back from their brief contact and led her to the settee where her book still sat. Moving it, he bid her sit next to him.

She slid onto the bench closer than she needed to.

"How were your travels?" She was eager to hear everything.

"Uneventful. Except for the cold."

"I meant how were the negotiations?" How could he mistake her? She cared not about his traveling conditions.

One look at his growing smile told her he had not misunderstood. "We met with success."

"Truly? The war is over?"

"I would not be so hasty. We eased tensions in Prague for now. Perhaps for certain. There is now an understanding between the people of Prague and the royals. But not everyone was happy about it." His gaze settled on some point in the distance.

"Who was unhappy?" What was this uneasy feeling in the pit of her stomach? She had hoped for better news.

"Jan Zizka. He is a prominent leader of the Hussite movement. So I don't think they will go quietly." Petr bit at his lower lip before turning his gaze toward his wife. "But for now, there is peace, though tenuous at best."

Did this bother Petr more than he betrayed? Lenka did not like it. "What do you think he will do?"

"Zizka has gone to Plzen to join with a preacher in the movement."

"That's so close to Karin and Pavel!" Lenka filled anew with worry. "What if . . . ?"

Petr put a hand on Lenka's. "No good can come from speculation. Pavel and Karin will make their own decisions. All we can do is make ours and hope the best for them."

Strapping on his sword, Pavel secured it at his waist. The weapon had belonged to his grandfather. It had served him well. Pavel only hoped it would do the same for him. The weight of the familiar weapon felt good. There had not been cause to wear it since coming to his parents' home and he had missed it.

Movement behind him warned that he was not alone. But Pavel did not need to look toward the sound to know there was no danger. The gentle footfalls were those of his Karin. Before he could turn, she was behind him, her head pressed to his back and her arms wrapped around his midsection.

Placing his arms over hers, he closed his eyes and reveled in the feel of her presence. She would be missed these next days, perhaps weeks or even months, while he was away.

Karin murmured something against his back he couldn't make out.

"Hmm?" he mumbled, turning so she was against his chest. He used a finger to tilt her chin up so he could look into her eyes. Half expecting tears, he was surprised to find none. Was she putting on a brave front? For him?

"I am going to miss these moments," she repeated. Her voice seemed small and timid, as if she had been afraid to speak it.

He slid his hand up to cup her face. "As will I, my love. As will I." Part of him wanted her to beg him to stay. But she would not. Not after their conversation last night. Pavel had surprised her in their bedchambers. There had been tears in her eyes then. It hurt his heart to remember the scene even now . . .

"Karin, are you hurt?" He fell on his knees in front of her.

"No." She tried to wave him away and turned her back to him as much as she could in the chair. "I am sorry . . . I just . . . " She choked back more sobs, unable to finish.

Pavel was silent for several moments. He knew what troubled her. How could he tell her that his heart hurt, too? Instead he reached up and gently, taking her arms in his hands, guided her down into his embrace.

She all but fell onto the floor next to him.

They remained in each other's arms for some time.

"It is all right, Karin. I understand."

"I know you have to go. And I support you. I just . . . it's difficult . . . "

He nodded against her shoulder. "I know."

She leaned back, taking his face in her hands. "Take me with you."

A smile tugged at the edge of his mouth. How he wished it were feasible. But he would not put her in harm's way. Not for his own selfish reasons. "It is not possible."

"Then give me a child."

It was an odd request. What could he say? So he just stared.

"I want something of our love to continue if anything happens to you." She was being driven by emotion and not reason.

"Karin, you know nothing would make me happier, but we talked of this. Bringing a child into a country torn apart by war . . . into the world as it is now . . . it's not what either of us wants."

She nodded, looking down at her lap. It almost seemed as if she was embarrassed by her request, by her emotions.

Pavel lifted her chin again so she could see the sincerity in his eyes. "I love you. And I will be thrilled to mark this world with our legacy. But it is not the right time."

Taking a deep, ragged breath, she met his gaze fully. "I know you are right. Forgive me."

"It is not necessary." He drew her closer to press a kiss to her forehead.

As he pulled back, she grabbed at his collar and jerked him to her for a full kiss. The kind of kiss that caused his heart to beat faster and his blood to race. It was a kiss that asked for more. And that, he was willing to give her.

"Pavel?"

His name on her lips forced him back to the present. Wanting to kick himself for being lost in a memory instead of cherishing this moment with her, he frowned.

"Did I upset you?" There was a meekness in her voice that cut into him.

"No. Not at all." He gave her his full attention. "I was just lost in a memory."

Her eyebrows knit together. "Oh?"

"A good memory. Of us." He offered her a wide grin.

"Ah." She returned his smile.

"And I will carry these memories with me until I return." He pressed a hand to his heart.

She placed a hand over his. "And I'll be waiting."

"Promise?" His lips moved closer to hers.

"Forever." She closed the distance between them. They embraced, lost in a kiss that would have to last them for many days to come.

CHAPTER 3
REUNITED

Radek rolled his sleeping mat. He'd not had a sound sleep these last several nights. He missed his bed and the safer surroundings of his solid home. It's not that he was unaccustomed to sharing his sleeping space or even to less luxurious bedding. Truth be told, he preferred to lay his back on a firmer surface. And he did not mind Zdenek's close presence. They had roomed together in Prague while attending lectures at Charles University. The man's daily habits had become second nature.

But Radek had been spoiled at the chateau—his own room with a rather large bed. Room to think, room to just be.

Everything was different now. That time was in the past.

Would they ever see Stepan again?

Zdenek coughed off to Radek's right, but Radek ignored it. His friend's lungs took a few minutes to get going. The coughing was just part of his morning routine.

Where had his thoughts been? Oh yes, Stepan. Once more, Radek envied that his friend had been able to choose which side of this conflict to fight on. Stepan had chosen long before this war began. Pavel had too. Maybe that's what he should have done. As it was, the side he would fight for had been all but thrust upon him. This did not seem to bother Zdenek, but he was much more laid back. Radek wanted to know he believed in what he was fighting for. Did he?

Something thrust against Radek's ribs. He held up a hand to push against the offending object.

Zdenek's elbow.

As Radek's hand clamped over Zdenek's arm, Radek met his eyes as they widened. Radek's other hand smoothed over his injured side. "What?"

Zdenek nodded off to the left. "The commander is coming. Should we stand?"

"I don't know." Radek was just as new to this as Zdenek.

"I think we should." Zdenek rose, maneuvering his head to catch a better glimpse of the man they would follow into battle.

Radek followed suit and got to his feet, but rather reluctantly. He did see the small contingency of men coming through the camp. They were led by a man—stout, broad, everything a great Czech military man should be. A beard covered his face and he had a patch over one eye. *What was the story behind that?*

He didn't have much time to think on it before Zdenek broke into his thoughts. "Radek, it's Pavel! Do you not see him?"

Radek cocked his head to the side and scanned the group following Commander Zizka. There, near the back, a blond head among the others. Was it? He narrowed his eyes to focus his vision and watched until the man's face came into view. It was! Pavel walked among the commander's men.

"Pavel!" Zdenek called out, stepping toward the group.

Radek reached out to stop him but not fast enough. Zdenek was already a few steps away. Pushing out a breath through his teeth, he seethed. What could he do but follow?

Pavel's head had turned.

Several Pavels.

And several men by other names.

It seemed as if all eyes were on them as they moved through the men packing their campsites. But they had gotten the attention of the Pavel they sought. He stopped, and turning, squinted his eyes in the direction of the men coming toward him. Radek was sure he would never forget the smile that broke across Pavel's face.

"Zdenek! Radek!" Pavel stepped to the left, closing the distance.

The two men each grabbed one of Pavel's arms.

"I cannot believe you are here," Pavel said, grasping their arms as if never to let go. "I feared what may have happened to you both."

"We were in Prague when Queen Sofia's mercenaries attacked." Zdenek spoke of it openly, but Radek knew it was not without reservation. "And we joined the fight. No one is going to oppress our people again."

Radek did not know what to say, so he remained silent.

Pavel's attention was on Zdenek, and he seemed not to notice.

"I am sorry to hear you were forced to endure such." Pavel's voice was low, his eyes sad. "But I am glad you have joined us."

Radek's stomach turned. Was he now a Hussite? It did not feel right to take on that title.

Looking back to the group Pavel had been walking with, Radek saw that the group had stopped to watch the display.

"Commander Zizka," Pavel addressed the man as he would a friend. How was that possible? Were all Hussites on such terms no matter their station?

Radek focused on what Pavel was saying.

"These are my dear friends. They have come to fight with us. I trust them with my life."

Commander Zizka sized each of them with his good eye before sticking out a hand toward them in turn. His grip was quite firm.

"Gentlemen," he said, nodding. "Any friend of Pavel's is welcome. Certainly a trusted friend."

"Thank you, Commander." Zdenek seemed rather struck by meeting the man. "We are proud to be of service."

Radek continued to maintain his silence, still not wanting to contribute anything he didn't mean. And he did not wish to speak what was on his mind. These men might not receive it well. How would his friends receive it?

"I planned to show these fine men the battle carts I commissioned. Would you care to join us?" His one eye searched their faces. Was he trying to discern their intentions? Their trustworthiness?

Radek did his best to appear compliant.

Were Pavel and Zdenek's eyes on him as well? It felt like it.

"I would be honored." Zdenek sounded confident in his loyalty.

Radek, unsure he could put forth such an assertive effort, nodded.

"Very well," Commander Zizka said, turning toward Pavel. "Shall we?"

"Of course." Pavel moved to follow the commander back to the waiting group, waving for Zdenek and Radek to follow.

Zdenek all but skipped after Pavel, but Radek could not help the heavy feeling that rested in the pit of his stomach. What was he going to do?

Dusk settled upon the Bornekov residence. Petr and Lenka supped in relative peace. There was always the lingering concern after their daughter's well-being, but she was as safe as could be, well within Hussite-controlled territory. Was she happy?

If he had to guess, Petr would say so. He hadn't had much time to watch her and Pavel together, but what he had seen assured him that what they shared was true and deep. There was no doubt Pavel would put her needs above his own, would give his life for her if need be. Still, though that reassured him, Lenka worried after their daughter. She was a mother. And nothing could change that.

Cutting across his beef and dumplings, Petr shifted his gaze to look at his wife. She was, likewise, distracting herself with her meal. In the flicker of the candles that lit the dining room, he saw sadness in her features.

"Tell me," he spoke, breaking the thick silence between them. "What say you to a turn about the gardens tomorrow?"

Lenka's eyes were on him then. Something played across her features. Confusion? Surprise?

It wasn't difficult to determine why. Since his return, he had shut himself in his study most days, recording all that had happened during the negotiations and regaining control on his business. It just now occurred to him that he had shut her out too.

"That would be nice." She reached for her goblet and took a long sip.

What should he say about his revelation? Should he apologize? How to begin? What to say? He never was good at these sorts of things.

A silence fell between them.

Perhaps he could just say what was on his heart. "Lenka, I . . ."

The massive door opened.

Why now? Petr's head drooped slightly before he redirected to face whomever came into the room. A manservant strode toward him. Tempted to give him a cross look, Petr forced a neutral expression onto his face. What could be so important it would not wait? He took a breath. His faithful manservant would not disturb him with anything less than the most critical affair.

Jiri came around to where Petr sat and leaned in as if he shared a great secret. "My lord, Mr. Matousek is here to see you."

What was the caretaker of their summer home doing here? He should be doing just that—caretaking the home.

Petr's eyes met Lenka's. She would not have heard Jiri's quiet notification, and he did not wish to alarm her further.

"This will only take a moment." With that, he stood, placing his napkin on the table and following Jiri to his solar where Jarek Matousek waited.

The man's clothes were disheveled and his hair wild. Had he come in a hurry? Petr paid little mind other than to make a mental note of it. He wanted to know what was going on. Now.

"Jarek," he said, dispensing with the pleasantries. He had not the time for them. "What brings you to my home at this hour?"

"My lord, we received the strangest declaration at the summer house today. I thought it best I bring it to you myself." The man's voice was as shaky as his hand. He reached into his shirt and pulled out a piece of paper. It had been crumpled at the edges where it had made contact with his clothing, but it was still largely untouched.

Petr took the paper from Jarek and opened it, moving to sit on a nearby chair. He was but a few words in when he jerked his head back up. "Who brought this to you?"

"'Twas a lawyer man, my lord." His reply was simple, but it caused warmth to drain from Petr's face.

This could not be right. A lawyer? What recourse did they have?

"What does it say?" came a voice from behind him. He jerked his head around. Lenka stood in the doorway. Had she followed him?

He was on his feet at once, folding the letter and moving to her. "My darling, it is not a matter to concern yourself with . . . "

"It has upset you. I want to know what it says." Lenka had a fire in her eyes. She was not going to back down.

"Jarek, would you excuse us?" Petr faced the man who still appeared rather harried from his trip. "There is fresh food in the kitchen. You remember where it is?"

"Yes, my lord. Thank you." The man moved past Lenka and out of the solar.

Petr shut the door behind him. Best to keep his and Lenka's conversation from curious ears. "Please, sit," he said to his wife, waving toward the sitting area.

She opened her mouth as though she was about to argue, but then closed it. Taking the few steps toward the settee, she planted herself there. Then her intense gaze rested on him, boring into him.

He felt the full weight of it. Sighing, he ran a hand through his hair. "Jarek received notice today that we are to vacate the summer house and its premises within the week."

Her eyes widened. "On whose authority? Who can order us off our own property?"

"Vlastik."

She shook her head. "I do not understand. How can he command us to do anything with our summer home? And why would he care? Does he not have enough properties of his own?"

Petr shrugged. "It is part of Karin's dowry we signed away. It's a contract. That property now legally belongs to Karin and Stepan. And Stepan, as its new owner, is demanding we vacate."

"But they never married." Her brows furrowed. Lenka's confusion was growing, not easing.

"According to the marriage contract, they are married. You know as well as I do that the ceremony is nothing more than a formality. The contract is what matters. And we signed one."

Lenka sat in silence. Was she trying to let it sink in? Yes, it was becoming obvious to her, as it was to him—they never considered the legalities of the contract.

"What are we to do? What does this mean for Karin?" Her voice came out hoarse, broken.

"We are going to find our own legal assistance. This cannot be the first time something like this has happened. And I do not think this means anything for Karin. She is beyond their reach. Even if she were not, I think Vlastik is out to inflict pain. I do not think he would truly see Karin as a fit bride for his son. Not after everything that has happened."

Lenka nodded. Her eyes were wide and her countenance downcast. How he hated bringing more worry into her world.

He stepped to where she sat, taking a seat next to her. "All will be well, my dear." His free hand reached for hers, intertwining their fingers. "Even should the worst come, we have not lost anything we could not afford to lose. Just a luxury. But I am not convinced that even that is gone."

She squeezed his hand. And he knew she was pulling what

strength she could from him. So, he set the letter down and gathered her into his arms.

Eva Valenta tucked her skirts as she bounced in the wagon. Her small family had packed their few precious possessions and headed for southwestern Bohemia. Father had heard there was safety in that region for Hussites—a congregating colony of sorts. She never imagined he would take up with the radical faith, but something about it rang true with him. And so here he was, ready to sacrifice everything to pursue that movement.

What would become of this Hussite movement? That remained to be seen. Eva feared putting her heart into something that may be gone with the next passing gust of wind. It was enough that her father had risked everything they had, their futures for the cause.

Her sister, Patricie, groaned beside her. She did not fare well on long trips. Even a ride to a nearby town was taxing on her stomach, much less traveling halfway across the Bohemian territory. Eva had done her best to steady her and keep her mind on other things, but nothing helped. The bumpier the road got, the sicker Patricie became.

"We will stop soon," Father promised.

Patricie nodded her thanks but continued to hold her arms across her midsection. She was a faint shade of green by now.

"Look, Patricie!" Eva pointed to the forest line in the distance. "A doe."

Her sister glanced in that direction and nodded, but it did nothing to quell her nausea. If only she had other things to turn her mind toward.

Eva herself had a hard time not thinking about the young man who had come to call on her so many weeks ago. His green eyes had lit up when she came to the door. She warmed at the memory. He had amused her, it was true. But in a good way. Had he ever courted a girl? Or even talked to a girl? The way he tripped over himself at the ball made her doubt as much.

"What are you smiling about?" It was Patricie's voice breaking into her thoughts.

"Nothing," Eva said, letting out a long breath. Truly it was nothing. Or at least it would come to nothing. He was of noble birth. A courtship between them would never be allowed.

"You are thinking about *him* again." It was not a question. Her sister knew her too well.

Eva nodded but did not look over. There was sadness in her heart she knew would be translating to her features.

Her sister's hand fell on her arm. It was her way of showing sympathy, as they both knew the match would never be. Their prospects were not as bad as some girls in the village, but their father's new obsession with the teachings of Jan Hus had not improved them. Certainly uprooting them and his growing business would eliminate any possibilities they might have had of making good matches. Now they had naught but their good looks and character to put them forth as marriage material. It was a hard truth, but a truth all the same.

"I think this is a good stopping place," Father said, indicating a nearby stream that had just come into view.

Eva and Patricie nodded.

It would feel good to wash off some of the dust from the road. Only to get back in the wagon and acquire more.

Still, she would revel in the few moments of having a clean face. A woman must not neglect the simple things in life. That is what her mother would say, were she here. Mother had not been with them for some years, not since the plague swept through town and claimed a life in almost every house in their village.

Father slowed the horses as they approached the stream. He jumped down and reached up to help his daughters out of the wagon.

Patricie seemed quite dizzy once on solid ground and had a difficult time finding her footing.

Eva was by her side, steadying her.

Father took the horses closer to the stream and Eva steered her sister toward the water as well.

Once they were almost to the stream's edge, Patricie released her hold on Eva and raced at the water, emptying the contents of her stomach just short of the stream.

Eva was soon beside her, holding her hair, offering as much comfort as she could.

When Patricie was done, she sat back and let out a loud sigh.

"You all right?" Eva continued to stroke her back.

Patricie nodded, turning to look at her sister. "Much better."

Eva nodded. They sat at the water's edge for several moments while the horses drank their fill and then commenced grazing.

After some time, Eva stood. "Let's wade." She jerked her head toward the stream and whispered to her sister as if it were a scandalous thing she suggested. After all, there were some benefits to being a simple merchant's daughter. Not having to stand on propriety was definitely one of them.

Their shoes were off in seconds and they plunged into the cool stream, holding their skirts up. It was a lost cause and they knew it, for soon they were splashing at each other.

By the time Father was calling for them, they were all but soaked. But they were no longer road-weary. They were happy and rejuvenated.

"Looks like you two had a time. Best get back on the road." Father held out a hand to help lift the first daughter into the wagon.

Eva stepped forward, still wringing out her skirt.

Patricie groaned, but came to the wagon to be hoisted up next.

"We need to pick up the pace," Father informed them.

Patricie's face drained of color.

Eva laid a hand on hers and squeezed it.

"Hopefully we'll catch up to Commander Zizka's army soon enough."

The massive house seemed almost cavernous. Baron Alexander Krejik walked the halls and heard nothing but the sound of his own footfalls. It would not have felt so empty, he was certain, if his son had not left to claim his role in this war. When Pavel was here, the walls echoed with laughter and merriment. Now all was silent.

Pavel's wife, Karin, kept to her room and the study. They would see her only at meals. Marketa longed for she and Karin to reach better terms than the simple politeness they now enjoyed, but that kind of relationship required time. Even he wished he could do something to help Karin feel more included. Maybe then these halls would not feel so empty.

It was not just Karin that had disappeared these last several days —he noted that his wife felt less at ease moving about the house. She, too, kept to her solitude. What had made her such a hermit? On occasion, she would walk out to the garden to see to its planting and tending, but that was the extent of her outings. This was not like her.

Alex felt it was up to him to do something. This was, for certain, out of his realm of comfort. He would much rather have gone off to war with Pavel if they would have him. But they would not. What did they need with an aged soldier? Something he would never tell his wife was that he had written to Commander Zizka offering his services along with Pavel's. The man was mindful of Alex's pride, insisting Alex could best serve their purposes at home while Pavel would be best utilized by Zizka's side. While Alex was pleased to have his son do his duty, he was saddened at his own apparent impotence in this arena.

Just then, Alex passed near the study. The door creaked. It drew his attention. And he saw Karin emerge, a couple of books in hand.

"Baron," she said, curtsying. "Forgive me, I did not see you."

"It is no matter." He offered her a smile, hoping to ease her anxiety. It did not seem to be working. "Did you find what you needed?"

"Did I . . . ?" She peered at him, confused.

He pointed at the books in her hands.

"Oh, yes." She let out a breath. "Your library is quite extensive."

"I am glad you are pleased." They were once again plunged into silence. He broke it. "And your rooms? Are you comfortable?"

"Yes, my lord. I am quite comfortable." She returned his smile then. It was a genuine smile as far as he could sense.

"Good, good. Have you had a chance to visit the garden this season? It promises to be every bit as beautiful as last year."

Karin gazed toward the window at the end of the hall as if she could see the garden a full story below from where she stood, several feet away from the window. "No, my lord. I have not had the pleasure."

He felt stuck. What should he do? Release her to return to her bedchambers and read? This was what she obviously intended to do. Or invite her on a stroll with him? And maybe, just maybe, get to know his son's wife a little better. Though it would push him out of his arena of comfort, he decided on the latter.

Sticking out his arm, he offered her his best smile. "Then I insist I have the honor to show it to you."

Karin's eyes met his and he saw a hesitation in her.

Still, she slid a hand into the crook of his elbow and returned his smile.

And so, leading her, he walked down the stairs and out of the house to his wife's most prized sanctuary.

They made simple conversation as they walked, and he discovered Karin was a lady who smiled easily and laughed heartily. He liked those attributes. She complimented the garden and its arrangement with such sincerity that he wished Marketa was there to hear it. Perhaps he would remember to share it with her later.

After some time in the garden, Alex escorted Karin back into the house and to her room. The dinner hour approached, and he was certain she would need to ready herself.

He did pause before releasing her hand. "Karin, you are free to move about the grounds and house as if it were your own. As you do not have your own house yet— a fact I hope to rectify soon enough —I do so hate to see you shut up in your rooms all the time."

She nodded, her gaze settled on the floor.

"We miss him, too," Alex said boldly, patting her hand.

Her eyes rose to meet his.

"I just mean to say that you are not alone."

Karin's head bobbed, and she bit her lip but did not speak.

Was she fighting tears? He saw moisture welling in her eyes. What could he do? What was appropriate? The tears came into being and fell down her face.

She leaned into his shoulder.

Had he offered it? Perhaps in his silence he had. He raised his opposite hand and patted her back. "It will be all right. God will protect him. We must have faith."

Karin nodded into his shoulder. "I know. It's just . . . not easy."

He nodded. This was beyond his level of comfort. Marketa always managed these sorts of things. And he certainly couldn't comfort Karin as he would his wife. But she was like a daughter. A daughter he never had. A daughter he had prayed for.

Closing his eyes, he imagined she was his blood daughter and embraced her, just allowing her to cry. He stroked her hair and whispered soothing words that made little sense. In time she did calm and then quiet.

Eventually she pulled back, wiping at her face.

And the spell was broken. She was not his daughter but his son's wife. Still, she was more somehow.

Their eyes met and he offered her a warm smile.

She did her best to turn her mouth upward, her eyes glistening. "Thank you. I didn't mean to—"

He shook his head. "Think nothing of it."

Karin nodded before pulling in a deep breath. "I think I better prepare for the evening meal."

"I will see you in the great hall, then." He released her hand and started to turn, but paused. "Just think about what I said."

Karin gave a slight bow of her head.

Then Alex walked away, back down the silent hall. He prayed this would be the beginning of a change in his home.

Pavel trailed behind Commander Zizka, eager to see these battle carts the commander had commissioned. They had spent a long morning finalizing their negotiations with the Royalist commander. Plzen was taken by negotiation instead of battle; they had fallen by choice. The Royalists granted them communion in both kinds—of bread and wine—and many Hussites were content to remain with those sanctions.

Zizka was not. It was no secret he'd had his eye on Usti for some time now. The Royalist commander granted safe passage to anyone wishing to leave Plzen. And they intended to leave—but not before Commander Zizka showed off his battle carts.

As they walked on, Pavel could make out a looming object in the distance. Still, it wasn't as massive as he had imagined. How could this simple wagon defend all their army? Chancing a glance at Zdenek and Radek, he tried to decipher if they were equally unimpressed. Their faces held neutral expressions.

"Come, come," Zizka said, waving the men closer. He seemed almost giddy.

So the men took the steps that would close the distance remaining between them and the war wagon.

"Please, have a look." Zizka raised an arm toward the wagon, inviting them to inspect it.

Pavel moved closer to the piece. Upon first glance, it appeared to be nothing more than a conventional wagon with raised sides.

Running his hand over the smoothed surface of the wood, he noted that the planking was about four feet off from the base of the unit. There were hinges on top of the side facing them and an extra board hanging down.

He twisted away and opened his mouth to inquire after its use when Zizka stepped toward them.

"This board can be raised like so." He hopped into the wagon and lifted the side panel to elongate the sidewall. There were small openings in the panel at about the level a man would be firing a crossbow or a hand cannon. In this way, he could do it with maximum protection, exposing only the parts of himself necessary to fire the weapon. Ingenious. Zizka then demonstrated how the side panel could be fixed into place for the duration of combat.

"This is a magnificent idea," one of the other soldiers in the group spoke up. "But how many men can fight from one of these?"

"I imagine there will be about sixteen soldiers associated with each wagon: crossbowmen, gunmen, soldiers with flails, shield men, and, of course, drivers." Zizka rattled off the list with such smoothness, Pavel had no doubt he had this all planned to the last detail.

But then, would one wagon truly make much of an impact against such an overwhelming foe?

"Excuse me, Commander," another nobleman spoke up. "Did you say *each* wagon?"

"Ah, yes. Yes, I did. My intention is to have several of these wagons linked together in a circle with the remaining soldiers and cavalry protected within the center." Zizka's eyes lit up and his mouth curved upward.

Pavel was starting to get the vision. If they could set up something like that, would it be impenetrable? If so, it could mean the war for them. "How will you create a solid barrier?"

"You see how these front wheels are projected out from the body?"

He nodded. It had not escaped him, but he had thought perhaps it was a design flaw.

"This is so we can lock one front wheel into place with the rear wheel of the next cart. Then we can chain them together for stability. We can then post armed soldiers with shields in the gap." Zizka moved around the cart as he explained it, trying to give the men a picture of what it would be like.

"But could not an enemy soldier gain access under the cart?" It was Radek that spoke.

Pavel was certain he had exposed a flaw in the plan.

All eyes were on Zizka.

The commander's face broke into a smile. "You think like a man of war, my boy." Zizka then came around to the extended side of the cart and reached underneath. Slung below the wagon was another hinged plank that fell as he released it. This closed off the space underneath and it even had the same firing slits pierced in it so soldiers could fire at the enemy from that position.

Pavel was eager to see the war wagons in action. Not that he was ready to rush into battle, but he felt more confident in their defensive position should they find themselves in combat in the near future. These were magnificent!

Zizka crossed his arms over his chest, which was visibly puffed out.

And rightfully so. This battle cart was everything he had said it would be.

"Any other questions?"

The men looked at one another and shook their heads.

Pavel sensed that the other men around him were, likewise, pleased.

"Then I shall bid us disperse for now. Collect your men and rally them together. Today will be a long one. We march north tomorrow." Zizka gazed over his group of chosen leaders, nodding to them and clapping several on the shoulder as they parted from the group.

Turning toward Zdenek and Radek, Pavel motioned them closer. "I would be honored to have you fight alongside me."

"We would not have it any other way." Zdenek's voice was bold and confident.

Radek simply nodded. Still a man of few words.

"I have been charged with leading the group from Plzen. We need to move through the camp and locate these men."

Zdenek and Radek nodded.

"My campsite is on the far east side of camp. We shall rally there." Pavel pointed in that direction.

Zdenek and Radek nodded again, exchanged a look, and then headed out into the camp on their errand.

Pavel thought he should join them in their task but then thought better of it. Perhaps he needed to take this time for solitude and prayer. He was going to be responsible for leading these men into a fight for their lives. Maybe not today, but soon. That weight lay rather heavy on his shoulders. And he could not bear it alone. Yes, prayer was going to be a necessary part of his role.

Stepan awoke, drawn to the light of the early morning rays slipping in through a crack in his curtains. It did not bother him. He welcomed the reminder that another day came in the midst of conflict. Everything was so twisted, and he felt it to his core.

Rising, he rang for his valet. The matter of dressing for the day was inconsequential. So routine, these things. They rather bored him.

Once the valet came and Stepan was prepared, he waved off the manservant while shifting his shirt collar. Need they be so high on the neck?

His father would be waiting for him to join him for breakfast in his study, but Stepan hesitated. Being with his father only left him more conflicted. It was as if his spirit could be as torn as their homeland.

But he could not escape this morning engagement. Nor did he

truly want to. As much as his father left his insides a twisted, cluttered mess, he desired the man's approval more than anything.

Taking a deep breath, Stepan made his way to his father's study. Just as he expected, his father sat at the table, already engrossed in his breakfast.

"*Dobry den*," Stepan said, taking his seat across from Vlastik.

A manservant stepped forward, offering to serve him from the platters of food on the table.

Vlastik made a grunting noise that resembled the Czech greeting but continued to focus on his food.

The two continued to eat in silence until Vlastik pushed his plate forward. Only then did he look across the table and meet Stepan's eyes.

"The Pope has made it official."

Stepan stopped chewing the bit of food in his mouth for a moment. Then he swallowed hard. "Official?"

Vlastik's countenance dropped as if he were rather bored with explaining things to Stepan. "He has declared a crusade."

What would this mean? There was already fighting. Loyal Royalists were already active, staging raids all over the Czech lands. What difference would this make?

Vlastik continued his explanation. "These skirmishes in Bohemia will now be an organized crusade to eliminate all of these heretics. It's a good thing, my boy."

"Could a unification of the Royalist forces lead to a unification of the Hussite forces?"

Vlastik's face fell. Then his eyebrows furrowed and his face reddened. "They are a disorganized band of misfits. Farmers. Merchants. Untrained, untried, and without any real direction. What hope do they have against a royal army?"

Stepan sank back into his chair. He had not realized his wondering had been out loud. And he certainly had not intended to anger his father.

After a few moments, he raised his eyes to meet Vlastik's. "Of course, Father. They will be defeated."

As the servants passed dinner entrees, Marketa could not help but study her daughter-in-law. This had become habit. What were this woman's thoughts and passions? It was clear Karin made her son happy. But what was it about her? Trying to remember that long-ago conversation when he spoke of Karin with such longing in his heart, Marketa attempted to gauge Karin's finer qualities from those he might have highlighted. Marketa's memory was not what it could be, however. And so, she was left with what she could observe about the young woman who had come to live in her home.

There were a few things she did know about Karin. The girl was polite, well mannered, and had at least a passing interest in reading. And she was a Hussite. That took courage. Pavel had said Karin even defied her family to follow her beliefs. The story got a little hazy when it came to the reasons she was sent to the chateau and the viscountess's plot to kill her. It seemed a bit melodramatic. But what a story!

On this night, however, something had changed. Karin and Alex conversed more easily. Not that Marketa could hear much of what was said. This table was ridiculous in its length and they would not speak up. For one, Karin was more soft-spoken than should be allowed at such a table. Alex did not help matters in that Marketa could only catch snatches of what was being said.

In the next moment, both Karin and Alex's eyes were upon her. Had she said something out loud? Surely not. Had one of them said something to her? Yes, perhaps that was it.

"I apologize," she said, dabbing her mouth with a napkin. "I did not hear the question."

"Karin and I were discussing your garden. It is magnificent. Well done." Alex raised his voice to an unnecessary level.

Marketa furrowed her brows. Why would he raise his voice so? She was not deaf, after all, just farther away than he had anticipated.

"Thank you," she all but yelled back. "But I assure you, there is no need to shout at me. Just speak up."

Alex and Karin exchanged a look. What was that about? More and more, people were doing that around her. She did not like it. Not one bit. But she must rise above it. Yes, instead of getting cross, she would just change the subject.

"Any word from Pavel?" She set her knife down and lifted her wine glass to her lips.

Karin met her eyes. "I received a letter just today. If you would like, I will share it after dinner." Was it her imagination or was Karin speaking a bit too loudly as well?

Either way, she let her mouth upturn and nodded. "Yes, that would be nice."

One of Karin's sweet smiles spread across her face. This must have been one of the things that endeared her to Pavel. Marketa could understand. She was enchanting.

Though the meal continued in relative silence, Marketa was unable to focus on anything but the letter forthcoming. She was all too eager to hear about Pavel's whereabouts. What was he doing? Was he safe? Would the letter bear bad news? Surely if anything was awry, they would have heard. Yes, she had no need to worry.

It was not long before the meal came to a close and the plates were cleared. Marketa focused on her husband who spoke.

"Shall . . . by . . . fireplace?"

She could not make out every word, but she gathered that he wished they all retire to the large solar.

Nodding, she pushed her chair back and stood.

The trio moved out of the dining hall and toward the nearby solar.

Karin excused herself to collect the letter.

This large solar was every bit as grandiose as any room in the house. Perhaps a little too grand for Marketa's taste. She would much rather be in one of the smaller rooms for a more intimate gathering. But this was what Alex had suggested.

Sitting on a blue velvet-clad chair, she ran a hand over the fabric. Had she never sat in this chair before? Was it new? Pushing this to the side, she focused on Alex.

He chose the settee nearby.

Marketa opened her mouth to speak but could not focus. She had nothing to do but wait for Karin and the contents of the letter.

"My dear, are you well?"

Eyes widened, she glanced at her husband.

His eyes were on her hands.

Only then did she notice she had been wringing them. Clasping them together, she laid them in her lap. "Yes, perhaps I am a little anxious."

Alex's eyes met hers. They were kind, understanding.

Karin stepped into the solar; cutting off whatever Alex might have wanted to say. She moved to sit on a chair near the settee. Then she paused and stepped to a chair closer to Marketa.

Why would Karin be so concerned where she sat? Did she feel the need to sit closer to Marketa? The baroness captured this thought and tucked it away for later; she did not want to shift her focus from the letter.

Licking her lips, she watched as Karin unfolded the paper and began reading the writing Marketa would have recognized anywhere.

"Dearest Karin . . . " The young woman paused and moved her hands down the paper. Did she skip personal things said between husband and his wife?

"We have started setting up our units. I am commanding a small contingency of men that includes, if you can believe it, Zdenek and Radek. Yes, my friends are alive and well and joined with our cause. They are with us in Plzen and part of my unit. More than that, they will be invaluable as I take on the weighty task of leading these men. Please continue to pray for me in this.

"I feel neither prepared nor equipped for this job, but I know He has called me and He will supply what I need. By the time you receive this letter, we will have marched for northern Bohemia. What lies before us, I cannot say. But I will carry you with me. Always. Give my parents my best. As for you, my darling . . . " Karin's voice trailed off, but she continued to read silently.

Marketa could not mistake the moisture welling in Karin's eyes. She must miss her husband. No one could blame her. Newlywed brides should not be asked to part with their beloved so soon after their nuptials. Pavel and Karin were being brave for sake of the cause. For the Czech people. For their religious freedom. Indeed a worthy cause. But at what cost, Marketa could not say.

Gazing at Karin's face, she saw that the young woman bore part of that pain even now. And Marketa hoped for both their sakes that this short absence would be the extent of their sacrifice.

CHAPTER 4
BATTLE

Sounds of the carts and horses moving over softer ground drowned out everything else. Pavel settled into his saddle and steeled himself for the journey ahead. It would be quite the journey to Usti, but they would stop with greater frequency for the sake of the women and children. And, because of the carts, they wouldn't cover ground as quickly.

He glanced ahead and to his right to where Commander Zizka led the group of misfits. From his proud stature upon his horse, one would never know he led untrained farmers and merchants, with but a handful of noblemen. These were the only trained men among his army. They had simple weapons—farm instruments altered and fitted for battle. A band of misfits indeed.

As Pavel watched, Zizka's posture altered. He leaned back and pulled on the reins. Pavel searched the horizon ahead. His heart sank into his stomach. An army marched straight for them, fitted into two columns. They appeared at least 2,000 strong.

Zizka turned to the south. Pavel's gaze followed. There were wooded hills there—good for defense. But they lay too far away. From the grimace on Zizka's face, he knew it too. The commander's eye searched the area, and Pavel could almost guess he was searching for some way to fortify their position. It was no use. They sat in the middle of a wide, flat river valley with naught but some empty fishing ponds.

Seconds later, Zizka began barking orders. This was a man of action. He lined the troops with one flank against a nearby dam. Next he arranged the twelve war wagons to cover their flank and rear. Then he focused on the men directly beneath him and issued orders to them.

"Rally the infantry," he said to one of the men. "Ready the troops. Pavel, assign men to the hand cannons inside the war wagons."

Pavel rushed off to fulfill the task he'd been given. The harried men were thick as goulash stew. He had to push his way through to get to the war wagons. Along the way, he grabbed what able-bodied men he came across who asserted they could work a hand cannon. Once the positions inside the war wagons were filled, and the soldiers with shields were in place in the gaps between the carts, Pavel stopped to breathe.

He scanned the coming army, and his stomach turned. There were so many of them. Now close enough for him to make out their uniforms, the bright red marked them as Royalists. They had been betrayed. Though they were promised safe retreat, it was not to be. He had to find Commander Zizka.

Locating the commander a second time proved more difficult. Zizka had taken up position on horseback just behind the war wagons. From there, he could look out across the approaching army.

"Commander," Pavel tried to get his attention. "What are your orders?"

Zizka's mouth was a thin line. The man grimaced. Yes, even he must know the situation was bleak. He peered down at Pavel. "You have seen the army?"

Pavel nodded, swallowing hard.

"Then you know they outnumber us five to one."

Pavel nodded again.

"But we have right on our side. We will stand strong."

"I am prepared to stand beside you and fight, Commander." Pavel gazed out across the crowd of people surrounding him. His eyes caught on the families. "But I think also of the women, the children."

Zizka closed his eye. Pavel could almost sense the war within him. Having someone voice it made it that much harder.

"Commander," Pavel said, his voice low and quiet. "As brave as our men are, I do not think we can win. We are too few and too unprepared."

Zizka nodded. Then, turning to his aide beside him, he said, "We must put up the white flag."

Pavel closed his eyes. He did not relish the fact that they were about to surrender, but it was the right thing. For the sake of the precious lives they guarded. *Lord, please guide our way. Keep us from harm.*

Not long after, Pavel saw, off to his right, the aide raise a white cloth on a long pole.

He breathed out a sigh. It was done. The rest was in God's hands.

And he prayed right up until the moment the enemy attacked.

Countess Bornekova paced in her bedchambers. Petr had gone after their legal adviser and left her in the massive manor. There were rumors that the fighting continued despite Petr and the other nobles' efforts toward peacemaking. And it continued to worry her.

They had received a letter from Karin after all this time. She was well and situated at the Krejik estate. Pavel had joined the Hussite efforts. This greatly concerned Lenka. Not only for his safety but also for Karin's well-being.

Pavel meant everything to her *katka,* and Lenka feared a bout of melancholia that might never end should something happen to him. Worst of all, there was nothing she could do to comfort her daughter from such a distance. Even were she by Karin's side, what could be done? What words could assuage her lonely heart?

A knock at the door drew her from her musings. Looking toward the barrier between herself and the harsh world beyond, she wondered whether or not to allow the intruder to enter her solitude. Sighing, she remembered her responsibilities that went far beyond her frayed emotions.

"Come," she called, stilling her movements. She folded her hands and raised her invisible mask, the one that would give nothing of her heart away.

The door opened to admit a manservant.

"My lady," he said, his voice lowered in apology as he stepped into her private sanctuary. "Forgive the intrusion. A messenger has come and insists he deliver his message to the lord or lady of the house."

She nodded, doing everything in her power not to betray her heightening concern. What could be so important to require such a stipulation? Had something happened to Petr? To Karin?

Instead of falling apart, she gathered her skirts and followed Jiri into the hall and down the grand staircase to the solar where the messenger awaited her.

The man stood where he must have been left, just inside the door of the solar. When Lenka entered, his eyes were on the far wall. But he glanced toward the door and the room's new occupant as she came into the space.

He bowed to Lenka. "Countess Bornekova."

She was not in the mood for these formalities, but she must endure them all the same. As he returned to his full height, looming several inches over her, she was ready for him to reveal his purpose.

"I understand you have a message for me?" She tried to sound bored, though everything in her cried in angst, anxious for the knowledge he possessed.

"Yes, my lady." He eyed the manservant.

"That will be all, Jiri." She dismissed him with a wave of her hand.

As Jiri stepped from the room, the messenger's shoulders relaxed, but he maintained a proper distance.

"I have a message from the Viscount Vlastik Dvorak and his son, Stepan Dvorak. They make formal request of the payment of the contracted dowry of 5000 Guldens in silver."

Lenka couldn't speak. Payment of the dowry? Shouldn't she have expected this? If they were demanding the Bornekovs remove themselves from the summerhouse, the dowry payment was the natural next step. Petr said they had only put forth in the contract what they could afford to lose. She hoped that was still the case.

Zdenek maneuvered until he got a clear shot with his crossbow. His efforts were met with success. As the battle waged, the Hussites saw the Royalist soldiers fall prey to their strong fortifications and careful aim. The war wagons proved every bit as valuable as Zizka hoped. They were the only reason there still was a Hussite camp. Of this, Zdenek was certain. Not only were the Hussites still there, they were inflicting a lot of damage into the attacking force with minimal casualties on their end.

Reloading his crossbow, Zdenek prepared to fire again. But he heard a cry coming from the opposite side of camp.

"Cavalry coming from the marsh! We need men to shore up that side of camp!"

Zdenek glanced around. His eyes locked with Radek's next to him.

"I'll cover this, you go." Radek jerked his head in the direction of the voice.

Nodding, Zdenek placed a hand on Radek's shoulder and moved across the camp. It surprised him how quickly he jumped into action once the battle was upon them. He had wondered if, after what had happened in Prague, he would hesitate in the midst of fighting. But once he knew what had to be done, his body took over and gave him what he needed to sustain him. It was as if he could do anything.

His foot caught on something and he almost tripped. Regaining his footing, he looked down to see what had gotten in his way. It was the pole with the white cloth. Without a second thought, he stepped over it and moved on.

Who were these soldiers that a white flag meant nothing to them? Had they no decency? But God had smiled upon the Hussites. Against all odds, the battle was turning in their favor. Now, if they could hold off this cavalry, they would win.

Zdenek jogged the rest of the way to the far end of the camp.

"What are our orders?" he asked the man standing next to him when he stopped. They all gazed across the swampland.

"A scout returned and said the cavalry's horses became mired in the muck. So the soldiers are coming on foot," the man said. He was a young man, much younger than Zdenek. The flail in his hand began to shake. Was the man trembling? Had he ever seen death?

As they watched, a group of armor clad men moved slowly in their direction through the swampy land. Their progress slowed. And slowed. They became stuck little by little.

"Come on, men! Let's finish them!" a voice cried.

The men around Zdenek rushed forward with their flails. Having no armor, the infantrymen moved with greater ease through the swampy area.

Zdenek was unable to move. He could not make himself rush after helpless soldiers, even if they would have struck him down in a heartbeat. Even if he had already killed men in this fight. Somehow, this was different.

As he recoiled, he spotted another soldier off to his left who was frozen to the spot. Making his way to the young man, Zdenek prepared to walk him back to the battle carts. They might be of more use there.

"Soldier, care to join me with a crossbow?" he said as he approached the figure.

The face that spun toward him betrayed features that, though dirt-marred, were delicate and fine. They were the visage of a young woman.

His heart skipped a beat.

It was not just any woman, but the woman from the ball—Eva.

Dawn streamed into the window. Shining on Karin's face, it brought her to consciousness. Opening her eyes, she became aware that a maidservant exited the room having already opened the drapes. How had she slept so long? It was customary for Karin to awaken and open the drapes before Nicol came in.

Karin felt a yawn coming and stretched out her limbs. Perhaps it was simply due to a long night of tossing and turning. She couldn't sleep quite as well without Pavel. There was just no adjusting to it.

"Good morning, my lady." Nicol stepped into the room, an emerald green gown draped across her arm. "I did not know if I would have to rouse you."

Karin offered her a smile. "I have managed to find the sunlight."

Nicol nodded.

The young woman was pleasant indeed. Theirs was not quite the up-and-down relationship she'd had with Mary. Nicol had a gentler personality, not as . . . colorful as Mary's, but perhaps not as interesting either. No matter, as long as they were more amicable than she had been with Mary and her spying ways at the chateau.

Sitting up in the bed, Karin's stomach rumbled and turned. Perhaps she should ask Nicol to order her a breakfast tray. She opened her mouth to do just that and then covered her lips with her hand. Perhaps the turning of her stomach was not hunger, but queasiness. Maybe breakfast could wait.

Karin slid out of bed and made her way to where Nicol stood

with the gown. Smiling despite the uneasiness, she allowed the girl to help her out of her nightdress and into her clothes. This gown was not one of her favorites, but as she gazed in the mirror, she mused that it complimented her eyes well. The shade was a perfect match. It also stood in stark contrast to her red hair—a nice juxtaposition.

Nicol then steered Karin to the vanity, where the maidservant began the task of taming her red locks. It was not an easy task, and Nicol had not the experience Mary seemed to. So, it took more time.

But today, the longer Karin sat, the queasier she became. Swallowing, she closed her eyes and tried to think on other things. Like Pavel. Where was he? Was he safe? Was he thinking of her? She would be counting down the days until she could see him again if only she knew when that was. And she wished she could write him but had no idea where to send such a missive. His letters had served to encourage and calm her, but there was no way for her to respond.

A knock at the door shattered her thoughts.

"Come," Karin called.

Another maidservant came with her morning tray.

"Thank you."

The woman set the tray on a nearby table while Nicol put the finishing touches on Karin's hairstyle. She had decided to braid and pin it up today. It was always nice to have it off of her shoulders, but it took so long to get it just right.

Once she was done, Nicol stepped to the tray and took the lid off. The smells of the food reached Karin's nose. She rushed to the chamber pot before she lost the entire contents of her stomach.

"My lady!" Nicol rushed over, holding the thick braid to the side and laying a hand on Karin's back. "Are you well?"

"Yes," she said, trying to retain some dignity. She sat up and attempted to gather herself. It was difficult with a churning stomach. Placing a hand over her midsection, she hoped the nausea would pass. "I must have eaten something that hasn't agreed with me."

"You've been having this happen a lot lately," the young girl commented, standing and walking to the water bowl. She returned with a wet cloth.

Taking it with gratitude, Karin pressed the cloth to the back of her neck. It was true. She had been plagued of late. But was it so often? Karin thought back over the last couple of weeks. There had been these bouts of sickness in the morning. Certainly she couldn't be getting bad food every night. Then she was struck with a random thought. Why had it not occurred to her before? She counted in her head. Yes . . . yes, that would be about right. Her heart sank.

She and Pavel had discussed this and decided to wait. What were they to do now? It was not possible to put this on him in the midst of war. And so, an occasion that should be celebrated together would be lamented in silence.

Karin was pregnant.

Gazing into the eyes of the one man in the world she was certain she would never see again, Eva's knees felt weak. Not only had Zdenek found her, she had been discovered, too. When the battle began, she had feared the worst. Then she noted how outnumbered they were. What could she do? Sit by and watch them be overcome? No, she did what any able-bodied daughter would do— she took her place among the men. After her father ran off into battle, she tucked her hair into a cap and tied on some of his clothes. Patricie had not been pleased, but Eva insisted that it must be so.

But here she stood; unable to do the very thing she had been determined to do—fight. And, finding herself wanting of the courage to attack these helpless men, she had been discovered by the one man whose opinion mattered more than it should.

She dipped her head, tearing her eyes away and staring at the ground. There were no words forthcoming.

"Eva." Zdenek found his voice after some moments.

Chancing a glance at him, she did not see disapproval in his eyes, but concern.

"You should not be here." There was no accusation in him; rather his voice was gentle, kind.

"The Royalists number is great. I had to do what I could to help." Would he understand? She hoped so. Her intentions and her follow-through were two different things. And that was laid bare before him. Did she seem foolish?

He placed a hand on her arm. His touch warmed her even through the thick cotton of the man's oversized shirt.

"We need to get you to safety." His voice was firm, his concern evident.

Eva nodded, her heart dropping. He must think her silly. She faced camp and allowed him to lead her back into the inner area where the women and children were huddled. But he did not loosen his hold on her arm. Of this, she took note.

They walked through the camp, dodging men running this way and that. But Eva could not help but feel as if they were the only two. All her attention was focused on the simple contact of his hand on her arm. She wanted to say something, anything. Yet her lips would not move.

At last, they arrived at the center of the camp.

"You must help with the women and children," Zdenek said, turning to face her. "Keep them safe. That is how you can best serve." His gaze wandered over her form, resting on her eyes. What was he not saying? Without another word, he turned to leave.

"But . . . " she started, and then thought better of it. Would she see him again? No, she had shown her true cowardice, and he wanted nothing further to do with her.

He stopped, turning back toward her. His eyes sought hers.

She was not used to someone gazing at her so intently.

Walking to her, he took her hand in his. Gone was the young man who had tripped over himself at the ball. This man was confident and collected. He was sure of himself and what he wanted. "I will find you once victory is ours."

From his tone, she knew it was a promise. She wanted to nod, but couldn't move, not even to breathe. As he released her hand and walked away, she drew in the breath her body was desperate for. Once she lost sight of him in the crowds of people moving about, the sounds of the battle returned. People shouting, hand cannons firing, cries of pain, and children screaming. That's where her attention went—to the children.

Turning, she moved into the thick of the women and children and was met with a myriad of facial expressions. Fear. Confusion. Exhaustion. Worn and worried, none of them were too sure about her. Remembering she appeared to them as a young man, she pulled her hat off, letting her hair fall. They may think her strange to be in men's clothing, but at least she was now clearly a woman.

What they needed more than anything was food. Had anyone seen to their physical needs this day? Eva searched until she found a cart full of foodstuffs, perhaps rations for the soldiers, but she took some for the huddled innocents.

As she distributed the much-needed food, Eva attempted to reassure the women and children, many of them huddled together as if fearful of the attacking forces breaking through. She offered them a smile and assurances that the Hussites prevailed.

Though her efforts were tireless and did not seem to make much of a difference, she continued to try to exude what confidence she could. Her feet tired and her arms ached, but she pushed on, moving between the cart and the crowd until at last everyone was fed. Then she continued to walk in their midst, encouraging them.

After some time, she felt a gentle hand upon her shoulder. She spun toward it and met the eyes of her sister.

"Patricie!" She all but collapsed into her arms.

"Eva, you must rest." Patricie lowered them to their knees gently, not able to bear the weight of her sister's body.

"I must continue to calm the women, the children. They are so frightened." Eva's gaze met her sister's bright eyes.

"Look at them," Patricie challenged her. "You cannot assuage them all. Their fear is greater than the words you offer."

Eva's head hung. Her sister was right. She had failed yet again.

"But you have fed their bellies, for which they are grateful." Patricie urged Eva to stand and attempted to move her sister to their wagon. "Here," she said, making a space in the back. "You must rest, sister dear. You look like you need it."

Eva shook her head in protest. "There are many still in need." But she could not deny that her body was exhausted from all her efforts.

"I shall see to them," Patricie offered. "You rest. Just for a moment."

"Just for a moment," Eva insisted. She watched as her sister moved back into the crowd of women and children, patting a head here, touching a shoulder there.

Eventually, she found her eyelids were heavy. Too heavy. So, she allowed them to close. And it was not long until she surrendered to the darkness on the edge of her consciousness.

Stepan's anger burned. Karin had been unfaithful to him. She lied to him. In the worst way possible. He watched, uncaring, as her body slid down the embankment. Racing after her, he stood over her limp form. Her movements betrayed her efforts to stand, but her body was injured. And he knew he had caught his prey.

Reaching down, he twisted her onto her back. She would face him in her final moments.

She blinked in the rain, but her eyes sought his. They were pleading, innocent.

But he knew the truth – she was not that innocent. No, she was a traitor and an instigator, a liar. So, he raised his sword above his head and with one swift movement, plunged it into her heart.

Stepan awoke with a start, heaving, covered in sweat, lost in the memory that would not release him. It took several minutes for him to realize where he was and to remember what had occurred that terrible day. He was safe, in his family's home in Cologne. His father had brought them here as a reprieve from the war.

Taking in more gulps of air, he noted the moonlight creeping in through his open drapes. And he remembered that he had retired early this evening. Begging off dinner due to a headache. Looking down, he saw that his sweat-soaked clothes were not, in fact, his nightclothes.

His eyes darted around the room as if the images from his dream would appear. Would Karin come through the door to haunt him for the things he had done? Or rather, for what he had attempted to do? He had not, in fact, done the deed. She was alive and whole.

He let out a long breath. Then he whispered thanks to God that He had stayed Stepan's hand. Not that Stepan had ever believed God was all that concerned with the goings on in the lives of humans. But, something had sent Pavel at just the right time to prevent Stepan from making the biggest mistake of his life. The near miss of which still plagued him.

As Stepan sat on the edge of the bed, he began removing his soaked garments. The air was cool against his bare skin. What was he to do? These nightmares were becoming more frequent. How could he convince his own mind that he was not to blame?

Jerking on his nightshirt, he grumbled to himself. *I refuse to take on the guilt for this!* He had not done anything wrong. The only thing he was at fault for was letting them go. This is what should torment him. They had wronged him and his father, and they deserved to be punished. Now, they were out there, probably contributing to the war effort. No doubt causing the deaths of Czechs loyal to the crown. Yes, this is where the guilt lay.

But when he lay back down and closed his eyes, Karin's face was before him yet again.

The fighting let up as night closed in. A heavy fog descended upon the camp, thick enough to disguise fellow soldiers from one another. It drove the enemy into a hasty cease-fire. Likewise, Pavel and his comrades stopped their own firing for lack of targets. Turning to Commander Zizka for further orders, they were met with a decision they did not expect—they would retreat into the cover of the darkness and fog.

Many grumbled as they wanted to stay and finish off the Royalist army, but Pavel knew that Zizka was leveraging their advantage. They had dealt a sound blow to an army against insurmountable odds already. Best not to tempt fate. Or, as he preferred to see it, lean too heavily on the graces of the Almighty. Yes, retreat was best. This day would forever be remembered by the Hussites as a great day. A battle that should have been a slaughter became a victory.

As they slipped away into the night, Pavel wondered after his friends. He had seen them but a few times during the battle. What had happened to them? It was not so much concern about their safety that plagued him. The Hussites had far too few casualties for him to be worried about that. No, the Hussites had been the cause of heavy losses this day.

But Pavel had noticed how the battle in Prague affected his friends. Would this battle forever taint them? Zdenek became frozen when he saw the advancing army. Would another fight break him completely? And what of Radek? He had grown all the more quiet of late. Never much of a talker, he was even less so now. What was happening in his head? It was difficult to say.

All of these things he used to occupy his mind so his thoughts would not dwell on the thing that made his heart ache: Karin. But as they marched through the foggy darkness, moving, almost creeping into the night, he had nothing more to distract him. How he missed her! Should he have allowed her to join the families that camped with them? No, that would have been selfish. It was dangerous for these women and children. Never had that been more evident than now. He would have a talk with Zizka about their presence in the camp.

The battlewagon in front of him stopped. What held it? Pavel maneuvered his horse around to the front of the cart. With a quick glance, he spotted what had occurred. One of the wheels was lodged in the muck of the marshy land. A driver had already dropped to the ground and worked to free it.

Pavel waved over several infantrymen as he dismounted. He instructed the men to assist him in pushing on the cart, leveraging it from its hampered state. They positioned themselves around the cart and pushed on Pavel's command. After some time of working at the wagon, it began to inch forward, creaking and groaning as it did so.

"Move, men!" Pavel called out. He shoved men farther away as he dove.

The cart crashed down.

Landing in the mud, Pavel barely had time to turn as a loosened flail flew straight toward him.

CHAPTER 5

INJURED

Petr had poured over books and papers for the better part of the night. His back and shoulders ached from the effort of holding his upper body in such an unnatural position. With naught but candlelight to illuminate his documents and writings, however, it couldn't be helped.

The door to his study creaked. He did not bother to look up. Servants attended to him throughout the night with tea and food as he had need. Perhaps another servant had been charged to bring him fresh tea.

Rustling fabric of large skirts drew his attention from his current writings on property rights. As he raised his eyes, his gaze was met not with a servant's weary look but with his wife's enchanting eyes.

Had she risen early, at this ungodly hour, and called for her maidservant to dress her for the day? He saw the remnants of sleep in her face. Her eyes drooped underneath heavy lids and her features betrayed her age today—the lines were deeper and her skin seemed to settle on her face. Had she slept at all last night?

"Lenka," he said as he straightened in his seat. He regretted the movement. His back protested and his shoulder muscles screamed in

79

pain. Closing his eyes against their collective outcry, he promised himself a hot soak later.

"You never came to bed," was all she said.

Nodding, he was careful to make slower movements. "I could not pull myself from my work." He waved a hand across his desk, indicating the piles of documents that had occupied him these last several hours.

"Is this not work our legal advisor should be doing?" Her brows knit together close to her eyes. He did not like to see her so concerned.

"Yes," he conceded, folding his hands together in front of his chest on the desktop. "But I cannot leave it all to him. I, too, need to be aware of the law."

Lenka sighed, nodding her head slowly, lips drawn into a tight line. Was there more she wanted to say? Did he want to hear it? His brain was quite over-taxed with the work it had accomplished. Perhaps too much. There was a throbbing behind his right eye. One of his massive headaches would not serve him well. He simply could not spend the next day or so in bed trying to rid himself of the confounded thing.

He did not realize he had brought a hand up to pinch the bridge of his nose against the pain until he saw Lenka's expression. Her raised brow and concerned eyes told him of her suspicions.

"You cannot deprive yourself of your rest." Her voice was gentle. Yes, she was rather concerned after his head pains.

He nodded. She was not wrong. She never was. If he did not love her so that would annoy him. Well, even more than it already did.

"I need just another hour and I'll retire." Then he remembered his promise. "*After* a hot bath."

She tilted her head to the side and gave him a serious look. He was not going to get that extra hour. As she opened her mouth, he prepared himself for a thorough scolding.

He was saved by a maidservant, come to deliver his fresh tea. He couldn't remember the last time he was so grateful for a servant's presence.

"Lida," Lenka said as the girl set the tray on a side table.

"Yes, my lady," the girl said as she curtsied.

"Please have a hot bath prepared for the Earl at once and have his valet lay out his night clothes." Lenka's tone did not invite dispute or discussion.

The young girl curtsied again and took her leave.

Lenka's gaze landed again on Petr. "Now, you may have ten minutes to tell me what you have learned. Then it's off to bed with you."

That was unexpected. Lenka did not make a habit of ordering him around. That did not change the wisdom of her words. So, he gathered his wits and let out a deep sigh. Leaning forward, he became aware of every muscle in his upper back.

"It doesn't seem there is a precedent. Unless our legal adviser can find something I've missed, it may be up to the judgment of the authorities."

"Isn't it always?"

"Yes and no. When there are laws to support a case, the judge has to observe them when making his decision. In our situation, however, if there are none to be found, the judge has more . . . discretion. I fear a judge could be swayed by the war or by Vlastik's money, position, and power. Who knows? Vlastik might even be able to bribe the judge." Petr watched Lenka's face.

As she absorbed what he said, her face fell and her eyes darkened. "That can't be legal!"

"It's not." He leaned back in his chair, rolling his shoulders into a more relaxed position, forcing his muscles to release. "But that doesn't mean it never happens. We are simpletons if we ignore the possibilities."

"So we are to count our property and money as lost?"

"I didn't say that. We will fight this in every appropriate way we can."

Lenka shook her head, lowering her face and putting a hand on her chin. She moved to one of the chairs on the other side of the desk and sat.

Petr stood, ignoring the tension in his muscles, and moved to her. "What is it?"

"Fighting. Everywhere there's fighting. It's too much. Our country is torn apart by war. Must our home be also?"

Against his better judgment and the increased throbbing in his head, he knelt on one knee in front of her. And, taking her hands in his, he rubbed the backs of her fingers.

"We will do what we must. If you would wish it, you can go to the summerhouse for a couple of months. I will send for you when it's over."

"No!" Lenka put a hand on his chest. "I want to stay with you. I will fight with you. By your side."

A warmth spread from his core. He did love this woman. Leaning forward, he pressed a brief kiss to her lips. And then the pounding in his head demanded attention. He pulled back, grimacing.

"Petr? Did I . . . ?" Lenka's brows furrowed, her forehead creasing.

"No, it's not you. It's this headache." He touched his fingers to his right temple.

"Then let's get you to your bedchambers." She stood and assisted him to his feet. And, arm-in-arm, they walked toward their chambers.

Zdenek scanned the camp. Where could she be? The number of women and children among the soldiers surprised him. This would not be in the months to come. It was inevitable. After this last battle, it was not feasible that they would continue with the camp. Zizka would find a safe place for them to remain, and he would insist they stay behind.

Radek spoke as he put out his bedroll, but Zdenek continued to eye the crowd. He hoped his friend's words were not important. Still, he heard the droning of his friend's voice, nagging at the back of his consciousness as he hunted.

Was she hiding from him? That did not seem likely. But it would reason that in this amount of time, he would have spotted her. Days had he searched. Since the battle's end.

"Zdenek!" Radek's insistent voice broke into his thoughts.

Only then did Zdenek turn to look at him.

Radek's face bore a stern expression. Had he known where Zdenek's mind was?

Zdenek shifted his focus to his own bedding. "I'm sorry. I did not hear you."

"I've been speaking of our plans. Will we stay with the camp?" Radek paced beside Zdenek.

What was with him? Something weighed on him. Was it this recent battle? No, it had been lingering long before. Zdenek just could not figure what. And he had not put in the effort to try. His thoughts had been on his own demons . . . and her.

"Zdenek?" This time Radek's voice was firm, louder.

"I apologize, friend. My thoughts are amiss today." He offered Radek a shrug and an apologetic look, but could do nothing further to assuage his guilt.

Radek rolled his eyes. "I know where your thoughts are. I only ask that you consider my question."

Zdenek thought hard. Radek's question. What was it? He had just asked. Their plans—he asked about their plans. Should they stay with the camp?

Meeting Radek's eyes, Zdenek stood. "I will give my life to defend the freedom of my people."

Radek crossed his arms, brows raised.

Zdenek focused on Radek's amused features. "And that means I will follow Commander Zizka. He is a sound leader, and I believe in him."

Radek's face fell. Was this not the answer he had expected? "And who are your people?" came his quiet voice. "The Hussites?"

Zdenek opened his mouth but paused before speaking. He supposed he was fighting on the side of the Hussites, but that's not how he saw it. His goal was to fight for Bohemia. And, as far as he could discern, Zizka and the Hussites were fighting for Bohemian rights and freedom. "I fight for the Czechs."

Radek sighed, glancing down at the ground and then back at Zdenek. Did he want to say more? If so, he held back. What stopped him?

Looking past Zdenek and into the crowd, he spoke, "I believe I have found what you are looking for." He nodded his head, indicating something just behind Zdenek.

Turning on the balls of his feet, Zdenek's eyes worked their way through the small gathering of people. There she was—Eva.

She moved from one side of the camp to the other, carrying a bucket of something. Water perhaps, as she was headed from the stream.

Making eye contact with Radek one more time, Zdenek then moved off in the direction of the girl who had so captivated him.

Zdenek closed the distance between them easily with his long legs. He was behind her in a matter of moments.

"Eva," he said, reaching to touch her arm. It was doubtful she would hear him amongst the crowd.

She jerked at his touch, sloshing water from her bucket as she spun and soaking him. Her face registered the shock she must have felt, and her hand flew to her open mouth.

"My lord, I apologize. I did not see you." She closed her eyes, and her cheeks colored. Was she embarrassed?

Zdenek stared at his drenched pants and raised his eyes to meet hers, laughing. "Do not worry yourself. I am uninjured. All is well."

Upon seeing his laughter, her face relaxed. But she did not smile. Something was amiss.

"May I walk you to your campsite?" His eyes settled on hers.

"I fear I now have no water for our meal." She peeked at him through long lashes. Such a bewitching sight.

"If I may, I would like to remedy that. After all, it is I who is responsible for your upturned bucket." Zdenek moved a step closer, indicating the bucket in her hands.

"As you wish," she said, nodding and turning back in the direction from which she had come.

He reached for the handle. As he grasped it, their fingers touched. "May I?"

She swallowed visibly.

Was he affecting her the way she affected him?

After a few brief moments, she nodded, relinquishing her hold on the vessel.

They walked in the direction of the stream, side by side. Along the way, their shoulders and arms brushed against each other in the thickness of the crowd.

A tingle traveled up Zdenek's arm and down his spine at each point of contact. How was he to make conversation with her? What did one say to such a maiden? Then he began to worry. Had they no commonalities?

Eva sniffled.

Zdenek turned and saw her wipe an errant tear.

Pausing, he laid a hand on her arm.

She halted but would not look at him.

"What has troubled you so, milady?" Brows furrowed, he watched her features as more tears came, but she remained silent. Stepping in front of her and lowering his head, he attempted to catch her eyes. They were wide and glassy, but they met his.

After some moments, she glanced around herself, and wiping at her tears, spoke, "My father is missing."

"Missing?"

"He never returned after the battle." This brought a fresh tear.

Zdenek took her hand in his. "We must go to Commander Zizka at once." Tugging at her, he moved toward the center of camp.

She stood her ground. "Patricie has already talked with one of his captains. Father is counted among the captured men."

Halting his movements, Zdenek felt his face fall as well as his heart. He knew all too well what that meant. Hussite prisoners would surely be sent to Kutna Hora to the silver mines. It was said this predominantly Catholic community took full advantage of the old silver mines and would throw the unfortunate captives down the shafts. Any not killed by the fall would die a slow death of hunger, dehydration, shock, and infection. Horrible. He felt sick.

Turning back to Eva, he wished with everything in him that he could gather her in his arms and comfort her. But that would not help.

Eva's eyes were on his as tears streaked down her face.

He worked to swallow past the lump in his throat. Was she looking to him for words of solace? What could he say? What could he do? Any words would seem hollow, empty in the light of such tragedy.

Unable to stop himself, he reached out and grazed the side of her face, wiping at the tears there.

She closed her eyes and leaned into his hand.

In the next moment, she stepped toward him, and he pulled her into his embrace before he could stop himself. Selfishly, he relished the feel of her. Could she sense that his heart was about to explode? But he remembered her tears and pressed a kiss to the top of her head.

"I'm sorry, Eva. I'm so sorry," he managed.

And those words seemed to be all that was necessary to release the floodgate.

She sobbed then, her body wracked and shuddering.

Still, he held her, wishing he could protect her from the harsh realities of the world and the truth of what her father would endure, and hold her forever.

Stepan gazed out the large window in the house's massive solar. From this vantage, he couldn't discern that he was anywhere but home. The landscapes in Cologne were not altogether different from what he was accustomed to in the Czech lands; sweeping lines of greenery created hillsides peaked with treetops. It was true this area was not quite as mountainous. Not only did this grand estate reside in Cologne, it was situated closer to the city as well. But no one would know that from where he stood. All he saw was lush greenery and peaceful nature.

It was just an illusion. All was in turmoil. Including his heart. He could not shake the images from his dream the previous night. Every time he closed his eyes, he watched in his mind's eye as he yet again plunged the sword into Karin's heart. And so, his eyes would open to find his hands sore and knuckles white from gripping whatever object happened to be nearby for him to steady himself.

Would he have? He had to believe that he would not. But the images coming from his mind were so powerful, so vivid; he began to doubt his own goodness. He began to fear what he was capable of.

A knock at the door interrupted his reverie. Glad for the distraction, he turned to see a household servant bowing.

"My lord, Professor Evzen has arrived and wishes to speak with you."

The manservant seemed to be working to maintain a veneer of calm. Was he fearful he had angered Stepan by his interruption?

"Please do send him in."

As the servant moved to leave, Stepan stepped away from the chair he leaned against and rubbed life back into his hands. He did not want the professor to see the effects of his terrifying daydreams.

Moments later, Professor Evzen was escorted into the parlor.

"*Dobry vecer*, Professor." Stepan tilted his head ever so slightly in the professor's direction.

"*Dobry vecer*." Evzen stepped further into the space. "It is good to see you."

"And you, Professor. I trust your journey was pleasant." Stepan spoke to the man in front of him, but his mind was still on the fading memory of his dream. Glancing around the room, he sought solace for his eyes, his thoughts. He couldn't focus.

"Yes, my lord. I cannot quite express my gratitude for your offer of sanctuary in the midst of all happening in Bohemia."

Stepan avoided Evzen's eyes. He could not see the man's expression. Nor did he truly care. These were simple pleasantries. And Stepan did so tire of pleasantries.

There were some moments of silence before the professor spoke again. "Shall we sit?"

Stepan looked back toward his mentor and, sighing deeply, nodded.

The men maneuvered around the furniture pieces in the center of the room to find places where they could converse with ease.

"Something troubles you," the professor said as they settled into their respective chairs. It was not a question.

Stepan took another deep breath and let it out through clenched teeth. Dare he share his dream? He had not told anyone of the true happenings between he, Pavel, and Karin that day. No, he had fabricated a tale, with true details woven in, for his father and whoever else needed to know. But no one knew he had almost . . .

Evzen ran a hand along the rich fabric on the settee. "You do not have to share. But you can trust me."

"It is nothing." Stepan shook his head and waved off the professor. "Nothing more than all this trouble with the Hussites."

Evzen nodded, but a quirked eyebrow told Stepan that his mentor knew there was something more behind Stepan's downcast affect.

Stepan chose to ignore it and push the conversation in this new direction. "I could never have imagined they would gain such support among the people or make such successes."

"Would you call a stalemate success?" Evzen questioned in the way he always did.

Stepan knew Evzen was pushing him to think harder. "When a

weak band of farmers goes up against a king's army, I would." Stepan's reply came out much harsher than he'd intended.

Evzen's eyes widened.

"And let us not forget they are courting Poland." Stepan dropped this information into Evzen's lap and shifted his gaze toward the window as if he could see all the way to the Polish border.

"Poland?" Evzen's tone was even.

This was new information he delivered. Stepan knew it. Yet the professor did not seem the least bit surprised. Was he doubtful of the veracity of the news?

"Yes—Poland." Stepan now focused on the professor, holding the man's gaze and leaning forward. "I found the evidence of it myself."

Then one of Evzen's eyebrows rose. There—he had gotten some reaction.

"So you are going on missions for the crown now?" The professor delivered this statement in that annoying way he had of asking a question without truly asking a question, but rather making a statement.

"Perhaps. I mean, yes. I mean . . . I am at the disposal of my king if he ever has need of my services. You know that."

Evzen nodded. "I do not think anyone could doubt that of you, my lord."

Stepan settled back into his seat, but he could not calm his racing heart. What was happening to him? He was loyal to the king. And he would do whatever was asked of him even. Even . . . The image of Karin from his dreams flashed across his consciousness. Yes, he could. He would . . . even kill.

Karin gazed out the window toward the east side of the baron's property. Yet her mind was not on the lush landscape before her, but on the delicacy of her situation. What was she to do? It was just impossible! If only she could write Pavel. No, that would not be ideal either. She did not wish to worry him. This was not the time to burden him with such a weight.

Looking down at her abdomen, yet unchanged by the child within, she found her hand already resting over the imagined swell. She closed her eyes and whispered a silent prayer in the midst of her confusion and dismay. This should be a happy time. And she *was* happy about this life growing inside of her.

But she was also fearful. Fearful of what it would mean for her and Pavel. What would life offer a child in the midst of the trials they faced? War. A country torn apart. A child is a gift to the world. The world should bring nothing but hope and promise to the new life entering it. She feared neither would be true.

Picking up the book in her lap, she focused on the words and tried not to think on the child. At least for the next half hour. Perhaps that would give her mind some peace. So she opened the book and pored over the words. Five minutes later, she found herself rereading the same paragraph for the fifth time. This would not do!

There was a sound . . . movement. Someone was in her bedchambers! She peered up to face the intruder and found herself looking at the figure of her husband. Frozen to the spot, she felt the warmth drain from her face. Was she looking at a ghost?

Her mouth moved, but no words came forth.

The figure of Pavel moved.

She shrank back into the chaise lounge, her hands clawing at the chair as if to pull further away from him. Why had she conjured this image of Pavel? Or was it truly a ghost? Had something happened to her beloved?

"Karin," he spoke.

Her heart nearly stopped beating.

The mirage continued to move toward her.

There was nowhere to run. No other choice. Karin utilized the only weapon she had at her disposal—the book. She threw it at the apparition.

It hit him and thudded to the floor.

He grunted when it struck him.

Jerking her head to meet his eyes, she read his shock as real as her own. Shouldn't the book have sailed through the ghostly figure? Now she faced the fact that he might truly be here.

"Pavel?" Her words came out as a gasp and her heart raced.

His face continued to betray his questioning concern. Was her behavior so strange?

Only then did she allow her eyes to take him in. His appearance was more haggard than she remembered. Sandy blond hair was mussed and clothes disheveled. And his arm was wrapped in a sling.

"Karin?" His voice was firm but his confusion evident.

With slow movements, she stood and took the steps needed to close the distance between them. Reaching forward with a shaking hand, she felt her fingertips graze his face. Once they made contact, Pavel let out a breath and pulled her into his embrace with his good arm.

She held to him tightly, burying her face in the crook of his neck. And she allowed her tears to come.

Pavel nuzzled the hair near her ear and whispered things she could not discern as he held her so tightly that she almost could not breathe.

But she didn't care. He was home. He was alive. She lingered for several moments, taking in his presence and relishing the feel of his arms.

At long last, Pavel loosened his hold and she released him to draw back.

"I can't believe you're here." Her eyes glazed with fresh tears.

Pavel wiped them with the pad of his thumb as the corners of his mouth angled. Leaning forward, he pressed a gentle kiss to her lips.

When he pulled back, her knees became weak and her head swam. In the span of a few moments, she had experienced fear, elation, joy, peace, and a rush of love so powerful it overflowed from her eyes.

"I think I need to sit down." She gripped Pavel's good arm.

He led her to the chaise she had earlier abandoned. As she sat, he took a place beside her, not releasing her hand.

Karin took several deep breaths. Would she ever gather her wits about her? Then she turned back toward her husband. Wanting to lose herself in his eyes, she sought out those blue orbs. The deeper she looked, the heavier the weight of guilt became. One of her hands flew to her midsection. Should she tell him? Her eyes fell. Only then did she truly notice his injured arm.

"You are hurt." Her eyes were on his, brows furrowed. "What happened?"

"It's nothing you need to concern yourself with." He reached forward and cupped her face. "I will heal. That is all you need to know."

She pulled away from his hand. "I want to know what happened."

He gazed at her for a few moments and sighed. Was he truly thinking of not telling her? At length, he spoke. "It was an accident with some of our weapons. My arm was injured."

"How exactly?"

"Karin, that is not important. I only want you to know that it happened, and I have been sent home to be seen by a doctor, to recover. Commander Zizka did not need me slowing them down and eating up rations when I could not fight." He laughed a little as if it was some kind of farce.

Karin did not laugh. "What manner of injury did you sustain?"

Pavel sighed again and gave her a long look. "It was from a flail."

"A flail? Did someone . . . ?"

"No." He held a hand up. "It came loose from a falling wagon and I raised my arm to block my face. The flail struck me and wrapped around my arm."

"Block your face?" It did not sound good. Pavel seemed quite nonchalant about the whole thing. What would have happened had he not reacted so fast? She twisted away and closed her eyes against the images that came, unbidden, into her mind.

Pavel lifted his hand to her face again, brushing her hair back. "I am all right, my love. Let us focus on what we do have. I am well. And we are afforded some time together."

Karin nodded but did not turn to face him or open her eyes as the ghastly impressions continued to plague her. A tear slipped free.

Moving closer, Pavel wrapped his free arm around her and drew her toward his body. "No, do not fear. God is with us, remember? It is He who holds our future, our wellbeing. He is the One who has our path laid out."

Karin leaned her head on his shoulder and nodded against him. But there was still fear in her heart. Could she trust God with her husband?

A call rang forth throughout the men at the stream. It was time to move on. Radek placed a hand on the saddle and checked the simple straps. Stretching out his back, he delayed resuming his place atop his steed for every second he could. For once he was there, it would be a while before they would stop to refresh the horses again.

He moved his hand along the flank of his companion. It was true he rather enjoyed the company of animals more than people. They never pushed for conversation or asked hard questions. No, his horse was content to just listen when he cared to speak. And it didn't matter how quiet he was or how much sense he made. If he wanted to start a thought out loud and finish it in his head, his horse did not care.

Now at the animal's face, he placed his hand between her eyes and let his palm slide down the length of her muzzle and graze the soft skin of her nostrils. The horse whickered in response and moved her nose against his hand to encourage him further. He obliged, moving his hand down her face once more before running his hand further down to give her strong, muscular neck a good pat.

"You missed your calling," he heard a voice behind him. "You should have been a stable boy."

Radek shot Zdenek a cold look. He knew his friend was only joking, but he was in no mood to be insulted for any reason.

"I did not mean . . . " Zdenek started, his features falling.

Radek waved him off as he continued to pat his steed. "It is all right."

"I do think we may get left if you spend any more time on your grooming." Zdenek motioned toward the retreating group, moving from their places all around them and heading east.

Radek sighed, watching the farmers, merchants, villagers—all well-meaning and impassioned men—as they moved on to follow Commander Zizka wherever he would lead them. And why shouldn't they?

He could think of several good reasons why not. And only a couple of reasons why they should. But those reasons seemed to outweigh the logic of the former. He, too, had committed to this commander, to these people—his people. Hadn't he?

So, he gripped the saddle and pulled himself up. Gathering the reins and nodding to Zdenek, he moved after the large group. He was fortunate to be on horseback. Many of the men were walking. At least most of the women and young children had places in wagons. But he was sure this caravan was a sight. And not an intimidating one. Truly they were no army.

Yet they had succeeded against a real army. That should not have happened. He could not deny that Zizka's leadership had proven effective. Maybe it was worth sticking around.

Radek stole a glance at his friend. Now there was a committed man. Even more so now that he had discovered the brunette in the ranks. What were the odds? But Zdenek was completely taken. Never mind that it would never, could never, be.

Zdenek glanced at him. Had he sensed Radek's eyes on him?

Either way, Radek offered him a smile, which Zdenek returned with some reluctance.

"What?" Zdenek's full smile became half-crooked.

"Nothing," Radek said, turning his attention back to his horse and the road ahead. "I only wondered how your talk with that brunette . . . what was her name? Ivana? Iva?"

"Eva." His face colored. "Eva. Her name is 'Eva'."

Radek stifled a laugh and nodded.

Zdenek remained silent.

"Well?"

"Well what?" Zdenek's eyes were trained forward and the color on his face deepened. Was he avoiding Radek's gaze? Radek could barely contain another bout of laughter.

"How was your walk the other day? You never did tell me." Radek did his best to make his voice sound as innocent as possible.

"It was . . . um . . . " Zdenek appeared as if he might hurt himself looking for the right words. "Nice."

"Nice?" Radek teased back. "Hmm. It's been a while since I had a 'nice' walk with a beautiful lady."

Just when Radek was certain there were no deeper shades of red for a person's face to turn, Zdenek proved him wrong. He could not stop the small laugh that escaped his lips.

Zdenek shot him a stern look and urged his horse a few paces ahead of Radek's.

Taking a deep breath, Radek enjoyed the last moments of laughter before his attentions returned to the present. And he again began to wonder why he was with this group at all. He did not have to make any decisions now, though. There would be rest and respite at their destination. In Usti.

CHAPTER 6
SECRETS

The doctor removed the last bandage on Pavel's arm. Karin sat nearby, her hands clinched in her lap. Now that the injuries were displayed, she fought a wave of nausea. That was becoming more and more difficult to do these days. But this fresh wave was for an altogether different reason. She saw the damage the flail had done. And it had been vicious.

His arm was a crisscross of scrapes among a myriad of bruises. There were the surface scrapes that did not bother her, but there were also the deeper wounds, where the flail had dug into his flesh with great force. She tried not to imagine these kinds of wounds on his face. He could have lost his eyes . . . or worse. No, she need not think on that.

"Whoever stitched these did a fair job," Dr. Doubek commented as he maneuvered Pavel's arm this way and that, checking it over.

Occasionally, Pavel would grimace, but no sound escaped. He was brave. Braver than she wanted him to be.

"Thank you. It was one of my friends. I'll have to forward your compliments. He did not even want to do it."

The doctor nodded as he continued to examine the arm. He twisted Pavel's arm in an odd angle.

Pavel sucked in a breath.

Karin almost jumped out of her seat. She was ready to come to his aid. Thankfully, she kept herself in the chair and neither Pavel nor the doctor noticed her movement. They were both focused on his injured arm.

"You will need to rest the arm. Keep it in the sling. Are you in any pain?"

Pavel glanced at Karin. Was he afraid to speak the truth in front of her? She could handle it. His eyes returned to the doctor's and he nodded.

"Nothing I cannot manage, but there is some amount of pain."

Her heart flipped in her chest. Why, she did not know. Of course he was in pain. How could he not be? So why did it bother her for him to voice it?

"I will give you a tea to help."

Karin had heard those words before. But she was determined he would get his tea. Regularly.

"And you need to keep this arm clean. Regular washing. But not in a bath—with a cloth. I'll put on fresh bandages today. I'll need to train your manservant on how to wrap your arm so you can put on clean bandages every few days."

"Doctor," Karin interjected. "I would like to change his bandages myself."

"You, my lady?" The doctor was skeptical and his features read it well. "This is a job better suited for his manservant."

Pavel's eyes met Karin's. "I don't want you to have to . . . "

"I insist," Karin said with an intensity she had not intended. And upon seeing their faces, she thought better of it.

Pavel was accustomed to her spirited nature, but she didn't want to disrespect him by showing the doctor she was not submissive. So, she softened her tone. "Please."

The doctor looked from Karin to Pavel and back to Karin. He

sighed. "I will at least insist the manservant be called to be shown as well."

Pavel nodded and Karin motioned to the maidservant picking up the old bandages stained with dark red that she should retrieve Pavel's valet.

Karin's stomach twisted anew as she got a look at the bandages in the girl's hands. So distracted was she that she almost missed Pavel's next question of the doctor.

" . . . I return to my unit?" Pavel trailed off.

Karin blinked several times. What did he say? How could he be so eager to rejoin his unit? He had just come home. He'd been here less than a day and already his thoughts were on returning? Her stomach sank. It did not help her nauseated feeling.

The doctor gave him a long look. Did he want to speak to the matter? All he said was, "I think you should give it three weeks to mend. Then we can check. But I think you will be able to use your arm at that time."

Pavel relaxed into his seat as if this was the information he truly needed. Not if he was going to ever be normal again. Not when could he and his wife resume normal activities. But when he could get back to his unit. The more she thought on it, the less she could contain the anger bubbling in her. At least it quelled the nausea.

The maidservant returned with Pavel's valet, and the doctor began cleaning Pavel's stitched wounds.

Karin tried to pay attention, but her vision blurred, blinded by emotion. Perhaps it was a good idea after all that the manservant was here to observe as well.

Pavel's eyes remained closed as they worked on his arm. How unpleasant was this for him? But she could not feel sympathy for him. Not when she was so angry and hurt.

Every few minutes, his eyelids would slide open and his eyes would meet hers. Then a smile would play at the corners of his lips. It tugged at her heart. He was a charmer. But she found herself looking away and avoiding those crystal blue orbs. Deep down, she wanted to be angry. It was better than the other emotions swirling beneath the surface.

Once the doctor declared his work complete, Pavel's arm was once again encased in bandages and held in place with a more adequate sling than before.

Pavel offered the doctor a tired smile. "Thanks."

"I'll be back," the doctor said. "Be mindful to rest and keep it clean. Especially if you want to get back to your unit sooner rather than later." Dr. Doubek stood.

"Yes, doctor." Pavel rose as well.

Karin found herself a little more unsteady than she expected but got to her feet as well. "Yes, thank you, doctor. We will be mindful of what you said."

Pavel's valet motioned toward the door and escorted the doctor out, leaving Pavel and Karin alone.

Karin glanced at Pavel.

His eyes were on her, his gaze intense.

She pivoted away and moved to the room's sole window. Standing off to the side, she leaned against the frame and let her hands graze the curtain. Karin felt more than heard him come up behind her.

He reached out a hand toward hers, grazing her skin and letting his fingers trace a trail down her forearm.

Karin moved a step away, looking into his face. How could he not understand?

His brows furrowed.

Perhaps he did understand.

"What is the matter, my love?"

Why did he have to woo her with his rich baritone and words of love? She fought the urge for her resolve to melt.

"What makes you think something is wrong?" Why was she playing games with him? Baiting him?

"I can see you are angry, Karin. Please talk to me." His voice was earnest, thick with emotion. Yet she could not let go of her right to be mad.

"Whatever could be the matter?" She challenged him, stopping her retreat and meeting him face to face. "You are ever so eager to return to your unit. To leave me behind again."

She watched his features. It was as if she had slapped him in the face. Perhaps because he knew she was right. Deflating into the chaise near the window, she fought tears. That would not serve her anger. And that's what she was. Angry.

There was silence for several, rather long moments as they squared off.

At long last, he moved toward her, taking a seat on the edge of the bed near the chaise. "You know that's not true. I don't want to leave you. I . . . the truth is I . . . ache for you when we are apart."

She glanced up to meet his eyes as if she could gauge the truth of his statement there. But her heart read his veracity better than her eyes did.

"You misunderstand," he continued. "If I am eager to rejoin my unit, it is in hopes to end this war and make our country once again safe for you, for us."

As much as she fought to hold on to her anger, it began to dissipate.

"Our people are out there . . . hurting, trying to survive. And I can help them. God has called me to help them. Can you understand that?" He stood and moved closer to her.

She wanted to retreat again, but found herself unable to move.

He reached down and touched her face. Only then did she realize she was crying.

"I just . . . " she started, but a wave of emotion overwhelmed her, threatening to crush her.

"What?" His voice was soft and gentle. His hand was tender as he slid onto the chaise's seat beside her and drew her to his chest with his good arm.

Then she cried openly. And she knew. She wasn't angry. Not truly. At least not at him. Maybe at this war that had torn their country, their world apart . . . and was tearing them apart. The emotions she had tried to smother came rushing to the surface. It was too much.

And Pavel held her as she fell apart.

But on the edge of her consciousness, she felt a nudging, an urging to trust. To turn over this fear, this worry, and all these feelings of helplessness to Him who is able to carry them.

Still, she resisted. No, she could handle these feelings. Especially now that she and Pavel were of one mind again. She might even get up the courage to tell him about the baby. Another time. For now, she would bask in his love.

Zdenek watched as Eva tilted her head back and laughed. He enjoyed watching her laugh. He enjoyed making her laugh. He just enjoyed her. And all the more as they spent time together. It seemed time was in ample supply since they had been in Usti.

Seated on blankets across from one another, they had been conversing with ease for most of the afternoon. Zdenek popped another bite of bread into his mouth. He smiled as Eva's laughter subsided and her gaze returned to him. Something passed between them in that moment. It started in the pit of his stomach and crept into his chest. It was a warmth that spread and tingled as it did so. But it soon permeated his whole being. He could get used to this feeling.

"Why are you looking at me like that?" Eva spoke up. Her cheeks colored. The brilliant pink on her fair skin set against her dark hair made her all the more attractive. He fought the urge to reach out and touch the side of her face where it was highlighted.

"Like what?" He was fearful he sounded drunk. Even to him, his words seemed slurred.

She giggled, her features becoming even more pink. "Like I'm a piece of chocolate to be devoured."

He stifled a laugh and looked at the ground. Was he so obvious? His own face warmed. Working to gather his thoughts, he knew he needed a response. And one that would not make her want to slap him.

"Zdenek?" her voice purred his name.

He closed his eyes against the emotions and sensations rushing through him. He had to think! She wanted an answer.

He raised his head and gazed at her. "Because, my lady, you . . ."

"There you are, Zdenek." Radek's voice interrupted him. He brought his horse to a halt, just short of Zdenek and Eva.

Zdenek was on his feet, his face warming even more. To have been interrupted during such a tender moment! As if Radek needed more to tease him about.

"Yes, seems you found me." Zdenek stole a glance toward Eva before turning his attention to Radek.

He did not miss the surprised confusion on her face. Was she surprised at his reaction? Was he wrong to react this way? Or did Radek surprise her? Maybe she only expected to be introduced.

"Radek, this is Eva." Zdenek reached over, offering a hand to help Eva to her feet. He could not help the tingling sensation in his skin where their hands met. He had to force himself to keep his attention on the present. "Eva, this is Radek."

Eva made a slight curtsy for Radek as he dismounted. "A pleasure, my lord."

My lord? Why was she acting so odd? Then Zdenek realized. She wasn't acting strangely at all. This was entirely appropriate. That made his heart drop.

Radek dipped his head in some semblance of a bow. "Likewise. But I believe we have met before."

"Yes. At the viscount's ball in Hradek Kralove." Eva was all politeness and rank with Radek. Why?

"Zdenek." Radek shifted his gaze back to his friend. "Commander Zizka wishes to speak with the unit commanders."

And now Radek was being a bit strange to disregard Eva's presence. How could he not know how important she was to Zdenek? He must know. All of his teasing certainly testified to that.

There was silence. Then Zdenek realized they were both looking at him—Radek with expectation, Eva with curiosity. He wanted so much to make this better, but he did not know how. Regardless, the commander called for his presence and he must go.

Turning to Eva, he said, "It has been a pleasure."

She nodded and curtsied toward him. But he did not miss the sadness that grazed her eyes.

"I shall see you again," he interjected.

Again, she nodded, but the fire in her had been extinguished. She moved back in the direction of her family's cart.

Radek's horse shifted. "Let her go. We are needed elsewhere."

Zdenek peered at Radek, unsure what his friend meant. But Zdenek did not push the issue. He simply nodded and about-faced to follow Radek.

The entire walk to where Zizka gathered the men was spent in silence. Radek did not seem to know what to say, and Zdenek certainly did not know.

What had just happened? One minute he and Eva were laughing, and the next they were not. And what's more, he seemed to have hurt her.

Radek came to a stop beside Zdenek and his attention refocused on his surroundings. They had arrived at Zizka's temporary home. He was even then speaking with his second-in-command as the others gathered around him. It was not long before one of the men alerted the commander that everyone was present.

"Thank you for coming," Zizka's voice boomed.

They could have been in the far reaches of the camp and still heard him. He hoped the commander was not planning on dispensing sensitive information. Glancing around, he noted that he seemed to be the only one bothered in the least by the man's volume.

"As you know, I have been charting Usti for defensive and strategic purposes. I have determined that it is not sufficient for our reasons. Therefore, we have no choice but to move our camp."

There were murmurs of dissatisfaction among the group. No one, it seemed, wanted to pack up and move again. But Zdenek knew they would do as they were told.

Zizka put his arms in the air. It served its purpose and the clamoring died down.

"A small town south from here, Tabor, will be much more suited to becoming a military center. There is already a gathering of Hussites there and the population continues to increase. The layout of the land is far more appropriate for what we seek."

The commander paused and the men commenced talking amongst themselves.

Zizka allowed them to, his face set, features firm. "I have every hope this will be a permanent placement for our camp."

The murmurs became those of excitement.

Zdenek remained silent. Every few seconds, someone would nudge his arm and make a comment in his direction. But he was too distracted to listen or respond.

What would happen with him and Eva? Once they arrived at Tabor, would the military then strike out on their own? Would the spark between him and Eva burn out before it had even had a chance? And why all this strangeness between Radek and Eva? The more he thought, the more questions he had.

Evening closed in on the Bornekov's stately home. Lenka's carriage pulled through the gate and toward the entrance so she could step out near the massive front door. Peaceful as it was, she relished this time of day and welcomed the close of another busy cycle of the sun.

She had been on her feet, it seemed, since before dawn. There were more things that would keep her still into the night.

Her thoughts remained on this evening's meeting. It had been her first. Would it be her last? Prudence begged she wait until Petr agreed to accompany her, but she long ago tired of his resistance. No, the time had come for her to find out what it meant to be a Hussite.

So, she attended one of the talks given by a leader of the local Utraquist movement. It had been rather . . . interesting. The speaker did not display the passion she'd come to expect from the more radical Hussites. Yes, it was true the Utraquists were not as extreme as the Taborites, the group Karin would surely find herself at home with. But would Lenka find agreement with them as well? She doubted it.

The Taborites wanted to bring an end to everything Lenka knew —not only the Catholic Church, but also the very manner in which her family lived. If they had their way, everyone would be equal. That was not possible. It was too far reaching and too much for Lenka to support.

Lenka made her way through the cavernous hallways toward the large solar. Petr was there, seated in his favorite chair, reading a missive of some sort. As she entered the room, he glanced up.

"How was the meeting?" He set the papers to the side.

"Different." She took her seat adjacent to his.

"Different?"

"Yes. The meeting was quite different from what I'd expected."

"Different? How?" Petr ran a hand along the arm of the chair.

"The speaker spoke only of communion of both kinds. And of peace with the Catholic Church."

Petr's brows rose.

"Yes. Imagine, Petr, peace." The words rushed out of her. "A Hussite faction seeking peace."

"It does sound incredible."

"But true. What if all Hussites could be convinced—?"

"Let's not make too much of this one speech by one man."

Lenka nodded, lowering her head. Her heart dropped, but her husband was right. She need not be impulsive. Raising her eyes to meet his once more, she found him staring at her. A longing had settled in his gaze. A longing for what she could not say. But it was fleeting. There for a moment and then gone.

"There has been word from Karin."

Lenka's body came to life. She sat straighter, and her limbs tingled.

Petr quirked a brow. "Here is yours. I have read mine." He extended his arm and pushed sealed papers toward her.

How had she missed them? They lay next to her chair.

With shaking fingers, she reached over and gathered the parchments. Moments later, she had broken the seal and began poring over the precious words.

Mother,

So much has happened, I scarcely know where to begin. Pavel has decided to join the fight for our freedom. I support him in this, but I worry. And so I am torn. Must it be this way? I want to encourage him in fighting for our cause. In fact, I long to believe in our cause enough to sacrifice even my husband. But I fear I do not. Does this make me a hypocrite? That I lack the kind of faith and trust in our Lord's sovereignty over even this matter? Of course He will take care of Pavel. Of course He will watch over us. He has walked with us through so much. But still my heart worries.

And that is only the beginning. There is more. My heart is heavy as I share the news I have held closest to my heart. Dearest Mother, I hold you in the strictest confidence as I count you among one of the precious few who know the following. I am with child . . .

A small sound erupted from Lenka's throat. Her hand flew to her mouth in an attempt to contain it, but not soon enough. As her eyes shot toward her husband, she was met with his dark orbs staring her down, his features chiseled with concern.

"Something amiss?"

Lenka did not trust herself to speak, so she shook her head.

Petr's furrowed brow told of his doubt in the veracity of her claim.

She lowered her hand to her lap and swallowed hard, putting on her calmest smile. "It is nothing, dear. Just some unexpected news."

Slowly dipping his head once, Petr hesitated before returning to his missive.

Once Lenka assured herself that he indeed had become occupied, she returned to the letter.

> . . . I know this should be happy news, but it is nothing of the sort. Pavel expressed a desire to wait until there was peace once again in our lands. And I agreed. How could this have happened? Was I so careless? Now I fear to burden him further would be unforgivable. He has returned home, wounded. It is too much! To think I almost lost him. A flail struck his arm. It could have been his heart! But I cannot share these things with him either. Oh, Mother, how am I to keep up this mask? This charade? Is there hope for me?
>
> I know God will watch over us, over me, over Pavel. But I fear I have too many doubts. My heart is a dark cloud. And I pray for sun.
>
> My prayers are with you and Father as well. May this letter find you in good health and in good spirits. Keep me in your heart and in your prayers. And hold my confidence, I beg of you.
>
> Until I see you again,

Your katka,
Karin

Lenka swallowed the tears welling within her. Stealing a glance at her husband, she assured herself that he was indeed engrossed in his papers. Laying the precious letter in her lap, Lenka let her eyes close and she took her daughter's requests to the only place she could.

Stepan moved through the halls of the large house he was becoming accustomed to. His footfalls echoed as he strode past the elaborately decorated rooms, and he moved with purpose toward his destination. There was one thing on his mind. He needed to speak with his father.

There was some amount of speed in his step but also determination. Would his father be pleased with his decision? Would that affect his plans?

It was no secret that Stepan longed for his father's approval. Or that he had gone to great lengths to secure it. Or that he had fallen short. Time after time. Was his father so difficult to please or was Stepan destined to forever disappoint?

If only he could know what it was his father expected of him. Then, perhaps, he could fulfill his purpose and release this burden. That, however, did not seem likely. He would ever be guessing and striving then.

Perhaps this time, he thought . . . yes, his father would be pleased this time.

Stepan found himself standing at the end of a great hall in front of a large mahogany door. He raised his fist and banged on the hard surface.

"Come," came his father's gruff voice from the other side of the sturdy wood frame.

He pushed the heavy door out of his way and entered the viscount's private solar. The man sat in a comfortable chair taking in some wine and staring out the window. His gaze diverted to Stepan as he entered.

Muttering something indistinguishable, Vlastik raised his tankard for the servant to refill.

Stepan attempted to hide his disappointment at his father's easy dismissal, but waited until his father's cup was filled and the viscount had taken a long swig. Only then did Vlastik turn his attention back to his son.

"My lord," Stepan offered him a slight bow. "I have come to inform you that I intend to take my leave of—."

"Oh?" Vlastik's eyebrows rose.

"It is my hope to join with Pope Martin's Crusade against the Hussites, Wycliffites, and all other heretics in Bohemia."

The viscount lowered his tankard. "I see." There was no mistaking the smile that touched his features.

Stepan's heart pounded. "Yes, Father, I will ride out at first light and join with the other crusaders gathering forces to enter the Czech lands."

Vlastik sat his cup down and stood, maneuvering over to Stepan. He met his son's gaze and gave him a hearty clap on the back. "I know you will make me proud, son."

"I will, Father."

Vlastik bobbed his head and moved back to his chair. "Sit." He waved an arm toward a nearby chair. "Share a drink with me. Our revenge over the Bornekovs is almost complete!"

Stepan worked to hide his confusion. He was about to risk his life in a cause he thought his father cared about, and yet Vlastik seemed more concerned about some legal battle with Karin's parents. It left a bitter taste in Stepan's mouth.

But he couldn't say any of that. So, he tried to speak simply when he found his voice, forcing his tone to remain even. "Yes, Father. I regret I cannot stay for that drink. I have many preparations to oversee."

"Of course you do. Fare thee well, my son." Vlastik raised his cup in the air and drained the remainder of the liquid.

"Yes, Father." Stepan bowed again before turning and taking his leave.

Karin stirred in her sleep. Something was not right. Her body was . . . something was not right. Then she felt it. Something in her stomach. It felt strange, yet wonderfully delightful at the same time. She opened her eyes and laid a hand over the almost indiscernible swell of her abdomen.

But as she moved her hand over her midsection, she felt nothing. Whatever it was had stopped. Snuggling back into the softness of the bed, she closed her eyes.

And there it was again. A whispery movement deep in her abdomen. Shifting onto her back, she placed both hands over her stomach and waited. A few minutes later, she was rewarded with the same sensation. If she had to describe it, she would say angel wings fluttered inside her. But she knew what it was. It was her baby. It was life.

The baby moved again, and she let out a small cry. She moved a hand to cover her mouth. With Pavel so near, she did not wish to wake him. But part of her wanted to. It was time to tell him, wasn't it?

Pavel shifted beside her. Whether from her movements or from the sound she had made, she did not know, but something had caused him to stir. In a state between sleep and wakefulness, he reached for her. Intertwining their fingers, she grasped his hand and tugged him closer. Her movements were as if by instinct. She was no longer thinking them through. Would she tell him?

He opened his eyes and he maneuvered closer to her in the darkness.

"Are you well?" came his concerned voice.

"Yes," her voice broke through tears.

His hand was immediately on her face.

"Why the tears, my love?"

"I'm just . . . so happy. I love you so much!" She moved her face to press a kiss to the palm of his hand.

He drew her face to his and kissed her lips.

What started out as a simple kiss, reaffirming their love, soon became more urgent, more wanting.

She needed, even wanted to tell him about the baby. They would share this happiness together. But as she pulled away to speak to him, his voice filled the space between them.

"Is it safe?"

Her heart sank. She knew what he meant—was it safe for them to be together and not risk a baby. And all their conversations about waiting came rushing back. All his words about not wanting to bring a baby into this war pressed into her mind. And she lost her resolve.

Her eyes slid shut and fresh moisture slid down her face. She was thankful he would not be able to see it in the dark.

"Yes, it's safe."

He pulled her to himself with his strong arm and snuggled her, pressing his face to her hair, her neck, and finally, his lips to her face. And she lost herself in the comfort his love brought her.

CHAPTER 7
PLANS

Eva was all too ready when they slowed the horses and carts at their final campsite in Tabor. It had not been a long journey from Usti to Tabor, but any trip in their rickety wagon felt ten times longer.

Hopping out of the driver's seat, Eva rubbed her lower back. Her bones continued to vibrate as if she were still rocking in the wooden vehicle. There must be a better way! Eva could feel every one of her twenty-eight years.

Patricie flung her upper body this way and that to stretch her joints. She made quite the spectacle. But it was a necessity. And Eva did not blame her. But she did laugh.

When Patricie shot her a sharp look, she quieted. Only because she knew her sister was not in the mood to be teased.

"Time to set up camp," Eva announced, giving Patricie a meaningful look while putting on her bravest smile. Getting right to work was not what Eva wanted either.

Patricie groaned.

Eva longed for their comfortable beds back in Hradek Kralove just as much Patricie did. They never knew how enjoyable those beds were or how good they had it until they were camping under the stars with this extra-large extended family of sorts.

The hard mats on the ground were a far cry from the hay-stuffed beds in their simple, yet fairly well off house. And ever since she and Patricie had assisted with the women and children after that first battle, they had become the designated camp go-to's, it seemed. They had not the time to meet so many needs.

But, she supposed, they were blessed to be a blessing. It put life into their otherwise dull days. And distracted them from their loss.

Although Eva was quite certain Patricie would rather her day be boring than to have so many hands reaching out. Eva did not mind so much. She did long for more respite from it all. And more time with Zdenek.

Where had that come from? After the way things went during their previous interaction, she was not sure she would, or should, see more of him. It was clear his friend did not think much of her.

And why should he? She was a merchant's daughter. Not of the proper station to be receiving such attentions from Zdenek, who had noble blood in his veins. Yes, she and Zdenek might ignore that fact when they were together because of the ease with which they conversed and the enjoyment they seemed to have with each other, but it remained a hard fact all the same. It was not likely his parents would ever accept her as a suitable choice as his bride.

Eva let out a heavy sigh as she continued to pull things from the wagon. She feared her heart might already be too involved. Perhaps it was best if she did not see him again.

"Are you dreaming of that tall man?" Patricie teased from the back of the cart.

Eva glanced in her direction. "Not for much longer. I promise."

Her tone must have given Patricie second thoughts about teasing her further as there were no other remarks.

Just as well. Eva sifted through their cooking wares to find the large pot. She would need to go to the stream and fetch water for dinner preparations.

And though she tried to fight them, tears moistened her eyes. Reaching up to brush them away, she let out a frustrated grunt. This just would not do.

A hand settled on her shoulder.

She jerked in that direction.

Patricie stared back at her. Sympathy marked her features. "He didn't deserve you anyway."

Eva grinned despite her tears and embraced her sister.

As they pulled apart, Patricie reached out for the pot. "I will fetch the water."

This was a surprise. Patricie did not mind hard work, but she hated making trips to the stream and carrying the large pot of water back, bearing such a load. Perhaps Patricie was giving her time to herself.

Eva handed over the pot.

Watching her sister walk toward the stream did not serve its intended purpose. She did not feel any better being alone. If possible, the emotions welled all the more. Feeling foolish, she questioned herself. How could she have let her heart get so attached? And so quickly? Hadn't she known all along this was the situation?

Facing the cart, she leaned forward, placing a hand on the side to steady herself while she wiped at her tears.

A hand fell on her shoulder again. Had Patricie heard her sniffles and returned to check on her?

"You don't have to baby me, Patricie. We need that water . . . " she said as she turned.

And found herself face to face with Zdenek. Her pulse quickened and she tried to take a step back, but with the cart behind her, there was nowhere to retreat.

"Eva, are you unwell?" His eyes were filled with concern.

She gazed at the ground, fighting fresh tears. Why did her heart have to twist in her chest even now?

"No, I . . . that is, I'm quite all right. I just . . . " She couldn't think of a way to finish that sentence, so she let it trail off, peering up into his face.

Zdenek's mouth was drawn, his eyebrows furrowed. His concern after her was certain, but there was something more. Sadness? A hand rose toward her, but it stopped just short of her face. It hung between them for a handful of seconds before it fell to his side.

"Please, Zdenek, I do not want you to feel as if you owe me anything. Least of all an explanation." Why would he not just leave? Then she could begin the process of getting over this whole nonsense.

His eyes searched hers, his gaze intense. He opened his mouth, but no words were forthcoming. In a bold move, he reached over and took her hand in his. "I think I owe you more than you think. You brought a part of me to life I did not know existed. Please do not make me go."

She was caught, pinned by his words. But the truth of who they were continued to stab at her heart. It did not matter what she wanted or what he thought about his feelings. "I must."

He nodded, releasing her hand and turning to walk away.

She watched him take the steps that would create distance between them, her heart lurching with each one. After several paces, she could not fight back the tears or her outburst any more.

"Zdenek, don't go!"

He spun, setting his eyes on hers. Only a breath passed before he closed the distance between them. Pulling her into his embrace, he claimed her lips in a moment that forever sealed the fate of her heart.

Stepan urged his horse forward. His first official mission for the sake of the crusade was both important and boring. He and a few others had been charged with escorting a ranking Hussite, Cenek, back to Prague after his stay with Sigismund in Breslau. Apparently, the king decided to curry favor with the man. Cenek's stay with Sigismund had no shortage of grandeur and fanfare.

"Do you think the king succeeded?"

Jerking toward the sound, Stepan noticed that one of the other noblemen had brought his horse alongside Stepan's. He glanced back at the carriage as if Cenek could hear their conversation. Then Stepan focused his attention forward again. "Perhaps we shouldn't be discussing such things."

"Perhaps," the man agreed. "But we must find something to talk about. We have a long journey ahead of us."

Stepan relaxed his shoulders. "I'm not sure I can say that I know much of why the king asked this—" Stepan took a breath, "—*heretic* to come to the palace when our goal is to see them all eliminated."

"No?" A smile spread across the man's face. "I think the king intends to subvert the movement from the inside."

Eyebrows knit together, Stepan considered those words. If fighting could be avoided, it would be best.

"Don't you think it is unnatural for the nobility to not support the king? Does it not go against everything in you? After all, he is our lord. I can't understand why these heretics resist him. The townspeople and peasants . . . they are ignorant, grasping at anything that could mean a better life. But these nobles that support this radical movement . . . "

The dark haired man continued, but Stepan became lost in his own thoughts. Pavel's commitment was rather curious. Why would he go against his birthright, against everything that made their society great, go against the king, and support these Hussites? It wasn't sane.

" . . . perhaps then, if these wayward nobles can be convinced to remove their support from the rebellious peasants and townsfolk, then this whole movement can be weakened."

Something eerie touched the edge of Stepan's awareness. A chill passed over the exposed skin on his neck. Except that the spring air was quite warm. He jerked his head around and spotted a nearby manservant, Cenek's servant, watching them. And he followed them a little too closely. But as Stepan's eyes connected with his, he drew back, pulling at his horse's reins.

Stepan's verbose companion continued to talk as if nothing were amiss. "I, for one, think it will all come to nothing. The king is gathering princes and mercenaries from all over the empire. And we will strike when the time is right. None of this will matter. We have God on our side. These blaspheming heretics will be wiped off the face of the earth."

Stepan glanced at the talkative young man but did not respond. Something unpleasant settled in his stomach. Was it because of Pavel and Karin? Did he fear for his former friends? His consideration for them stayed his hand once. Would it affect his ability to fight now?

Karin watched the morning unfold before her. She drew her shawl more tightly around herself. After last night, she needed time and space to think. So, as her husband slept, she crept out of their bedroom and found a place in the gardens. The sun had just begun to peek over the horizon when she took a seat on the bench among the baroness's tender buds and blooms. A veritable blanket of color was displayed before her.

And now, as the sky opened to greet the sun's approach, it, too, became the most breathtaking display of color and wonder. Her breath caught. She could see this every day and never stop marveling at God's creativity. In fact, she had seen many a sunrise and basked in its beauty. But not of late. No, since becoming a married woman, the early morning hours found her at peace in the arms of her husband. And since the baby, she had not seen such early hours in quite some time. So she relished this day.

Her eyes slid closed and she whispered a prayer of gratitude to her Maker, the same Creator who had unrolled the scene before her.

If only He could still her troubled heart as easily as He stilled the waters during the great storm in her favorite story of Jesus.

But was He truly capable? Even yet, did He care to? Perhaps a God who was busy making magic in the sky and working out all of life in the heavens and the earth couldn't care about her aching heart. This is what her mind told her. Her heart knew better. Yet, it seemed too difficult to just trust Him.

"Good morning."

The voice behind her caused her to startle. Spinning around, she found herself looking into the eyes of her mother-in-law.

Breath heaving, Karin placed a hand over her heart in an attempt to still it. "Good morning, Baroness. I did not know you were . . . that is, I did not expect anyone to be . . . " Karin took a deep breath. "You surprised me."

A smile spread across the woman's face. "I can see that, my dear. I came seeking the same thing you have." She winked as she swept an arm over the garden.

Karin's gaze followed her gesture. She let out a breath as her lips widened into a smile. "Yes. The gardens are quite peaceful. A good place to think."

Her mother-in-law nodded and came around to sit next to Karin. There was laughter in her eyes, and her expression warmed and soothed Karin.

"Must I insist again that you call me Marketa?"

Karin let out a quick breath and nodded. "My apologies. It is difficult for me."

"I understand." Marketa let her gaze drift over the horizon. Perhaps she, too, was taking in the glorious play of colors across the sky. Then she refocused on Karin. "Still, I must insist."

"As you wish." Karin relaxed, the woman's presence easing her anxious thoughts. "Marketa."

The baroness nodded. She leaned over to touch a bloom nearby. "The garden will be in its full glory in a matter of days now."

Karin nodded and stretched the last bits of sleep from her arms. "I think so. I am quite eager for it."

"So, tell me, Karin—and you can be honest—did you come out here for the sunrise? Or for the garden?"

"Can it not be both?"

Marketa's eyes met Karin's and held them. She was silent for a moment. "I suppose. It is difficult to imagine my garden can rival such a vision. One of God's paintings." Marketa's gaze rested on the rising sun.

Karin's eyes shifted in that direction as well. "Do you think we are instilled with the desire to create beauty? Because God creates such beautiful things?"

"I know we are." Marketa's words were sure. "I believe every good thing in me comes from Him. Everything I create and give birth to is a piece of my soul crying out to Him."

Why did she have to use those words? Karin became silent. What about the child within her? Truly it was from God. Weren't all babies? But the timing seemed all wrong. It was difficult to see this baby as a blessing when there was such turmoil. When she couldn't even bring herself to admit its existence to Pavel.

Feeling eyes on her, she glanced at her mother-in-law. Marketa watched her with warmth in her features—a warmth that put Karin at ease. How did she do that? Karin sighed. There was nothing to fear here.

Then the smile on Marketa's face dropped. And her mouth became drawn. Was something amiss? And then she spoke. "I know what you are hiding from my son."

It was not an accusation. Marketa's words were kind and gentle.

The warmth drained from Karin's face. What could she know? How could she know?

Marketa's eyes pinned Karin.

"Whatever do you mean?" Karin managed a light-hearted laugh. There was no more to say. She had to get out of there, had to escape.

Before she said something she would regret. "If you will excuse me, I think the chill in the air has become too much."

Gathering her skirts, she rose and moved toward the house. Perhaps she could draw attention away from whatever Marketa thought she knew. She couldn't know the truth. Could she?

Stepping into the house, Karin released her skirts and smoothed a hand over them.

"Karin."

The sound of her name caused her to startle once again. She spun to see that Marketa had followed her in. Her hand flew to her chest, heaving great breaths from her fright.

"Karin," Marketa said, lowering her voice. "May we speak in private?"

As much as Karin wanted to refuse, she dare not. So she took a deep breath and nodded.

The baroness stepped around her, leading Karin down the hall and into her private cabinet. Once Karin was inside the room, the baroness shut the door and maneuvered toward the seating area.

Turning to face Karin, she beckoned her daughter-in-law to join her.

Karin's steps were slow as she closed the space between them. Her nerves were a jumbled mess as she took her seat. Her hands shook and she clasped them together to still them.

Marketa sat as well, facing Karin. Her features remained neutral, unreadable.

Karin swallowed hard. *Why wouldn't she say something?* Licking her lips, Karin searched for an excuse. "Baroness . . . Marketa, I am sorry if I have given you the impression that I . . . "

Marketa waved off her comment. "I know about the child."

Karin couldn't have been more surprised than if the baroness had slapped her. The shock left her tongue-tied. But Marketa simply waited for Karin to find her wits.

"How?" was all Karin could say.

"Come now," Marketa said in that same calm, gentle voice. "Mothers know these things."

Karin still struggled to breathe. Would she faint for lack of ability to collect air into her lungs?

"Please breathe, dear." Marketa leaned over and placed a hand on Karin's. "You have nothing to fear."

That did little to put Karin at ease. If Marketa knew, who else might?

"For heaven's sake, Karin, you're turning blue. Now start breathing or I'll have to call for the salts."

Karin nodded, forcing a breath into her lungs so deeply it hurt and then pushing the breath out harder than she thought possible. Again and again she did so until she felt more stable and less light-headed.

"Now then. That's better." Marketa patted Karin's small, pale hand before withdrawing her own.

They sat in silence. Karin did not know what to say or where to begin.

"What do you intend to do about it?" Marketa spoke into the silence.

"I . . . I do not know." Karin fought to stay grounded. Her head spun.

"Might I ask why you feel the need to keep this information from Pavel? If I know my son, and I think I do, he would be happy about the prospect of a baby. He loves you so. Unless . . . " Her gaze fell for a moment. "Are you not happy?"

"No, it's nothing like that," Karin assured her.

Marketa let out a breath. Had she feared Karin might attempt something drastic?

"It is true I have mixed feelings. We had not . . . planned on having a child so soon."

"These things are not something that falls on a schedule." Marketa offered Karin a knowing smile.

"And Pavel, he . . . you see, he . . ." Karin struggled with what to share with her mother-in-law. How much could she trust the woman?

Marketa already knew Karin's secret, and whether Karin trusted her or not, her mother-in-law had the ability to betray her. So, she might as well bare all in hopes she was truly the ally she appeared to be.

"The truth is that Pavel voiced he does not wish to bring a child into this war. He wants to wait until things are more stable."

"Is not that a nice thought!" exclaimed Marketa. "What a dream to be able to plan when your children come. What a plan to think they will come into a perfect world free from strife."

Karin let out a breath and a laugh despite herself. "And so, I have not wanted to put more of a burden on him than he already carries. Especially as he is so determined to fight. I don't wish to distract him."

"My dear, his attentions are already divided. Whenever he is away from you, his heart is torn. I have seen it."

Karin allowed that truth to sink in.

"And it is a noble thought to not place a burden on him, but perhaps this knowledge will not be a burden, but a source of hope, something more to fight for."

That had not occurred to Karin. Something stirred within her, somewhat of a tingling sensation. Perhaps her own source of hope . . . hope that she was safe to share this news with Pavel after all. And that made her excited. The excitement spread to her face and the corners of her mouth widened.

"Does that mean what I think?" Marketa asked, eyebrow quirked.

Karin nodded, closing her eyes briefly. She allowed herself to imagine what it would be like to tell him—to see the joy in his eyes. The sensations in her body began to build. Including a twinge. It was a strange twinge. Something in her abdomen. Was the baby just as excited as she? Placing her hands on her midsection, she wished she could share even this moment with Pavel.

The twinge became something more. It caused her to catch her breath. It was more . . . painful. The world around her started to blur. Pain overwhelmed her. In the next moment, her mother-in-law stood beside her.

"Is everything all right?"

"Yes," Karin said with a confidence she wasn't sure she felt. "It's just the baby moving."

Marketa frowned, appearing doubtful. "I still think we should get you to bed."

"I need to speak with Pavel," Karin argued.

"There will be plenty of time for that." Marketa took Karin's arm, helping her to her feet. "For now, we need to get your feet up."

As Karin stood, her head began to swim and there was an intense heat underneath her. Pain ripped through her. She almost lost her balance.

Marketa attempted to steady her. It took a moment, but they were able to keep themselves on their feet.

Karin looked at her mother-in-law. "Thank you. Perhaps I am unwell. Maybe I should lay down."

Marketa nodded. "I think we best get you back into this chair. I don't know if I can get you to your room myself."

As much as she wanted to argue, Karin relented. And with Marketa's help, she eased back into her seat. She tried to breathe through the increasingly painful twinges.

Marketa gasped.

Looking in her direction, Karin saw Marketa becoming pale, one hand on her chest, one on her mouth. She stared at the floor near Karin's feet.

"What is . . .?" Karin tried to talk, but it was difficult. So, she gripped the armrests and pulled herself forward enough to see what had upset Marketa. There, at Karin's feet, the floor was dark with red. Karin was confused. What could have caused such a mess?

Fighting through a thick cloud to try to make sense of it, she saw that the hems of her skirts were stained as well. But the pain and the darkness swirling closer and closer prevented her from making a clear connection. Was she going to faint?

"Don't . . . tell . . . Pav . . . " was all she could manage before the darkness overtook her.

The time had come. There had been much ado about how they would proceed in the legal realms of their dispute. But an agreement had been reached. And Petr traveled to Kutna Hora. A small court convened here.

Vlastik preferred to be heard by the king's court. But Petr had no hopes that would be a fair trial. The likelihood of the king's council being paid off was high. Not that it wouldn't happen here. Still, Petr had better odds in this smaller court of the people. However, Vlastik had still insisted on a town controlled by Royalists.

So, here he was, prepared to defend himself with his legal advisor by his side. Looking at the man as they rode into the quaint village, he noted the confidence on the man's face. By all appearances, the man had already won. Petr wished he could take comfort in that.

He scanned the area. The town bustled with activity. Red markings of the Royalist garb were rather abundant and it unnerved him. It seemed as if he should hide for some reason. Flashes of the patrol coming to his home—and his fear for Karin—filled his mind.

Shaking his head, he attempted to clear the images. This was not the place or time. He had a task to complete that would require all his concentration. In a matter of minutes, he would be facing down his old friend.

Moving through the town, he sought out a building that could hold the magistrate and court proceedings. His advisor seemed to know where they were going. And so Petr had no choice but to follow.

After some moments, they stopped at a rather nondescript structure. He never would have picked it out to be anything more than a merchant's home. But his lawyer dismounted, so he followed suit. All the while, he searched for his friend-turned-enemy and worked to push down the sense of foreboding welling up in him.

"Shall we?" the advisor said, motioning toward the door.

Petr nodded, falling in step with the man.

They stepped into the modest building. Within, it opened to a large room. A handful of men were already gathered in the space, but Vlastik was not among them.

Their conversation died when the door closed. The men looked toward Petr as he approached. The best-dressed man in the group was soon introduced as the judge, and the rest were members of the court—the bailiff and the judge's record keeper. Another finely dressed man introduced himself as a representative for Vlastik. His words came out as if honey dripped from his tongue.

Petr's eyes narrowed. It seemed rather suspicious that the man representing Vlastik would find time to speak with the judge before he and his aide could arrive.

"If there are no objections, I think we should get started." The judge took his place behind a large table.

Petr's mouth opened, and then closed as the bailiff and record keeper took their places. Finally, he found his voice. "Shall we not wait for the viscount?"

Vlastik's representative exchanged a knowing look with the judge and stifled a laugh. "Earl Bornekov, you did know the viscount would not be appearing before the court, did you not?"

Petr stared at the man.

His aide put a hand on his arm. Should he step back and be silent? He could not contain himself. "No, I did not."

The opposing lawyer's eyes became wider. "You cannot have thought a man of his position would risk journeying into Bohemia during a time such as this."

Warmth crept into Petr's face. Why shouldn't he? Was this some kind of game to Vlastik? And then he knew. It was. Vlastik had played him. He sat in his grand house somewhere in a foreign land—Germany probably—laughing about this whole affair.

Vlastik's legal representative would report back, and they would have even more sport over the matter.

Petr wanted to storm out. He wanted to show this man how little he cared for their game. But this matter was not a game to him. No more than this conflict was to the Hussites.

But, just like Vlastik, Sigismund seemed to think it was a game. He had tried to play the Hussites against each other when he invited Cenek to Breslau and courted favor with him.

What Sigismund hadn't known was that Cenek would be just as two-faced. Cenek had returned to a unified Prague and called for councilors, magistrates, university masters, delegates, and Hussite priests from all around Prague and Bohemia to meet and come to one accord. Then he had taken back the Hradcany. Now the tables were turned.

Petr raised his eyes to the judge. He would bring an end to Vlastik's game too. He would show the man that he was not to be trifled with.

Radek walked through the village on his way back to camp. *So, this is Tabor.* Commander Zizka had spoken so well of this place. He talked of the people's commitment to the movement and of their devotion. So far, it didn't measure up.

"*Dobry den*, brother," a man passing by nodded to Radek.

Brother? Who was this person, and why did he address Radek so informally? This was only one of many things he did not understand about this town and these Hussites. They had been warned that the Taborites were Hussites through and through. Extremists. Although what that would mean, he had not known.

Radek approached camp to find a massive gathering of the farmers-turned-soldiers surrounding Commander Zizka and a man he did not recognize. From his ornate attire, Radek would guess him to be a priest.

"Welcome to Tabor," the man said to the group.

As Radek joined the crowd, he scanned for Zdenek. Where was he? The crowd pressed in, and he became doubtful he would find his friend.

Just then, however, he caught sight of Zdenek's dark blond hair out of the corner of his eye. He stood farther to the right with *her*— Eva. Radek frowned. When would Zdenek understand his cavorting with that girl was inappropriate?

Zdenek slipped a hand around Eva's waist.

Radek fumed. Folding his arms across his chest, he shifted his attention to the priest. He would have to deal with Zdenek later.

"In Tabor, we live in a community of grace and giving, just as the Lord Jesus Christ commanded. We, working as one, give to anyone who has need. So, we ask that you, too, bring all your belongings to the center of the village so that they can be distributed."

Had he heard correctly? Everyone was to give up his or her possessions? And just who decided who deserved what? Was it this rather finely dressed priest? He did not like this. Not one bit.

Zizka spoke up. "We are, of course, not asking you to give up your weapons and your bed mats." He shot a sideways glance at the priest.

The man hesitated, giving Zizka a long look. "Of course not."

Radek was thankful that all he had in his possession were his sword, clothing, bed mat, and horse—all useful for battle-readiness. Nothing that he would be required to give up.

But hadn't Zdenek's 'friend' and her family packed all they owned in a wagon and brought it with them? They would have to sacrifice much. He chanced a glance in her direction. She shifted her weight and peered up at Zdenek. Her features betrayed her uneasiness.

Radek could not stop the sly smile that broke across his features.

CHAPTER 8

STRUGGLES

Pavel awoke with a start. Something was wrong. He could feel it in his gut. Turning toward Karin, he needed to assure himself she was well. But her place in the bed was cold and empty.

He sat upright and his heart dropped. What happened to her? She was in trouble. He knew it.

Jerking the covers off, he flung himself out of the bed and raced to the door, not caring that he was in naught but his nightclothes. How long had she been gone? From the light streaming in through the crack in the curtain, he saw that it was well into morning.

He fought the urge to cry out for her. Stepping into the hall, he heard the distant sounds of servants moving about. Turning his head to the right and then to the left, he tried to plan his next course of action. Where to start?

Think! He attempted to calm himself. In all likelihood, she had risen early and gone for a turn about the gardens or for something to read in the library. But the sick feeling in his gut told him there was more to her disappearance. That feeling was louder than his ability to quiet it.

Still, he took a moment to breathe. It would do neither of them any good for him to be thrown into a fit of panic.

The library. He would look there first. Then the gardens. As he made his way to the library, he glanced into various rooms along the way. They were all dark and empty. At last, he arrived at the library. It, too, was darkened except for the thin stream of light coming in through a drawn curtain. He flung it open and glanced about the room.

She was not here.

The back staircase was the fastest route to the gardens. He all but flew down the stairs. For certain, his feet skipped some of the steps on the way.

Once outside, he didn't relish the fresh air or the picturesque landscape. He moved with purpose through the gardens.

No Karin. Where could she be?

Sitting on the bench in the center of the gardens, he put his head in his hand. He had to calm himself. Perhaps she was conversing in a solar with his mother or some such nonsense. There was no need to get so worked up.

Standing, he moved back to the house. He strode back in through the main entrance, garnering a rather strange look from a manservant. Was he such an odd sight, up and about in his nightshirt? Pavel ignored it.

But as he moved in the direction of the large solar, he almost ran over his father.

"Pavel, where have you been?" Alex asked, a worried look on his face. This did not serve to quell the rising anxiety in Pavel.

"I have been searching for Karin. Is everything all right?"

Alex's face was solemn as he placed a hand on Pavel's shoulder. "I'm afraid Karin has taken ill."

"Taken ill?" Pavel wanted to move, to go to her, toward something. But he knew not where to go, so he stood where he was as if a feral cat ready to pounce on the next thing that moved. "Where is she? I must see her!"

"Yes, yes." Alex flinched at the force of Pavel's emotions. "I will take you to her." Alex indicated the main staircase, searching Pavel's face as he did so.

Pavel paid his father's scrutiny little mind. He cared for his father dearly, but right now, the man was an obstacle in the way of getting to Karin.

As they moved through the house, Pavel was surprised to be taken back upstairs and even more so when they stopped outside his and Karin's bedchambers. The same room he occupied perhaps fifteen minutes prior.

He reached for the door latch, but it turned and his mother stepped out. Pavel attempted to get around his mother and into the bedchambers, but Marketa blocked him.

"Pavel," she tried to still him.

He refused to be deterred.

She placed her hands on his arms, gripping his good arm with a surprising amount of strength. "Pavel."

That drew his attention.

"Pavel," Marketa started again. "There is something I need to tell you."

He gave the door another long look before dragging his full focus to her.

Her eyes whisked over his face.

"What is it, Mother? What's going on with Karin?"

Marketa exchanged a meaningful look with Alex.

Pavel's father nodded.

Still, Marketa remained quiet, almost as if she was unsure what to say.

"Mother, I am unnerved by your silence. Is Karin well?" His eyes stung with unshed tears. What was he going to do? If he didn't have Karin . . . *Dear Father, be with me. Don't let this be it.*

Marketa's hands on his arms softened. "Karin will be fine. She has taken ill. But she will be fine."

Pavel breathed a prayer of gratitude. "Can I . . . see her?"

"Right now the maidservants are getting her into a fresh night-dress. You'll be able to see her soon."

"I am her husband. Surely, I can be with her while . . . "

"I beg you, Pavel. Trust me in this." Marketa rubbed his good arm.

He was confused. And still quite concerned. Why was it best he not be in the room while she was changed?

"The doctor has been called." Alex took a step toward Pavel.

"The doctor has been . . . ? But mother said Karin was going to be fine. So the doctor hasn't seen her?"

Marketa and Alex exchanged another long look.

Pavel became all the more frustrated. It was more and more clear that he was being kept in the dark.

"Call it mother's intuition," Marketa said, turning back to Pavel.

"Mother, if you know something you're not telling me, I want you to. I need to know what is happening."

Pavel's gaze shifted between his parents. Alex's eyes were on Marketa. It almost seemed as if he was encouraging Marketa to continue. But Marketa's expression did not change.

"Pavel, all I can tell you is that it is a delicate issue. The doctor will know what to do to get her back to full health, but I do not think she is in any danger."

Looking into his mother's eyes, he tried to gauge the truthfulness of her statement. How forthcoming was she? Something still nagged at the back of his mind. Perhaps it was just this unnerving situation.

He nodded, letting his shoulders drop.

When he glanced at his father, however, the man was still somewhat unsettled. But should he expect any father to be otherwise?

The three of them remained in the hall in silence for the next several moments until a maidservant opened the door.

Pavel was on her like a wild dog on a helpless squirrel. "Is the lady ready to receive?"

The girl looked up at her master with wide eyes and replied in a sheepish voice, "Yes, my lord."

The small-framed servant girl stepped out of the way and Pavel raced into the room. It barely registered in Pavel's mind that the girl carried some sort of linens. A dress, perhaps.

Once in the room, his eyes sought out his bride. There she lay, paler than he ever thought possible, her red-gold hair the only thing breaking up the white of the bed linens. He all but fell on the bed beside her.

Her eyes fluttered open.

"Karin!"

She did not smile. Tears filled her eyes.

"What's wrong?" His voice was not much more than a whisper.

He watched her as tears continued to roll down the sides of her face. She did not bother to wipe them away.

"Please, talk to me." He became less sure of himself with each passing second.

Her small, white hands reached up to him.

He captured them with his good hand and held them both to his chest.

"Please," she pleaded. "Please don't ask me questions. Please just hold me."

He was confused and even more concerned than ever, but he released her hands and maneuvered his body in an attempt to slide under the covers next to her.

"No!" came her sharp admonishment.

He jerked back as if he had hurt her.

"Did I . . . ?"

"No." She shook her head, a small movement. "Can you just hold me? Now? As you are?"

It took him a moment to understand what she was asking. It would be much easier if they were both in the bed. But that was not what she wanted. So, he slid his good arm underneath her back and lifted her upper body toward his.

She wrapped her arms around his shoulders and tucked her face into the crook of his neck. It soon became quite moist with her tears.

But he held her still, wishing he could stroke her back or the long red-blond tresses that fell over his arm, but she seemed too weak to hold herself up.

What had happened to her? Whatever it took, he would find out.

But she had asked him not to question her now and he would respect that. As much as it was killing him inside, he would respect that.

He relished the feel of her warm, breathing body in his arms. She was alive. His mother had said she was going to be well. And, in the end, that was all that mattered.

Zdenek pushed his horse forward, weary. The battle, if one could call it that, began just before dawn. And it had ended quickly. Zizka took his men to raid the town of Vozice, near Tabor. Their surprise attack served them well. The soldiers in Vozice made a hasty retreat, leaving the royal castle to the Hussite warriors. But not before the Hussites took their share of prisoners.

As their campsite in Tabor came into view, Zdenek urged his horse to go faster. He longed to catch even a glimpse of Eva and his arms ached to hold her.

She and her sister had been through much. First to have their father captured, then to be all but forced to hand over their possessions 'for the common good.' Despite everything, she had been brave. As they relieved them of their things, she had watched without shedding a single tear. Patricie had been choked up. Perhaps that's why Eva had been so strong. For her sister.

Now riding into camp, he searched for his beloved. She rushed out of her makeshift tent. Had she heard the approaching horses?

Pulling the reins to the right, he directed the horse in her direction. Stopping just short of where she stood, he dismounted, and caring not who watched, he took her hand in his and pressed a kiss to the side of her face, though he longed to taste her lips.

"You are safe!" Her hand touched his cheek.

He nodded, taking her in as if he hadn't seen her in weeks, rather than a few hours.

Looking over his shoulder, she watched the others as they came into camp. Her eyes darkened.

Turning, he noted she saw the Royalist prisoners. He shifted his focus back to her. "All is well. These prisoners will mean salvation for your father!"

Her eyes met his again, now wide and intense. "What?"

"Commander Zizka intends to make a trade. These prisoners for the Hussites captured at Sudomer."

Eva's lips parted as if to speak, but nothing came forth. Then she closed her mouth. Tears brimmed in her eyes.

"Can this be true? Could he still be alive?"

"The commander believes so. There is hope." Zdenek tipped her chin with his finger before wiping a tear.

She threw her arms around him. "Thank God!"

Zdenek was all too happy to bring his arms around her and return her embrace. "Yes, thank God."

Stepan jerked awake. Shaking his head, he tried to bring himself to some semblance of alertness. He could not keep doing this. What would the other men think of his startled awakenings? He would just have to ensure his sleep be more restful at night.

Yet he could not deny that when he closed his eyes in the evening the screams of pain and agony filled his mind. And nothing could block them.

He had been stationed in Kutna Hora for weeks now. And he had since faced the suffering of the Hussites in a way he never imagined. The cries of terror as they were thrown down the shafts, the sickening cracks when they landed, and the cries of pain for those who weren't silenced altogether. Did it truly bother him this much?

Whose side was he on? Why should the suffering of a few heretics distress him?

Moving toward a well, he drew a bucket of water. Drinking his fill, he then splashed some cool liquid on his face.

A hand landed on his shoulder and he jumped, hand on the hilt of his sword. But as he spun to face his attacker, he found himself eye to eye with one of the other soldiers. What was his name again? Dominik. Yes, he had arrived the same time as Stepan.

Dominik held his hands in the air. "Sorry, friend. I did not intend to startle you."

Stepan nodded, relaxing his arms and removing his hand from his sword. "All is well."

"I think we're all a bit skittish these days. But the emperor will overcome."

Unmoving, Stepan wished he could agree. Was he uncertain? Or was it because he didn't want to see his friends tortured and killed in the way he had witnessed so many others meet their end?

He didn't know what to think. The Royalists had lost the Hradcany to Cenek; the man who pretended to side with Sigismund turned out to have other intentions. Cenek, so it was told, had relieved the presiding lieutenants, his own relatives even, from their posts and placed his own guards, loyal to the Hussite cause, in their place. And so, without any resistance, he had managed to capture the fortified castle.

"What do you think of this manifesto everyone is talking about?" Dominik asked as he leaned down to take a drink.

"What?"

"The declaration from the Hussites? Surely you have heard . . . " Dominik's eyebrows knit together.

Stepan shook his head. He had been much too tired these last few days to keep up with much of anything.

"Seems the heretics have been spreading around these accusations and some four articles of their faith. Let me see if I can remember . . . " Dominik glanced upward while his memory worked.

"Freedom of preaching, in Czech no less, communion of both kinds .. . "

"Of course." Stepan smirked.

"Of course," Dominik agreed. "They demanded the clergy live free of materialism and the denial that they are heretics."

"And they think Sigismund will agree to these things?"

Dominik shrugged. "It doesn't matter what they think. He won't."

Stepan stared off into the distance. The Hussites asked too much. Yet again. Over-reaching. If peace were ever to be found, there would have to be compromise. And it didn't seem as if either side was ready for that. The war would continue. So would the screams.

Eva sat for a much needed break. The fact that their possessions were taken did not mean the women and children had stopped looking to her and Patricie. Only now, they were not as able to give it.

But Eva was always ready with a kind smile and a word of encouragement. And the need for those things was great. At least, the demands on her time made it seem so.

Patricie had taken everything to heart. She had yet to recover from the loss of their possessions. Perhaps it was because of their father's absence. These things certainly did not mean so much to Patricie except that they were Father's and they reminded her of him.

The bucket at Eva's feet called to her. Time to get back to work. She rose and moved toward the stream, smiling and waving at those she passed.

Though their introduction to the Taborite community had been difficult, there were some things she did like. In particular, their desire that all people be equal. No lords, no peasants ... everyone the same. Zdenek's attentions were not frowned upon. Except by his friend, Radek. That, she could not help.

Zdenek had taken full advantage of their circumstances and

continued to see her daily. Anything seemed possible. And perhaps it was. In Tabor.

Could they always stay here, then?

Everyone around her rushed about. She didn't notice until the third person ran past, nearly knocking her down.

"*Prominte prosime!*" the man said, reaching out to help her regain her balance.

"Is something amiss?" Eva picked up the bucket she had let loose of in the mishap.

"Commander Zizka has returned! With some of our Hussite brethren who were captured!"

Captured Hussites? Would her father be among them?

"Where? When?"

"Right now," the man called over his shoulder. "At the town center."

Should she go after Patricie? Where would she even find her sister? Might Patricie have heard the news? Eva had to think so, for she could not stop herself from grabbing up her skirt and following the man into the heart of Tabor.

What Eva found was a thick crowd with reunions already in progress. Husbands and wives embraced, brothers and sisters celebrated . . . but where was Father?

She wandered around the town center, looking for any sign of her dear father or her sister.

A hand grabbed for her arm and pulled at her.

Then she was looking up at Zdenek's tall frame.

She wrapped her arms around his midsection.

He embraced her as well. And she soon felt his warm breath on her ear. "We have recovered your father!"

Eva buried her face into Zdenek's chest. Her heart was sure to burst.

"Come," Zdenek pulled back, tugging at her arm. He led her through the crowd, keeping her close to his body, safe, protected. Was there anywhere she'd rather be?

As the people thinned, she was able to see around Zdenek. Her father and Patricie were watching as she approached.

She released Zdenek's hand and rushed around him, throwing herself into her father's arms.

Her father—a man once dead now brought back to life! She kissed the side of his face as she pulled back.

Father reached around her and grasped Zdenek's arm, giving it a shake. Something meaningful passed in the gaze the two men shared.

And all was right with the world. If only for this one moment.

The massive door flung open and Petr stormed inside. Lenka bit her lower lip as she watched him march past and farther into their home. She didn't have to guess which way the court had ruled. Her heart fell. How could this have happened? What had they done wrong?

But she knew. They had entered into an agreement, pushed Karin into something she didn't want, and this is what they deserved. Lenka hung her head, ashamed for the role she played in the whole affair.

Glancing around, her eyes caught a couple of the servants looking at her. Of course they knew. What was there to do but remove herself to her room? No longer to be the spectacle she had clearly become.

Gathering her skirts, she spun and moved through the hall. Petr would no doubt be in his solar, so she decided to climb the back stairway to the second floor. Doing so took her near her personal cabinet. The sounds of movement within alerted her that Petr had escaped there instead.

Turning to give him privacy, she halted when he called out.

"Lenka? Is that you?"

"Yes, my lord."

There was a pause. And Lenka wondered if he had heard her. She opened her mouth, preparing to speak again. But his voice rose from within.

"Come, come."

Lenka swallowed hard. She did not enjoy being around her husband when he was in one of his fouler moods. He did have a temper, and when it flared, it could be destructive. Steeling herself, she stepped forward and through the doorway of the small parlor.

Petr stood within, facing her as she entered. Hands behind his back, shoulders squared, he appeared as if he had been expecting her. But she knew better. He had been pacing.

His searching eyes claimed hers. They were almost frantic.

She forced her breath to come slowly.

Petr drew a breath in and pushed it out. "It's gone. All of it. Gone."

Lenka resisted the urge to close her eyes but held his.

"Do you want to know how?"

She started to speak, but her voice was weak. Clearing her throat, she tried again. "How?"

"The judge wouldn't listen. Paid off by Vlastik, no doubt." Petr broke eye contact, looking away.

The weight of the decision fell on Lenka—their property, their money . . . lost. But it was more than that. Vlastik had chipped at Petr's pride. That was the worst of it. How could she get that back? She wasn't sure she could.

"Did you hear me?"

Looking back at her husband, Lenka was struck by the wildness in his eyes. It left her with only a timid reply, "Yes."

"Will you not speak then?"

Emptiness. That's all there was in her—a void. And it stung. "I . . . I don't know that I have the words to—"

"I just need you to say something."

The emptiness became sadness. And it overcame her. There were no words.

Petr nodded, dropping his head. Then he walked past her, out of the parlor, and down the hall.

Lenka closed her eyes as the sounds of his footfalls faded into the distance. She had failed him.

The horses were laden with battle supplies. All was prepared. The men and their wives readied themselves to march out. Prague needed them. Bohemia needed them and they would go.

But how Zdenek hated to leave Eva behind. It had taken some doing to convince her not to come with them but to remain in Tabor. He needed to know she was safe.

With her father's return and Patricie to look after, she should stay. And she'd had no reasonable argument against it.

Even now, he walked his horse to her tent. She stood, arms wrapped around herself as if chilled despite the somewhat warm spring air. And he wanted to once again pull her into his embrace, but one glance to where her father lay dozing made him think otherwise. So he took her hand instead.

"It is time."

She nodded.

"I shall think of you often."

"And I you." Only then did she raise her eyes to meet his. "I wish you would let me come with you."

He sighed. "It is better for you to stay. Better for your father. For Patricie. For me."

She nodded again, looking toward the ground and shuffling her feet.

"What if something were to happen to you? I would never forgive myself."

"What if something happens to you?" Her eyes flashed.

He didn't answer for a moment. "That is the way of war."

Her hand squeezed his.

Zdenek pivoted to mount his steed, but she held fast to his hand. It gave him pause. He glanced back.

Her eyes pleaded.

And he could no more deny her a proper farewell than he could halt his own breath. Pulling her toward himself, he leaned over her, hovering for a moment.

She tilted her face upward, lips parted and eyes closing.

He breathed in the scent of her, trying to take in every part of this moment. Then his eyes slid closed and his lips came down on hers.

The kiss was sweet and pure, but he soon became desperate to show her, to pour out his love for her. He resisted the urge to pull her fully against him. Instead, his fingers came up to graze the sides of her face.

"Zdenek!" a voice called out. It disrupted his reverie.

And he pulled himself from his dream and from her lips. But his eyes remained on her face.

Her eyes welled with emotion.

"Zdenek, come! They're leaving us behind."

Now he could discern it was Radek calling to him. Looking over his shoulder, he spotted his friend not too far away, leaning over the pommel of his saddle. He shot Radek a glare through narrowed eyes.

Then he shifted his focus to Eva. Self-conscious all of a sudden, he raised a shaky hand to caress her cheek.

She put a hand over his.

And then he pulled away, raising himself onto his horse.

"Now can we go?" came Radek's strained voice.

Zdenek didn't answer. His eyes were still on Eva. But he turned his horse in the direction of the others and dug his heels into the horse's flank. And he was off. Would he ever see her again?

CHAPTER 9
FEARS

Gazing at the approaching dawn did not bring Karin joy. It brought dread. Another day came. Would she have to face the reality of what happened? Couldn't it all go away?

Pavel slumbered next to her, still on top of the covers. He had held her until sleep claimed him. But in the night, he released his hold.

And she welcomed it. The solitude.

She had stared out the window the entirety of the night as her body was wracked with pain. Would it ever end?

Moving her legs to slide out of the bed, her body protested. But she pushed through the pain. Now on trembling legs, she leaned on the wall until she became certain her legs would hold her.

Then she stepped toward the window. Her only hope of alleviating this sadness, if only for a moment, would be perhaps to gaze upon the world beyond. Outside of this room, outside of herself.

She stumbled more than once on the short walk across the room, but she was soon pulling at the drapes to widen her view, desperate for solace for her soul.

Heaving from the simple effort, she managed to move one of the massive window coverings to the side. And, leaning on the opening, she filled her eyes with what lay beyond. A gray haze covered everything as if a cloud covered the sun. But the sky was clear. Still, the world beyond the window was not as it should be.

Why? How could it not be? When she needed it so desperately?

"Karin?"

It was Pavel. The bed linens shuffled and the mattress shifted.

Karin drew in a deep breath but did not turn to face him.

His feet padded on the floor. "Karin?"

She closed her eyes. Must she face him?

"Karin!" This time his voice was startled, concerned. "You're bleeding!"

Still, she did not speak. How could she? What would she say?

"Karin." His hands were on her arms. His face was in her hair. "Is it your time?"

She did not move. Nor did she answer. Best to let him believe it so.

"Are you in pain?" Hands rubbed her arms.

Her eyes fixed in the distance, she continued to deny him a response.

"Karin?" He attempted to turn her.

She stiffened her body, refusing to be moved.

"Are you well? Shall I send for the doctor?"

Holding a hand up, she pressed his body away from hers. "No. I am well."

He stepped back but grasped her hand.

Why did her body cry out against his? She wanted him to go.

"Why won't you talk to me?"

She looked at him, but her heart did not light up when their eyes met.

His eyes were wide. "Something is wrong."

Glancing out the window, she spoke firmly, "I told you, I am well."

He rubbed her hand caught between his. A silent moment stretched out between them.

She pulled her hand from his grasp.

Another moment.

Pavel reached forth, fingers nearing the side of her face.

Karin turned her head away.

He swallowed audibly.

More silence.

"If you won't tell me what is wrong, I will insist upon the doctor." Pavel's voice was firm.

Karin twisted to face him, perhaps a little too fast. Her body cried out. "As I said—I am well."

She could not miss the hurt in his eyes. And she jerked away before he could see her tears. "Just go." But as her shoulders shook, she was certain he would know she cried.

His hands were on her shoulders once more. "Karin, I—"

Raising her arms, she flung his hands away. "Just go!"

There were several more moments of silence followed by the door being shut. Karin was alone.

And she sank to the floor. What had she done?

Petr grumbled. He had been in a foul mood for the last couple of weeks. The decision about the land took more out of him than he'd expected. Most days found him hunkering about the halls of the house, not truly headed anywhere.

He did not see Lenka except at meals. Even then, she remained quiet, reserved. Should it pain him that their last interaction had been so harsh? It didn't. How could she not provide better support? How could she go mute when he needed her words more than ever?

A growl escaped his throat. He wanted to strike out at something, anything. But nothing presented itself as a suitable target. Would he lash out at his wife were he to come across her in his pacing?

What had he expected her to say? He closed his eyes as realization washed over him. And he hated it. There was nothing she could have said. Nothing that would soothe him in any real way. No, he had baited her. Was he only upset now that she didn't take it?

Putting his head in his hands, he let out a breath. He had to find her.

Stepping into action, he moved toward the stairs. Moments later, he approached her cabinet. He softened his footfalls as he drew near the opened door, straining to listen for movement.

Paper rustled and his wife's soft sniffles were audible through the stillness. Moving closer, he peered into the room. Lenka's form was at her desk, silhouetted against the light of the window. Her hands worked a quill across the flat surface.

This did not disturb him. The unmistakable sounds of her contained sobs did. As he watched on, she paused, and held her hand to her lips as her shoulders shook. And at once, his heart softened. It no longer mattered who should have said what.

Pressing into the room, he cleared his throat.

Lenka's head jerked in his direction. She twisted her body toward him in the seat while blotting at her eyes.

"My lord?" She didn't meet his eyes. Head down, she seemed to be examining her hands where they lay in her lap.

How was he to break this tension? Selfishly he wished she would, but it fell on his shoulders. As well it should.

"Lenka, I . . . " he started, but no more words came.

Her eyes lifted to his, glazed with emotion. Something pulled at his heart.

"Are you well?" Not much of a start.

She again peered at her hands. "Yes. I am writing Karin. She should know of the happenings in Prague."

He nodded. "What will you tell her?" Avoiding the subject. Why did he act this way?

"Of the challenge issued to Sigismund by the Hussite nobles now that the armistice has expired."

Petr swallowed hard. His personal efforts to make this peace agreement had been fervent. And he'd had every hope the peace would lead to a lasting truce. It had not. The nobles, previously hesitant to oppose Sigismund, seemed to no longer have such trepidations once Cenek double-crossed the Holy Roman Emperor.

"Do you think she knows that a Hussite officer has been sent to Poland?"

The Taborites were probably well aware of everything happening within the Czech lands. But it brought Lenka some amount of comfort to write these things to Karin, to have some news to share. So he shrugged.

His heart hardened as he considered anew the ramifications of the Hussite revolutionaries courting Poland, even offering the Bohemian crown to King Wladyslaw II. How would he respond? What would it mean for their country? Would Poland become involved?

Even so, Cenek did not wait for a response. He proved himself to be as two-faced toward the Hussites as he had been toward Sigismund. For some simple words of fine promises of peace, Cenek had handed the Hradcany back to the Royalists. And the Hussites were again left to defend Prague without the benefit of either fortified castle.

"Perhaps I should not tell her," Lenka said, breaking into his thoughts.

He looked up and saw her gazing out the window.

"If she doesn't know, perhaps that is better. And if she does, there is no need to remind her."

Lenka met his eyes. They stared at one another across the space.

"Karin will want to know how you are doing, how we are faring, and how the trial ended."

Long eyelashes fell over Lenka's green orbs. Karin's were so like her mother's.

"What will you tell her?" He held his breath.

"I haven't found the words." Lenka's voice was not much more than a whisper.

Petr closed the distance between them with slow, careful steps. Then he stood beside the desk looking down at his wife. "Would you tell her we are well? That though there are trials we cannot win, we will stand together?"

Lenka gazed up at him, her eyes glassy.

"And that her father is sorry for any hurt he has caused her mother?"

A tear escaped. Petr reached forward and wiped it away with his fingertips. Reaching for Lenka's hands, he drew her to stand.

"Will you tell her that for me?"

She nodded. "Yes. If that is your wish, my lord."

"Most sincerely." He pulled her into his embrace.

Radek yawned and stretched. Mounting his horse for another long day of riding was the last thing he wanted to do. The way Commander Zizka pushed them yesterday had been almost inhuman. But thinking about the men on foot made Radek ache all the more. They were committed to this cause. And for a committed man, it must seem like nothing.

Yet for Radek, his body was sore. Groaning, he rolled over, yearning for just a few more minutes of peaceful rest. Movement nearby caught his attention. Zdenek. Up and ready to go. Had he been so easily converted? Because of that girl?

"Almost time to go." Zdenek eyed his friend. Since when did Zdenek become an early riser?

Answering with a grunt, Radek turned away.

"Come now." Zdenek knelt by Radek's side. "We have much ground to cover."

"I can only imagine," Radek grumbled. But he sat up all the same. It was no use being difficult. His predicament wasn't Zdenek's fault.

Zdenek returned to his horse, tying his bedroll to the back of the saddle.

Radek forced himself to stand and do the same. When he pivoted to face Zdenek, he noticed his friend had been watching. It gave him pause.

"Forgive me, I only worry that something may be amiss." Zdenek's eyes were on Radek, sincere, concerned.

Radek ran a hand through his hair and looked into the distance. "It's just that I . . . I don't know that I fit in here."

"What do you mean? Of course you do. Just as much as I—"

"No, I don't." His voice was firm.

It silenced Zdenek.

They stared at each other as if squaring off.

"I don't know what I'm saying." Radek shifted his gaze to sweep over the camp. "I can't explain it."

There was no more time for further thoughts, however, as the men around them began to move as one. Those with horses took to their saddles, and the rest gathered their things and struck out behind them.

"We can talk more later," Zdenek said as he grabbed for the pommel of his saddle.

Radek nodded, watching his friend mount. Then he did the same.

They rode in silence. Perhaps because of the noise of the group's movement, perhaps because neither knew what to say. Radek certainly didn't. So he watched the scenery of his beloved homeland as it passed by. For the most part, though, he thought of the choices he had made—the ones he'd had control of and the ones he hadn't. And how he ended up here.

As they neared the Sazava River, their contingency came to a halt. He and Zdenek exchanged a look as they maneuvered their horses closer to the front. Close enough, at least, to see what lay before them.

Once Radek was clear of most of the horsemen in front of him, he saw why they had come to such a drastic stop. There, between the

Hussites and the river, stood no less than four hundred cavalrymen and a large number of infantry.

His shoulders tightened, his muscles readying for battle. All the while, his stomach lurched. Could he fight another battle for a cause he did not believe in?

Radek sought out Zdenek amongst the pressing group. Where was he? While Radek might not be able to rally to the Hussite cause, he would be able to fight for his friend.

The Taborite cavalrymen began shifting around him and one of the captains motioned to him. "You're with me."

What could he do but obey? Moving toward the back of the group, this smaller contingency of men, some on horseback, some on foot, moved with careful steps in a wide arc to the northwest. Radek saw that the plan was to flank the Royalist army while Zizka and the rest of the Taborites detained them fighting.

While they moved around, Radek heard the first clashes of weapons. And he hoped his friend would be safe. The small group had little trouble making their way to their destination. They now stood between the Royalist army and the small town behind them.

Radek readied himself to attack the enemy cavalry from behind, but he was given other orders.

"All right, men, burn it." The leader met their surprised gazes.

But the other men moved to do so at once.

Radek remained as he was. Burn it? This was a town full of houses. Where people lived. Women. Children. How could they?

His commanding officer glared at him and grabbed a torch held by one of the infantrymen. "Did you hear me?" He thrust the torch toward Radek.

"Yes, sir." Radek took it and moved to the first house, but he heard the screams of the townsfolk as they fled their homes and was, again, helpless to do anything.

The captain came from behind, grabbed the torch, and shoved it through the now vacant home's open window.

Radek stared after the flames as they lit and licked at the air, expanding as they breathed. When he shifted his eyes, he met the intense gaze of the captain.

"This is what we have to do to keep the Royalists from regrouping. I hope you will not disobey orders again, soldier." There was a roughness to the man's voice, but Radek thought he heard the slightest hint of sympathy as well.

In the next moment, the captain rallied his troops to attack the Royalist army from the flank. But as they gathered to do so, they could only watch as the Royalist soldiers retreated. Zizka had them on the run. And as the commander pursued them, Radek and the others joined in.

The pursuit led them to a walled monastery where the Royalist army took refuge. Radek, still numbed from the actions of his comrades-in-arms, watched as his fellow soldiers made a valiant effort to storm the structure. Still, something inside of him cried out that this, too, was wrong.

After several moments, it ended. Just as quickly as it had started, it was over. Zizka and his captains worked to pull the Hussites back.

Radek knew why. These Royalist soldiers had not succeeded in their task to stop Zizka, they had only been a distraction. His goal, his priority, was Prague. And go to Prague they would.

Truly, this skirmish had done much more than that. It had scarred Radek deeper than he cared to admit. What had he gotten himself into?

Marketa stepped into the bedchambers of her son and daughter-in-law. It had been days since she had been here. The last time was the day . . . it had been days.

Karin sat on the chaise lounge near the window. Wrapped in a blanket, she gazed out the nearby window. But the curtains were almost completely drawn, open not much more than a hand's width. Just enough to bring adequate light into the room.

Karin didn't even glance in her direction as Marketa came into the room. Did she not notice someone had intruded on her space? Did she assume it was her maidservant? Or was she somewhere else entirely? Yes, Marketa knew that look. She knew that pain all too well.

The baroness cleared her throat, not wanting to further intrude on Karin without her knowledge. Karin continued to stare out the sliver of window she had visual access to. It was not until Karin reached for the tea on her side table that she glanced in Marketa's direction.

Karin raised an eyebrow upon seeing her mother-in-law but made no other acknowledgement of the woman's presence. She went back to gazing out the window.

Marketa let silence fall in the room again. She closed her eyes and prayed. How was she to reach out to her daughter-in-law? To best love her? To best help her through this? Had there been anyone there for her? Her husband. She'd had Alex. And here Karin suffered in silence, without her husband's knowing support.

The baroness had watched these last few days as Pavel reached out to Karin only to be pushed away. Yes, Pavel suffered too. Did he harbor feelings of rejection? This thing drove a wedge between them. It was still early, but Marketa saw it.

Even now, Pavel should be here with her. But she had, yet again, pushed him away. Had he gone to the family chapel? Or out riding? These were the things he did to clear his mind, to re-center. But he should know the truth. Forced to deal without all of the information, he'd had to resort to what he did know. He'd been given half-truths and asked to accept it as the whole story. Yes, Marketa felt for her son.

And she blamed herself. She had only tried to respect Karin's wishes when she remained silent that day when Pavel questioned her. But she had been wrong. He deserved to know.

Marketa swayed, light-headed. Her knee joints were stiff. She had been standing in the silence with her thoughts for quite some time. If she didn't bend her knees or sit soon, she would faint.

She moved farther into the room and chose a chair not far from Karin. Easing into the seat, she felt the blood flow through her legs again. And her head stopped swimming.

She gazed out the window with Karin, but there was precious little she could see from the thin sliver of opening afforded from her angle.

"Beautiful day," she commented. Would that spark some reaction?

Karin nodded numbly.

"The garden has come into its full bloom."

Karin made a noise that sounded akin to a grunt.

"You can't stay like this, Karin." Marketa softened her voice.

No response.

"Please talk to me." Should she go to her daughter-in-law? Touch her? Marketa stared at the back of Karin's head, her hair, long since in need of brushing, falling down her back in a tangled mass.

Silence fell over the room once more. There was nothing left. The time had come. Marketa peered heavenward and said a prayer for strength and guidance. Then she drew in a deep breath before breaking the stillness.

"Karin, I know this pain you are going through. I know it's—"

"How could you?" Karin's eyes were on her. There was that spark.

Marketa blinked.

Karin shook her head and fixed her gaze out the window again.

"I know," Marketa began again, her voice firmer, more set. "Because I had three babies I never got to hold."

Karin twisted toward Marketa, but her eyes were no longer burning coals. They were glassy. And soft. "Truly?"

Marketa felt moisture on her face as she nodded. "Pavel is a promised child. A blessing. The doctor said he was my last chance, and I never prayed so hard for anything in my life."

Karin's eyes stayed on Marketa's. Was she trying to wrap her mind around the truth of it?

Marketa wanted to run, wanted to hide. She longed to retreat into her pain, not bare it and stay here, an open, vulnerable wound.

"Why does it hurt so?" Karin's voice broke.

"Because it was a life. Because it was yours."

Karin nodded. "Does the pain ever go away?"

"No," Marketa said as she sighed. She wished she could tell Karin something different. But she needed the truth. "Because you have a tender heart that loves deeply."

Fresh tears trailed Karin's cheeks.

"But the pain will not always be so sharp. In time, it will ache. And then, it will dull."

Karin leaned her head on the back of the chaise and closed her eyes. "Will I ever feel whole again?"

"Of course you will. God is the One Who makes you complete. And He can heal this wound. If you let Him."

"It's so hard to trust Him when He's allowed such pain into my life."

Marketa considered that. "But none of that means He doesn't have a plan in your pain. I'm certain that's what trust is about."

Karin nodded.

"And He has given you the same blessing He gave me all those years ago—Pavel. Remember, he lost a child too. But he doesn't know. Don't you think he deserves to? Deserves to mourn? To comfort you and to be comforted?"

Karin's tears were flowing. "I . . . I can't. I don't know how. Can you . . . ?"

Marketa shook her head. "I would take that burden from you in a heartbeat if I thought it would make things easier. It will not. It will only make things harder between you."

Karin shut her eyes but nodded.

"I will do something for you."

Karin's eyes flew open. A question in them for her mother-in-law.

"I will pray with you."

Karin sniffled as more tears came. She covered her face with her hands.

Marketa got to her feet, moved to the lounger, sat on the edge, and pulled Karin into her embrace. She held her precious daughter-in-law while she cried, wiping Karin's tears. And then together they prayed.

The evening settled over Prague. What a day it had been! And so glorious the reception they had received! Zdenek smiled to himself as he remembered the faces of the people as they welcomed Commander Zizka's Taborite army. Their last hope. It was a grand feeling.

And the feast that had been prepared! Zdenek had not seen food and drink like that in many months. Most of the peasants among them had never been treated thusly. And it became obvious they were quite overwhelmed by the gifts bestowed upon them.

Zdenek had not seen Radek for much of the evening. He disappeared soon after the meal commenced. But now Zdenek wandered, looking for his friend. Prepared to resign his search, he spotted Radek a block away outside of a monastery, arms folded.

The building stood strong and tall, rising above the street with its proud stone structure. Yet as he neared Radek, Zdenek became less sure as to why his friend would be staring at this one lone building.

"Radek," he said, his voice soft, not wanting to startle him.

His friend didn't seem to register that anyone had spoken.

Zdenek moved closer and spoke louder. "Radek."

At last turning his head, Radek acknowledged Zdenek. But he soon went back to his watch over the silent building.

Zdenek came up beside him. "Have you a new fascination with architecture?"

A gentle laugh escaped Radek's throat.

That put Zdenek at ease.

Radek let out a long breath. "Just thinking." Was there a sadness in his voice?

"Yes?" Zdenek crossed his arms, mimicking Radek's posture.

Looking at him, Radek said, "I don't think you would understand."

"We've been through a lot together. I think you might be surprised."

Radek's gaze moved back toward the structure. He pursed his lips but remained quiet for several moments before he spoke. "Today I was ordered to participate in burning peoples' homes."

Zdenek's breath caught. He knew Zizka commanded some of the troops to set fire to the town, but he hadn't truly thought about it that way. Maybe he hadn't wanted to.

"And I . . . I couldn't do it." His face fell.

"You disobeyed orders?" Zdenek managed.

Radek's eyes flashed as he turned on Zdenek. "Yes! And I'd do it again. Wouldn't you?"

Zdenek couldn't answer. Would he? "I . . . I think I would."

"That's a problem, Zdenek. If you don't *know* you would disobey the wrong order—"

The sound of horseshoes clomping on the ground nearby interrupted their conversation. Turning toward the noise, they spotted a couple of men on horseback and a group of women walking in their direction.

As the men drew nearer, Zdenek saw on their faces that they were surprised to find two Taborite soldiers out in the evening.

"*Dobry vecer*, sirs," one of the horsemen said. "What finds you away from the feast this evening?"

"Just out for some fresh air." Zdenek offered the man one of his winning smiles.

"Commander Zizka is rounding up the men. We will make camp for the night on an island north of the city."

"But not the women?" Zdenek indicated the group with his hand.

"No, the women will be housed in the monastery."

"Then we will detain you no longer." Radek inserted himself between Zdenek and the man before turning to walk back to the celebration hall.

Zdenek nodded toward the soldier on horseback, who was already ushering women into the monastery, and moved to follow Radek.

As he departed, however, he thought he caught a glimpse of familiar dark brown hair. But as he took a second look, he didn't see anything of the sort. It was probably nothing. Many Czech women had long, dark brown hair. Perhaps just wishful thinking. Besides, Eva was safe, miles away from here.

Stepan watched as another round of troops entered the camp at Kutna Hora. And not one of them was Czech. More and more they poured in, foreigners all. Wasn't there something to be said for the Czech people handling their own problems?

Dominik shifted beside him. "I don't like it."

Had he just heard Stepan's thoughts? Stepan stared at him, eyebrow arched.

"What?" Dominik gave him a long stare. Then he lowered his voice. "My father says this will not be good for any of us."

"Oh?" The only thing Stepan's father had worried about was getting rid of the heretics. But Stepan didn't like the idea of the foreigners dealing with Czech problems. The Czechs should be dealing with the Czechs.

"My father speaks of how weak-handed Wenceslaus was and how much freedom that gave the nobility. He fears a conquered Prague would usher in a strengthened crown. Maybe even an influx of . . . Germans." Dominik looked away toward a group of German mercenaries nearby and scowled.

Stepan could relate. He did not want Germans occupying and despoiling Prague and the rest of the Bohemian lands.

"Either way, my friend, it is time to go to Mass." Dominik elbowed Stepan and jerked his head in the direction of the town's cathedral.

They walked together through the town, among the gathering crowd. But, upon arrival, they found their own seats in the section set apart for the nobility.

Stepan enjoyed many things in the world. Mass was not one of them. Yet it was important for his faith that he attend. So he endured the songs and homily, knowing his presence in the church pleased Almighty God.

The priest gave his usual indictments of the Hussites and their heresy, proclaiming that all who joined the crusade against them would gain forgiveness for their sins and exemption from purgatory.

Even without such promises, Stepan would fight. But he could not deny that these assurances warmed his heart and made him feel more secure.

They took proper communion before the close of the service. And Stepan thanked God for the like-mindedness of those around him. This communion of both kinds was ridiculous on the face of it. Yet it was the one thing those Hussites refused to relinquish above all else. If only they cared as much about peace.

As they exited the cathedral, Dominik placed a hand on Stepan's arm and drew him to the side. He glanced around as if ensuring no one was close enough to overhear. Then he spoke. "Stepan, I hope I am not wrong in thinking we are of the same mind."

"I think so." Stepan's eyes moved between Dominik's and the hand on his arm.

Dominik removed his hand. "There are a group of nobles that have started to talk."

"Talk?"

Dominik licked his lips. "Yes, we hope to petition Emperor Sigismund about discharging these foreign soldiers."

Stepan mouth tightened into a thin line and he spun to walk away. "I can tell you what he will say."

Reaching out a hand to stop him, Dominik continued, "We have something to offer him that he won't refuse."

Looking back over his shoulder, Stepan's eyebrow went up. "What could we possibly offer the emperor?"

"The crown of Bohemia."

CHAPTER 10
MANEUVERS

Zdenek moved toward the small grouping of men. He had been summoned, but he knew not why. These men were Zizka's captains and higher-ranking soldiers. Why was he here? As he drew near, he noticed that Zizka was in the center, standing at a table with papers stretched out.

Trying to approach without being heard or seen proved impossible. Several of the men glanced up.

Including Zizka.

Zdenek found himself looking directly into the face of the massive commander.

"Zdenek, so glad you could join us." Zizka waved him further in.

How did Zizka know his name? Could he have remembered it from when Pavel introduced them? He had so many men under his command. Either way, he felt honored.

He came closer so he could see the map.

The man's huge paw of a hand was on the west bank of the Vlatava River near the castle to the northwest of Prague.

"I have learned that a large convoy will be coming through to resupply the Hradcany. It is unclear how many soldiers will escort the wagons or how many wagons will be in the train. But one thing is for certain: we must take it. Shutting off supplies to the Hradcany and starving them out will be the best way to take it. No direct assault."

The men murmured and nodded amongst themselves.

"Next," he said as he motioned toward the other castle, the Vysehrad, "the moat we had constructed to defend the New Town from the Vysehrad has been partially filled in during fighting. A new moat must be dug. Deeper, wider, and farther north. The women, children, and priests will do this. I have other plans for our troops."

Zdenek looked at Zizka expectantly. What was that next plan?

"We will then besiege the Hradcany. This will force Sigismund to act. I will not sit and wait for him to attack. It is cowardice to let the emperor make the first move."

Zdenek's eyes widened. Provoking the emperor? He thought maybe it would be best to focus on the city's defenses, but perhaps Zizka was right. After all, he was the military genius and a more practiced soldier. His plans seemed sound. And they always proved effective. Thus far.

"Any questions?"

The men eyed each other, but no one opened his mouth.

"Good, I shall have you three take your units and prepare them to go with me to surprise the convoy. And you," he pointed to one of his captains. "Your unit will oversee the rebuilding of the moat. All the remaining soldiers will take up positions around the Hradcany with hand cannons, preparing for our siege."

The men took their orders and were dismissed.

"Zdenek, please remain." Zizka moved toward him.

Turning to his commander, Zdenek watched the man for any sign that he had displeased him. "Of course, Commander. What might I do for you?"

"You have proven yourself to be a valuable member of my army. And quite loyal."

"Yes, sir." Zdenek thought about his conversation with Radek but pushed it from his mind.

"I need someone I can trust to take care of the supplies and foodstuffs we will receive from the convoy." Zizka's one eye searched Zdenek's face. "It's not something I can trust to anyone. There is a deep seed of greed hiding in many. I need someone who is selfless."

"Commander, I am honored you would think of me, and I promise I will do my best to deserve that trust." Zdenek raised his shoulders and puffed out his chest.

A smile tugged at Zizka's lips. "That's what I wanted to hear."

Stepan urged his horse forward. They made such slow progress; he wasn't surprised his horse kept falling behind. Probably falling asleep. He had been charged with escorting the supply train to the Hradcany. It was beneath him to be sure, but he would fulfill whatever task was levied upon him. If that included walking these wagons to the castle, so be it.

Taking in the scenery around him, he couldn't imagine how it was that these lands were torn apart by war and bloodshed. Or that these grounds were soon to be witness to such a crusade as this country had never known. But it was coming. And he intended to be on the winning side.

The wind rushed past him. He enjoyed the breeze—something to break the monotony of the day. As the wind died down though, he thought he heard . . . perhaps.

He held his hand up to halt the wagons. After several moments that felt like an eternity, they came to a stop.

Tilting his head to the side, he strained his ears, listening for anything out of place. All he heard was the distant rustling of trees and grasses. He prepared to lower his hand and get the convoy moving again when the world collapsed around them.

They were rushed from the east.

Blast those Hussites! How did they know?

Drawing his sword, Stepan called out, "Prepare yourselves, men!"

The men drew their weapons, but they were shaking.

One glance at the horde of Hussites headed their way and Stepan knew they were outnumbered.

"Stand and fight!" he urged his men.

But as the Hussites came closer, one by one the men escorting the convoy lost their nerve and fled.

Stepan was at a loss. He should stay and defend the emperor's supplies, but what could one man do against such an army? Surely he would be killed.

When he decided to flee, it was too late. The first of the Hussites was upon him, grasping at his horse. He kicked at the man, desperate for freedom.

Strong hands grabbed his leg and Stepan drew back his sword. He stared into the man's determined eyes once before running him through. Then Stepan could not tear his eyes away from the man's wide-eyed look of horror.

Shaking, he pushed the man away from his sword with his foot and dug his heels into his horse's flanks, praying that by some miracle he could escape. He galloped away and did not stop for hours. And even then he could hear the sounds of the horde and see those eyes . . . those big, brown, horrified eyes.

The world was still and quiet. Lenka gazed out her window from the top floor of the massive structure. Nothing seemed amiss on the grounds of the Bornekov estate. Every tree, every flower had its place. And all remained at peace.

All but the chaos within. As much as the world displayed a tranquil order, it mocked her. She was anything but peaceful. Another wave of emotion welled within and threatened to spill over. These last months had been the most trying of her life, yet she thought she might take them all again if only she knew her daughter was well.

There had been no word from Karin in weeks. The news of her pregnancy thrilled Lenka, now it loomed like a dark cloud. Why no response to her letter? Why no news of the pregnancy? Lenka's heart constricted. Something wasn't right.

Had something happened to Karin? To the baby? Or had she simply become distracted? Settled well within the boundaries of Hussite controlled land, she wasn't in much danger. But she mentioned Pavel's injury. Had his situation become dire? Had he returned to the fighting?

The lack of information limited Lenka. The tightness in her chest became more intense. She swallowed hard. What was she to do?

Movement behind her alerted her to the presence of another in her room, but she did not turn.

"My lady, are you in need of anything else?"

Sharka, her faithful maidservant. A welcome distraction.

Lenka turned. "I wish to go into the village."

Sharka curtsied and moved toward the door.

"Sharka?"

The younger woman paused and shifted to look at her mistress.

"Your mother, do you write to her often?"

"No, milady."

Lenka's brows furrowed. Was she expecting something of Karin that was not typical? As for Lenka, the letters to her own mother had been rather frequent until her mother's death.

Sharka must have noted Lenka's concerned expression. "My mother is one of your cooks. We have no need of letters."

Lenka's confusion melted into embarrassment. This information should not take Lenka by surprise. And it didn't. Not truly. In her musings, it had been forgotten. But now Sharka's mother's face appeared in Lenka's mind. Her kind eyes looking up as her plump hands continued hard at work. "Yes, of course."

Sharka nodded and curtsied before she took her leave. She would notify the stablemen the carriage needed to be readied for their mistress.

The only recourse Lenka had seemed to be information. Could she seek out the Hussites in the Utraquist sect and divine if they had any news of Tabor? Perhaps of Commander Zizka's army?

One thing was certain—she could no longer pace in her rooms and wonder.

Pavel returned from yet another ride through the hills of Tabor. If only his mind could be as clear as the mountain streams where he had watered his horse and refreshed his own sweat-soaked face. He had been able to see all the way to the bottom of the stream. He couldn't see two inches in front of him in this situation with Karin.

What had happened to her? That day . . . that horrible day. Something happened and everything changed. Lady problems were not discussed; he did not feel the freedom to ask. Not even his parents, who clearly knew more than he.

And so they were at an impasse. He kept reaching out to Karin and she kept pushing him away. His heart ached for her, longed for the connection they once knew. Would they ever know it again?

He flexed his injured arm, no longer in a sling. The doctor cleared him to return to his unit by the week's end. And he was eager to get back to the front, to bring hope and healing to his homeland. But could he leave when he and Karin were at odds? He didn't know. Nor did he know what good it would do to stay.

Dismounting, he gave the horse a good, firm pat on her back as the stable hand took her by the reins and led her away. He continued on toward the house. Perhaps what he needed to clear his mind was some time in the chapel. He redirected his feet in that direction. And was intercepted by his mother. She stood in the stairway, awaiting him. How long had she been there?

"How was your ride, dear?"

"Refreshing," he lied.

Her frown betrayed that she knew he was being less than truthful.

He ran a hand through his short hair, bleached a lighter shade of blond by longer hours in the sun.

"It was invigorating." There, that was truthful.

She reached forward and fingered the collar of his shirt, attempting to brush dirt off his doublet. It had been a while since she had mothered him in such a way, so he indulged her.

"I'm headed to the chapel for solitude and prayer."

Marketa's face opened into a pleasant smile. "Why not go and see if Karin would care for some company?"

Pavel sighed. "I can tell you, Mother, that she would not."

Marketa laid her hands on his shoulders, nodding. "I know things have been . . . difficult . . . between you and Karin."

"Mother, I'd rather not discuss—"

The baroness held her hands up. "And I don't want to get involved."

"I think you are already 'involved'." Pavel resisted the urge to roll his eyes.

Marketa continued, "I just think things are not what they seem. Keep reaching out, Pavel. I know how much you love her."

Pavel leveled his gaze on his mother and opened his mouth to respond, but she held up a hand in front of his mouth.

"Just . . . think about what I said." She leaned forward and planted a kiss on the side of his face before turning and moving down the hall.

And Pavel watched her go, more confused than ever. Rather, more torn than ever. Of course he wanted to go to Karin. But could his heart take more rejection? Could he bear it if she sent him away again? He longed to pull her into his embrace, press kisses to her lips, and hear her say they would be all right. If only she would let him.

But she would not, so he moved in the direction of the chapel.

Yes, prayers, and then he would retire to the separate chamber he had been keeping.

As his footsteps drew him closer to the sanctuary of the small chapel, something gave him pause. He turned and glanced at the stairs that would carry him to the second level. To Karin.

She was so close. But so far away.

Should he risk it? Risk his heart? For her?

His eyes slid closed. *Lord, my heart is weak. And it is wounded. What would you have me do?*

For the first time in days, he filled with a sense of hope. And he imagined that perhaps things could be different. Even if they could not be the same, maybe they could be better. And that was something he was willing to fight for. For her.

He took several long strides toward the stairs, and with determination, he mounted the stairway, even taking some of the steps in twos.

His heart raced with exertion and emotion by the time he stood outside the chambers he once shared with Karin.

He raised a hand to knock. And paused. A small voice warned that he asked for more hurt, that nothing would be different. But he knew he had received an answer to his simple prayer. And he would trust that.

Pavel landed his hand on the door three times.

"Come!" He heard from the other side of the door. It was Karin's voice, strong and sure. This was different.

Praying it was a good sign, he worked the latch and swung the door open.

As the interior of the room became visible, he drank in the sight of his wife as if she were water in a desert. It had been a couple of days since he had seen her. And even longer since her eyes had searched out his as they did in this moment.

He fought the urge to rush to her and gather her in his arms. That might be too much too soon.

Stepping all the way into the room, he noticed the curtains had been pushed back and that she was dressed, no longer in her nightshift.

She offered him a smile. More than that, he saw the smile reflected in her eyes. Could it be his Karin had come back to him? There was a stinging behind his eyes and nose as he fought tears of joy.

"You have your sling off," she said. Only then did he realize they had been squaring off in silence.

"Yes. Doctor Doubek came a few days ago. He said I should be able to return to the front by week's end."

"Oh." Her face fell.

Why had he brought that up? Of course she didn't need to hear that. He anticipated a flare of anger, or for the distance to fall back between them, or for her to find a reason to dismiss him.

Her eyes rose to meet his again. "Then we must make the most of the next couple of days." She offered him a smile. A genuine smile!

Surely his heart had wings. Pavel stepped farther into the room, unable to keep himself from closing the distance between them.

She watched him as if she expected him to pounce on her at any second. But as he neared, she adjusted her legs to make space for him to sit on the chaise.

He took the seat, his hands itching to touch her, but he forced them to remain at his side. Not an easy task.

Karin continued to search his eyes as if she sought the answer to some question.

He silently begged her to ask it. If that's what she needed to close this gap, he was prepared to answer anything.

Then she reached for his hands. The contact of her slender hands on his was not nearly enough to quench his thirsty soul. But it caused heat to shoot through his arms.

Did he flinch? She gave him an odd look and said, "I'm sorry. Did I hurt your arm?"

"No, not at all." He squeezed her smaller hands.

She shifted her gaze down to their hands and intertwined their fingers. As she leaned forward, her hair was so close. How he longed to plunge his hands into those red waves!

Everything about her intoxicated him anew. He was lost to her. Completely.

"Pavel," she started.

He worked to focus on what she said. It was difficult amid the myriad of sensations and emotions coursing through him.

"There is something I need to tell you."

She lifted her face so that her eyes met his. Those green orbs were glassed over, but she held back her tears.

His heart was moved for her struggle. With boldness, he lifted one of his hands to cup the side of her face. "You can tell me anything. You know that."

She nodded, closing her eyes and leaning into his hand. "This . . . this is not going to be easy."

His heart was so full of love. There was nothing she could say that would be harder than what they had already faced. He thanked God they seemed to be on the mend. "Just say it, my love. I promise, I'll catch you if you fall."

Her eyes held his. Then she began to speak. "Pavel, we were blessed with a miracle. A child. But—"

"A child?" His thoughts raced. They had been so careful. But it was not a sure way to avoid pregnancy. This was not what they had planned . . . but a baby . . . his and Karin's baby. His heart swelled. "Karin, that's wonderful, I know we were not quite ready—"

Tears welled in her eyes and she gripped his hands a little too tightly. "Pavel, that's not all."

"What?" A feeling of dread settled in his stomach.

"That day . . . that horrible day when I . . . " Her mouth clamped tight and tears escaped. "It was because I lost the baby."

The words that poured from her mouth were not real. How could he be taken to such heights only to be dropped down to earth again? Not even to the mountaintops where he had been, but in some deep dark pit. His heart, having just swelled to epic proportions, exploded. And it was as if he bled all over the place.

Karin's mouth moved, but he couldn't make out her words. He shook his head. And all of a sudden, he needed to talk. But how to get her to stop talking?

Placing a finger on her lips brought her to silence. He closed his eyes against the pain that now coursed through him. "Why . . . why did you not tell me?"

She was crying now. "I don't know. My reasons made sense at the time. But they all seem so weak now. It wasn't part of our plan. I didn't want to put an extra burden on you. What can I say to help you understand? I was scared. For you. For what it would mean for you."

So, she hadn't trusted him. That was the whole of it.

He extricated his hand and stood, moving away from the chaise. Pausing, he turned. "And you? You are healing well?"

"I . . . yes." Was there something confusing about his question?

Pavel nodded. Silence fell again, and he was left to deal with the emotions she had just handed him. He moved toward the door.

"Please, Pavel, do not do this," she whimpered.

He refocused his gaze on her.

"Do not shut me out. Listen to me. I built a wall around my heart and all it did was bring more hurt, more pain. It did not bring healing. We are stronger together than we are apart."

Her words began to penetrate the emotional fog around his brain.

"We need to work through this together," she said through her tears. "Trust me, I know. This will pull us apart or strengthen us. That decision is in your hands."

Her words trailed off as she shook with sobs. And he watched her cry. Helpless. Reaching out to him.

Lord, I am not strong enough.

But God was strong enough for the both of them.

He closed the distance between them once again and gathered her in his arms as they mourned the loss of their child together.

Zdenek pushed his horse harder. The army did not lag, but his horse had slowed its steps. Perhaps a clump of grass caught her eye. Admonishing the animal with a tug on the reins and a squeeze with his legs, he felt the mare move ahead.

The general mood around him proved to be somewhat somber. Why would today be any different? They faced many enemy combatants by this time. And no matter the odds, they had prevailed. Was it the skill of their commander? The passion of their cause? Or did God truly fight with them? Zdenek did not know. But he would continue to follow this great man and support his brothers in their struggle for freedom. These questions about God would wait.

Marching out of the heart of Prague, the unit of misfits-turned-soldiers approached their destination. The Hradcany loomed before them, high above the city. Turrets and spires were visible above the castle's walls. The structure had always been beautiful to him, striking in its architecture and lines.

Radek grunted beside him and Zdenek wondered after him. His friend had become increasingly more vocal these last weeks.

Zdenek's gaze leveled on Radek's features.

Radek's brows furrowed and his mouth formed a thin line.

"Something troubles you?" Though why Zdenek asked, he did not know.

Radek maintained his displeasure at the conflict within the Bohemian lands and at their continued participation in the fighting.

"Never. I never could have imagined in all my life I would march on the great Hradcany, the jewel of Prague." His voice was gruff, his words coming out in harsh tones.

Zdenek remained silent. In truth, the reality of their attack today became more and more difficult to absorb. Even more so as they approached the castle. His memory echoed with stories of the great Czech kings who had called this their home. Were their actions treacherous?

A tingle ran down the back of his neck. Shifting his eyes, he found Radek staring at him.

"You feel it too, don't you?"

Zdenek wanted to shrug him off. What could he say to stop these questions within himself? He had a job to do. They had committed to fight, and they couldn't stop now because of some nostalgia for a fairytale.

But he couldn't hide from Radek. So, he nodded, letting his gaze fix on the castle before them.

"Then what are we doing?" Radek lowered his voice to a whisper, his words still rough as he leaned toward his friend.

Zdenek lingered in his thoughts for only a moment more. "Everything has changed."

Radek raised an eyebrow and regained his upright posture.

"And we cannot act as though it hasn't." He met Radek's wide eyes. "Look around you. Our brothers fight for their freedom, for their God. And yet we debate the value of a building. Are not their lives more valuable?"

Radek's gaze dropped. And Zdenek thought Radek's hands tightened on the reins. Were his knuckles turning white?

"Radek?" he prodded.

"So be it," Radek ground out. He did not turn toward Zdenek, did not look up. Digging his heels into his horse's side, he pushed ahead of Zdenek.

"Radek . . . " Zdenek called.

But Radek did not stop.

CHAPTER 11
REGRETS

Karin knelt next to Pavel. Wasn't she cried out? Surely there were no more tears. But in the solemnness of the moment, her heart stilled.

Pavel reached for her hand closest to him and intertwined their fingers.

She peered at him, next to her at the altar.

His eyes were closed and his brow furrowed. Did he seek the Lord so fervently? Perhaps he could pray for the both of them. She wanted to pray. But the words would not come. Not even in the silence of her thoughts. Was there too much sadness?

Turning back to the altar, she examined her fingers, intermixed with Pavel's, and studied the wood grain of the surface in front of her. She gazed up at the stained glass windows depicting scenes from Christ's life.

Her eyes caught on the Nativity. And the loss of her child slammed into her heart anew. Still, no tears came, only the hurt.

But Mary kept all these things and pondered them in her heart.

She glanced at the artist's depiction of Mary. What had it been like for her? To know that her baby would taste death in her lifetime?

To hold the Christ child and know He would be sacrificed? *Could* she comprehend that?

But it had been part of a plan. A bigger plan. A plan Mary couldn't see. She just had to trust. And if Mary could trust God in the midst of that, perhaps Karin could trust God now. That He would hold her and sustain her, and then see her through it.

Then Karin found words for prayer. And fresh tears.

The attack on the Hradcany continued. Radek oscillated between taking a post among the Hussite revolutionaries and watching, stricken, as their hand cannons inflicted serious damage on the structure he had almost prized above their lives. How long could it last? How long could the Royalists in the castle withstand it?

Their food stores certainly dwindled. How their fears must rise as well. The Hussites had such fervor about themselves. They behaved as if possessed. Madness had overtaken them. Would they allow any of the soldiers in the castle to live?

Studying the faces of the men around him, he found cause to doubt.

Swallowing hard, he shifted his attention back toward the stone walls. What was that? There was movement off to the far south side of the structure. Yes, men crept around the exterior. Narrowing his eyes to hone his vision, he searched for any sign of weapons. He saw none. In fact, the men came with their hands stretched out and away from their bodies. As if they prepared to capitulate.

In that moment, others began to notice. A loud cry erupted from behind him—someone called for the Hussites to attack the small band of defenseless Royalists.

"No!" Radek pushed his horse into motion, placing himself in front of the exposed men. Raising his voice to the most extremes it would stretch, he shouted. "These men are unarmed. Would you strike at those who wish to surrender?"

Radek's eyes widened as he took in the scene. Hand cannons aimed at him, arrows pointed at his heart. Never had he been so anxious. But he would not leave these men vulnerable.

Zizka appeared from the midst of the menacing weapons, urging his own horse to Radek's position. "What is this?"

Radek swallowed hard. Would Zizka be his salvation or his end? The commander proved to be every bit as intimidating as the mass of weapons combined.

By some miracle, Radek found his voice. "These men are not attacking us. They are giving themselves up."

Zizka's hard gaze drifted from Radek's face to the soldiers behind him. "What say you?"

The men glanced at one another and some paled, clearly terrified.

One stepped forward. His voice trembled when he spoke, "It is true. We are defecting."

Zizka's eye bore into the man. Could he see through to his heart? From the intensity of his stare, Radek began to believe so.

At long last, Zizka jerked his head in the direction of the Hussite army.

Radek let out a breath, yet he resisted the urge to relax his shoulders. He retained the most rigid stance he could manage.

The Royalist soldiers still did not move.

Radek nodded at them, hoping to assure them all was well.

Watching Radek, but cutting eyes back to Zizka, the men moved past the two looming figures on horseback and toward the Hussite soldiers, who had lowered their weapons.

The relief that washed over Radek could not be denied. But as he watched the men move into the mass of peasants and farmers, his heart sank. Why should it be so? These men, the ones who had joined the Hussite army, they had followed Radek's lead. Once loyal to the king, now they became lost in this sea of misfits. Was there any sense in it? Yet Radek had assisted them.

Did they belong? How could they? Would *he* ever truly belong?

Radek knew what he had to do.

Lenka stilled her shaking leg, clasping her hands in her lap. The Utraquist priest droned on. He did so tend to pontificate. Had he not already made his point? And now he had spent the last hour restating it numerous times. She did not remember being so anxious the other evening when she first attended the meeting. Or was it because she had not so desperately sought vital information at that time?

Closing her eyes, she attempted to pray. Yet her thoughts scattered and darted from her prayerful words to Karin to God to the happenings in Tabor and so on and so forth. How did one manage such a divided mind?

When she opened her eyes, the priest had finished his lengthy oration and was praying. She bowed her head once more, not finding any more concentration.

Lenka did thank God when the man's supplication was brought to a close and the meeting dismissed. She was on her feet in a moment, moving forward amid the crowd.

The Utraquist priest spoke with a couple of the Hussites nearby who approached him.

Pushing her way through the shifting of bodies, Lenka moved as fast as she could. At last, she shoved between two conversing women and arrived at the front.

But the priest was no longer there. Where had he gone?

She spun, searching for any sign of his red hair.

He was amid the thick of the crowd now. Not far from where she had just come. If she had but stayed where she was, he would have walked by her.

Lenka let out a grumbled sigh and began maneuvering her way back through the gathering of people that had started to disperse.

As she came near the priest, it became apparent he moved toward his carriage.

"Please," she called out, quite out of breath and out of patience. "Wait!"

The man did not stop, nor did he so much as flinch in response. He advanced on a carriage, speaking to the manservant who opened the door.

"Father!" she spoke out louder than a lady of polite society should dare.

But he turned. And his eyes met hers.

She let out a breath.

The priest's brow quirked. "Yes, my child?"

Encouraged, she went to him. Much easier now that he remained in one spot.

"Father, I am Countess Lenka Bornekova. I confess, I am new to your gathering."

He offered her a smile. "It is no matter, child. All must find truth in their own time."

Lenka nodded and thought of Petr. Had he come to the truth yet? Or was he still seeking? It was no matter. She was here for Karin. "I have come to ask if you know anything of the situation in Tabor."

His brow creased. "Why do you seek information about Tabor? Are you a Taborite?"

Lenka recoiled at the intensity of his eyes. He glared at her as if he spoke of some sin. Weren't the Taborites and the Utraquists all Hussites? "No, Father, my daughter is staying just outside of Tabor. I am concerned after her safety."

The priest's gaze softened, but only slightly. He reached his hands toward her and she placed her hand on his. "Trust God. He is the only one who can know of her fate."

Shaking her head, Lenka wondered if she had understood him. Did he not know of the conditions in Tabor? Or would he not disclose them? Lenka opened her mouth but he shook her hand before releasing it. Then he turned and stepped up into his carriage, leaving her standing by the wayside. More confused than ever.

Stepan tossed and turned. The screams and cries of the Hussite prisoners being thrown down the shafts proved too much. Their horror. So many suffering, falling to their deaths. Those that survived starving, dying, in pain, calling for reprieve.

Eyes open, he felt his limbs twisted in the sheets and his night-clothes drenched in sweat. It was the same night after night. How much more could he take?

Extricating his arms and legs from the bed linens, he sat on the edge of the thin mattress, resting his head in his hands. Why should he care about what happened to these Hussites? These heretics? Didn't the end justify the means? This was war after all. And they were the enemy.

As much as he tried to convince himself of these things, his body continued to tremble. He wiped at his forehead with the back of his hand and realized it was a cold sweat. Odd. His body had seemed rather heated. But now he found it chilled.

Then he noticed that the drapes in his room had been opened. A breeze flew through his room, cooling the space. He would close them soon enough. But first he needed some water.

He walked to the basin and poured water into its generous bowl, splashing some on his face. The chill in the air became more biting, but he felt more human.

Moving to the window, he reached forth to close it. But as he neared the opening, he spotted a hand on the windowsill. Was someone climbing in?

Making a quick scan of the room, he searched for his sword. Where could it be? He couldn't spot it anywhere—not with his clothes or by the bed where he left it. What was this?

Whoever scaled the outer wall pulled himself up until his head was visible. But through the darkness, Stepan could only make out a silhouette. A man for certain, he moved at an odd pace. Slow, almost creeping. Perhaps because he thought Stepan to still be abed, sleeping.

Stepan glanced around the room for anything he might use as a weapon. He grabbed the pitcher beside the basin and held it at the ready, standing a few feet away from the window.

The man cleared the windowsill and now stood in the narrow opening.

Stepan gasped. His sword was stuck through the center of the man's body. How was this possible?

Jumping down into the room and into the moonlight, the man became clearer to Stepan. And he became afraid. It was not his nose or his mouth that struck Stepan but his horrified dark brown eyes.

And they were coming for him.

The man lurched toward Stepan, his movements gross and hunkering.

Stepan dodged the man's swing but stumbled back, losing his footing and falling.

Clomping forward, the ghostly figure continued its pursuit while Stepan scooted rearward, filled with terror, trying to escape his own doom at the hands of his victim.

Stepan bumped into the stand holding the basin. It came crashing down, preventing him from any further movement backward. He was trapped.

The figure pulled Stepan's sword from his own body, his dark red blood glinting in the moonlight when he held the weapon over his head.

Raising the pitcher helplessly in front of himself, Stepan could do nothing more as the man thrust the sword toward his heart.

Stepan startled awake, his limbs twisted in the sheets and his nightclothes soaked with sweat. He gasped for air, unable for several moments to take a full breath.

It was a dream. A bad dream, but a dream nonetheless. Was this a dream? He looked at the window—closed. Glancing next to the bed, he spotted his sword, sitting just where he had left it. Taking a deep breath, he untangled himself from the bed linens. Lying back down, he tried to shake himself free from the images of the terrible nightmare.

But when he closed his eyes, all he saw were those deep brown horrified eyes staring into his soul.

Pavel readied his things. There was sadness in his heart and slowness to his movements. He did not relish leaving Karin. It was too soon.

Having found one another again, they still mourned. But he had no choice. His arm had healed, and he had no real reason to stay other than his desire to be with Karin. And so he found himself once again torn between his wife and his duty to his country.

A small hand pressed against his shoulder and he let out a sigh. He knew it was Karin.

"All will be well, Pavel."

He twisted to face her, gathering her in his embrace.

They remained for some time in silence while he drew strength from her.

Then she pulled back only enough to look up at him. Her eyes were glassy, but no tears came forth. Did she hold them back for his sake?

Cupping her face, he grazed the side of it with his lips before pressing them to her mouth.

She accepted his kiss, tilting her head to deepen the contact, her arms wrapping around his waist.

As they broke apart, he laid his forehead on hers. "I do not wish to be parted from you."

Karin made a soft sound. "I know, but you must. It is time."

He nodded, reluctantly pulling away. It stabbed at his heart the way she hugged her arms to herself as he did so.

Slinging his parcel around his shoulder, he turned to her once again. Reaching a hand for hers, he whispered, "Will you see me out?"

She hesitated, then nodded, slipping her hand into his.

They walked out to the stables where Pavel's horse had already been saddled. His parents waited there as well.

Pavel released Karin's hand only long enough to bid his parents farewell, embracing each one in turn. His mother held on to him a bit longer than necessary.

Patting her shoulder, he attempted to reassure her all would be well. But could he truly offer such assurances?

His father took his mother's arm, drawing her from the embrace, and stepped to the side. Pavel caught his eyes and nodded. Not only was he grateful for his father's careful consideration, he placed the well-being of his precious wife in his father's hands.

Turning his attention to his beloved, Pavel drew Karin to the horse. He traced a finger down the side of her face as if he could memorize her features more vividly than he already had.

"Your visage will be my constant companion until I return to you."

Karin's mouth tugged upward. "Your smile will be mine."

He leaned in to kiss her once more. This was not the most fevered, passionate kiss they had shared. Not with his parents looking on. Rather it was sweet, tender, filled with hope and promise.

When he pulled back this time, Pavel allowed his fingers to linger on her face but a handful of seconds before he broke all contact with her and mounted his steed. But as she stepped away, he sought her face. It would be for naught—merely serving to delay him further. Still, he could not stop himself.

But she would not turn. Even as she reached his mother, Karin would not face him.

And he understood. She had met the limits of her strength.

So he urged the horse onward, keeping his eyes on the horizon.

Petr sat at his massive desk, hunkered over a few papers. He had ordered the summerhouse be vacated and surrendered to Vlastik. Now, there was the matter of the money. Where was he to pull that from?

Running a hand across his forehead, he attempted to soothe the soreness. It ached from hours of concentration. He did not see an easy answer. Closing his eyes, he steepled his fingers and took a deep breath. No good could come from working himself into complete frustration.

The door creaked. He opened his eyes and diverted his attention in that direction.

A manservant came toward him bearing a letter.

Petr leaned forward to receive it. As the servant approached, he saw two letters—one addressed to him and one for Lenka. And they were in Karin's hand. Lenka would be relieved. She had been in quite an unsettled state these last couple of weeks.

Nodding to the manservant, Petr dismissed him.

The younger man stepped into the hall and Petr settled back into his chair, opening his letter.

Scanning, he noted Karin's handwriting appeared rushed. What could have caused that? As he continued to look over the letter, one word stood out among the others and gave him pause: *baby*. He focused on the sentences around the word.

...I have lost the baby. And I am...

Lost the baby? Was Karin pregnant?

At that moment, Lenka burst into the room, breaths heaving. Had she been running?

Lenka stepped toward his desk, holding her letter out to him. "Karin mislabeled the letters. This is yours."

Petr met her eyes, brows furrowed.

Lenka waved the letter in her hand, holding out her other hand to collect her misdirected letter. She peered down at his hands, bearing the opened letter. Her eyes widened.

Had Karin and Lenka been keeping something from him? He glanced at the paper and then at Lenka. There was no mistaking the look of guilt in her eyes.

She leaned over, stretching across the desk to remove the letter from his hands.

He pulled it out of her reach and rose. "What is this?"

Lenka pulled her arm back as if stung. "I do not know what you mean, my lord."

"No? Karin speaks of a baby. Did you know she was pregnant?"

He watched his wife's face closely as her lips became a thin line. Was she choosing her words even then? Another story?

"I want the truth. What are you hiding?"

Lenka's features softened and she opened her mouth, then closed it, her brow wrinkling. "Did you say '*was* pregnant'?"

Petr glanced down at the paper. And his heart was sad as he realized what he had read. "Yes," he said gently. "She lost the baby."

The letter fell from her grasp as Lenka's hands flew to her chest. When she did speak, her words came out in spurts. "Is she . . . Karin . . . is she . . . all right? I mean, she must be, she wrote to us." One of Lenka's hands searched behind for a chair.

Coming around the desk, Petr helped his wife sit.

Her breath came in gasps, but it was becoming more even.

"I did not read the entirety of the letter." Petr spoke as he moved a hand along Lenka's arm. "Only enough."

Lenka nodded, her eyes forward, focused on the wall. "H-how did it happen?"

Petr opened his mouth to tell her he didn't know, but she spoke again.

"Was there an accident?" Her eyes were on his.

"I think we had better read the letter."

She stared into his eyes for several moments before nodding. It was a slight, jerking movement, but an ascent all the same.

Petr pulled another chair closer to Lenka and sat, gathering the letter from his desk and preparing to read. But something stopped him.

"What?" Lenka all but cried out, her hand on her mouth. "What do you see?"

"No." His hand was on her arm then, attempting to calm her. "It's not that."

There was a question in her eyes.

Petr retracted his arm and let out a deep sigh before meeting her eyes again. "I cannot overlook that you hid this pregnancy from me. Did you not think I deserved to know? To celebrate with you?"

Lenka's eyes watered. "Yes, my lord. But it was at Karin's request. She pled with me to keep her secret."

"Why? Why the secrecy?" Karin and her secrets.

"She did not tell Pavel. He was not ready for a family. And so, she did not wish him to know."

A familiar sensation sprang to life within him. A fire. The burn of anger. "Karin and her headstrong ideals," he grumbled. "And you continue to give into her diversions."

Lenka's face fell.

"Will she never grow up?"

He eyed his wife.

She recoiled from his scrutiny.

Throwing his arms up, he surrendered. "Here is your letter. I will continue to play along as you see fit." He thrust the paper toward her as he stood. "If you decide I need to know more details about the well-being of my daughter, I trust you will inform me."

Lenka opened her mouth, but he turned and walked out of the room.

Karin moved the paper closer to her face. The years had not been many, still they had worn away some of the lines from the writings. How sad. And this had been one of her favorites.

Laying the papers in her lap, she gazed over the garden. It didn't matter how many times she read Hus's teachings, there was always something new to glean. Especially when she and Pavel were able to discuss them. How she missed him!

"Mind if I join you?"

She didn't need to twist around to discern that the owner of the voice was her mother-in-law. But turn she did and offered Marketa a smile. "Please."

The baroness joined Karin on the bench, giving her arm a squeeze as she did so. "How are you today?"

"I am well." Karin let out a long breath. "As well as I can be."

"We shall pray for a safe return. And soon."

Karin nodded, looking down at her lap.

Marketa put a hand on the papers. "What is this?"

"Some of the early teachings of Jan Hus. My favorites, I must admit."

The baroness's face betrayed a small smile. "He was a good man."

Karin nodded.

Marketa cricked her neck to look more closely at the writings. "These must have been while you were but a girl!"

"Yes, they were. I didn't read them until much later."

"I imagine so." Marketa met her eyes.

"Even then, I had to hide them." Karin tucked an errant hair behind her ear, squinting in the ever-brightening sunlight. Mid-morning was approaching.

"How did you come by them?" Marketa's voice was calm, level, not pushing or probing, but curious.

Karin had not spoken of these things in quite some time. The years her parents feared the Hussite movement and forbade their daughter have any involvement in it.

"I had a friend. Her brother had become a follower of Jan Hus. And he supplied us with the teachings. There were others that became influenced because of him as well. We would pass the writings to one another in secret. Until my father found out. He tried to put a stop to it. Only…"

Marketa waited, watching Karin with kind eyes.

"Only I wouldn't give it up. You know the rest. He sent me to the chateau. I met Pavel, and our story had a happy ending." Karin gazed at the horizon. If only everyone's story had been so happy.

"What happened to your friends?"

Karin dropped her head. "My friend and her brother were found by a patrol. They were taken. I do not know what became of them. The others, I cannot say."

"That must have been difficult—to go against your parents and to watch others face consequences that could be yours."

Karin nodded, fingering the edges of the papers. Memories flooded her mind. Her father's anger born of fear, her mother's helpless anxiety . . . all because of her choices. Had she done the right thing? But she had. She had followed her faith and her heart. And God had blessed her—with Pavel.

God, please keep him safe. Bring him back to me.

Karin looked toward her mother-in-law. "I apologize. I do not know where my mind has gone."

"There is no need." Marketa laid a hand on Karin's. "Why don't we pray together for Pavel's safety?"

Karin sniffed. Were tears close behind? "I would like that."

The day was clear and bright. Why shouldn't it be? It would have been a good day for hunting, Radek mused. A hunter would have been able to see his prey for a great distance. That's what they should be doing—rising early for a hunting outing. Not dragging themselves from a restless night to meet the emperor and his Royalist troops in battle. Everything was wrong.

Why were Czechs fighting Czechs? And was he on the right side? This question had plagued him from the time he picked up his sword to defend Prague so many months ago. And he still wasn't certain *that* had been the right course of action.

Yet here he was, next to Zdenek, marching into another battle. Was he prepared to kill more of his brethren? One thing he did know —Zdenek would follow orders. And he did want to keep his friend safe. But how long would that be enough?

Looking ahead, he spotted the line of Royalist soldiers at the ready. How long had they been there? The scouts had reported to Commander Zizka that morning that they were here, in formation, prepared to do battle. And Zizka had been all too eager to engage the emperor.

Turning to his dear friend, Radek raised his voice to be heard over the many sounds of the people and horses moving around them. "Zdenek!"

His friend's head turned toward him, eyebrows raised.

"Let us keep toward the rear. Provide reinforcements." A weak reason, he knew. But he longed to remain out of the fight as long as possible and to keep his friend from involvement if he could.

Zdenek's brows furrowed. "Reinforcements? Are we not best utilized at the front?"

"Trust me in this." Radek hoped he would.

Zdenek didn't seem ready to, but, after some moments, he nodded and pulled back on his horse's reins. They moved farther back in formation.

Were they cowards? One look at Zdenek's face and it was clear he thought so. But Radek would have no guilt over it. He focused his mind on their forward momentum.

"Radek," Zdenek broke into the silence that had befallen them.

Taking in a long breath, Radek steeled himself. Would Zdenek want to move back to the front lines? "Yes?"

Zdenek glanced around them. Did he fear eavesdroppers? The men around them were all in their own conversations. When he spoke again, Zdenek's voice was lowered to the point Radek had to strain to hear him. "Do you ever wonder about the Hussites?"

Radek's heart skipped a beat. Did Zdenek struggle as he did? That would change everything! But he had to be careful. He must not be mistaken. Clearing his throat, he kept his eyes forward, but said, "Yes. I do."

Zdenek's eyes were on him. He could feel it. But he would offer nothing further. No, his friend would need to do the talking.

"I've never put much weight on religion," Zdenek said with a sigh.

Religion? Where was this conversation going? Radek peered at his friend. "I thought your father . . ."

Zdenek nodded. "I know." Zdenek's head jerked from side to side as if his father would appear from the crowd of soldiers or perhaps had spies among them. Then he drew in a long breath. "That is why I have never trusted in religion. Because of my father."

Radek's eyes widened.

"And I thought God must be a fabrication just as any other ritual of the church."

As much as Radek wanted to warn Zdenek that he walked the line of blasphemy, he could not. Dare he? Because Zdenek spoke what he feared to? Did *he* truly believe in an Almighty God?

"But as I have watched Pavel . . . and the Hussites . . . it has given me reason to wonder."

Radek could not help but turn curious eyes on his friend. What wonderings did he speak of?

"There is no reason they should prosper. By all counts of reasoning, the Royalist armies should have beaten them back and stomped out the Hussite movement altogether. Unless . . ."

Should he ask? Could he not? "Unless what?"

"Unless God is with them."

Radek fought to retain a neutral face. Surely he was not hearing this.

"My friend, you cannot deny that what we have witnessed is beyond explanation. The deliverance at Plzen, the progress in Prague, the very fact that the Hussite movement grows in strength each day . . . "

"Stop," Radek said, his voice more harsh than he intended. He just needed Zdenek to stop talking.

When he glanced at his friend, Zdenek's brows were furrowed.

"It's just . . . a bit much."

Zdenek nodded. "More than I should have said as we march into battle. Your thoughts are elsewhere. Yes, this is best left for another time."

Radek relaxed a little as Zdenek shifted his attention to the front of the line. The group came to a halt, and Commander Zizka called to his men. But try as he might, Radek could not see the large man from their position at the back of the group.

From all around him, a thunderous cry rose from the Hussites, and they rushed forward. He did not need to hear the clash of metal to know they had engaged the enemy. But move forward they did as the Taborites engaged the Royalists.

The battle raged on for some time. Decidedly, it was the Hussite army that gained ground. And then, without warning or cause, there was a massive shift in that same direction. As if the Royalist army had given way.

Radek glanced at Zdenek. His friend's face read the confusion he felt. What had happened?

But they continued to move with the Hussites. Before long, it became apparent the army was no longer fighting, but rather pursuing the retreating Royalists.

Zdenek pressed through the men to move further up the ranks.

Radek called out to him, but it was no use.

Zdenek soon disappeared in the shuffle of bodies and horses.

Should he follow his friend? Dodging infantrymen and other horses proved a difficult task.

When at long last he found Zdenek once again, he was riding alongside one of the captains, caught in conversation.

Just then, Commander Zizka called a halt to their movement. And collectively, the Hussites slowed to a stop. Only then was Radek able to pull his steed alongside Zdenek's.

"What happened?" Radek whispered.

Zdenek kept his eyes focused on Zizka, but leaned toward Radek. "No one seems to know. One minute the Royalists were fighting, the next they are retreating. It makes no sense."

"And we are no longer pursuing them?" Radek wasn't complaining. It was just that he was surprised Zizka would not continue to track them down.

"I suppose it's that we will not catch them, and in the meantime, we leave Prague vulnerable."

Radek nodded. Now he did care about Prague. No matter what was going on between the factions in his country, he did not want to see the city decimated. And he was certain that was exactly what would happen should Sigismund's mercenaries get their hands on it. Not the Czechs in his army but the foreigners. They cared little about the Czech's Golden Prague.

Commander Zizka must have ordered the Taborites to begin movement back to the city. The men around him shuffled and turned back in the direction they had come.

Radek, too, shifted his horse.

The road back to Prague seemed to stretch out longer than the journey to the battlefront. Perhaps it was the confusion at their apparent lack of victory that lengthened their trip. They would not be returning the victors they had intended.

Nearly halfway along their route, a messenger came to meet them and spoke in hushed tones to Zizka.

At that point, Radek was close enough to the commander to see his reaction.

Zizka's body tightened and his face became a mask.

But Radek had seen enough of the man to know that this did not mean good things.

The message had been overheard and was being whispered throughout the group. It reached Zdenek first. And Radek watched his reaction as well. His mouth became a thin line and his eyes darkened.

"What is it?" Radek was intent on an answer.

"The whole thing seems to have been a trick. Sigismund used the battle as a ploy to sneak in a supply convoy to the Hradcany while we were distracted."

It sunk into Radek's brain. He couldn't help but think it was rather clever. But then he realized what it meant for the Hussites. They would not be able to starve out the Hradcany before the main crusading Royalist army was sure to arrive. And they needed that stronghold, that castle to be sure to hold the city. What would Zizka do now?

CHAPTER 12

DANGER

Pavel awoke with a start, covered in sweat. Why? Why did he have to leave? How could he have not seen it?

Sitting up, he glanced at his friends nearby, resting peacefully. He drew his knees to his chest. *Oh, God, why?*

Just after his arrival in Prague, Zizka told him that he received reports of Ulrich of Rozmberk. The man had begun causing trouble in Tabor. Zizka had, just that morning, sent a group of men back to Tabor. This, he assured Pavel, would bring an end to Rozmberk's challenge.

Pavel was not so certain. What would become of his parents? Of Karin? Should he have spun his horse on its heels and returned?

His head dropped into his hands, thoughts so clouded he could not pray. But prayer is what he sought. For that was where he found strength.

Not tonight.

"Is something amiss?"

Pavel turned toward the soft voice to his left.

Zdenek stared up at him from his bed mat.

"I did not mean to disturb you," Pavel whispered. "Please go back to sleep, friend."

Zdenek shifted to prop his head up. "It is not you. I find it difficult to sleep, as hot as it has been."

Pavel nodded. "Radek does not seem to have the same problem."

Zdenek peered at the man lying to his other side. "Him? He could sleep in a thorn bush."

Pavel chuckled.

Silence fell between them.

Zdenek opened his mouth, but closed it.

What did he want to say? Why would he not just say it? Pavel stretched his legs.

Then Zdenek found his voice. "Have you always been a Hussite?"

What a question. Pavel's eyes met Zdenek's. He chose his words carefully. "In my heart, yes. I have always questioned some things in the church."

"Why?"

Zdenek was rather curious for the late hour, Pavel mused. But he wasn't bothered by it. Pavel took a deep breath and let it out. "I suppose because I knew God. And I knew His truth didn't line up with what I heard."

Zdenek looked to the ground for a moment. "That is a rather curious thing."

"What is?"

"What you said—that you 'knew God'. How does one 'know God'?"

What do I say? How do I explain something like this? "The same way you know anyone else. Through time, conversation, study."

"Conversation?"

"That's what prayer is." Pavel leveled his eyes on Zdenek's. "A conversation with God."

"You mean to say that God talks back to you?" Zdenek's face was a mixture of confusion, skepticism, and fear.

"Sometimes." Pavel shrugged. "But not the way you think."

Zdenek's brow furrowed.

"It's difficult to explain."

"If one cannot explain it, how does one convert anyone?"

That was a good question. So Pavel attempted to answer this unexplainable thing. "There are many things about God that have to be taken by faith."

Zdenek became quiet.

Were these questions the product of his time with the Hussites? Was this a sign Zdenek might be ready to take a step of faith? Pavel opened his mouth to speak further but was cut off by Zdenek.

"My father spoke often of faith." Zdenek's gaze was focused on the ground, almost as if he peered through the grass to something beyond.

Even if Pavel had something to say, he sensed it was time to listen.

"But he had little to show for it." Zdenek sat up then, crossing his legs in front of himself and looking off into the distance.

Pavel was tempted to peek at what he seemed so drawn to but kept his eyes on his friend.

"He was a hard man. Never satisfied with anything I ever did. I wasn't *good* enough. Not for his God."

What damage had this man done?

"So I decided I wanted nothing to do with this man's God." Zdenek met Pavel's eyes then.

How should Pavel respond? He should, shouldn't he?

Zdenek stood. "I'll be back."

Pavel watched as Zdenek walked off in search of privacy. Did he seek to relieve himself? Or just to have some quiet moments? Would Zdenek ever be able to accept the idea of a loving, gracious God?

Eva sat on her mattress, legs curled underneath her. Glancing across the space between her bed and the one next to it at her roommate, Apolena, she couldn't help but smile. The girl had become a dear friend. She had helped Eva during this transition, being away from Father and Patricie, and had assisted Eva in her efforts to remain hidden from Zdenek.

Eva hadn't wanted to lie, but he would have been displeased if he had known she came with the Taborite soldiers to Prague despite his insistence she remain in Tabor. But she had to be near him and wanted to participate in this cause.

The Hussite movement had become important to her. As much as she had loathed her father's decision to pack up everything and follow Commander Zizka, she had begun to understand. The commander was wise, and brave, and cared deeply about Bohemia and its people. And the Taborite women had only deepened her resolve.

"What are you thinking?" Apolena gave her a sly smile. "Your Zdenek?"

Eva plunged her face into her shoulder. "He's not truly *my* Zdenek." Her face warmed and she plucked at the fabric of her nightdress.

"But you care for him. And he cares for you, no?" Apolena ducked her head, catching Eva's eyes.

If possible, Eva's face heated even more. "Yes."

"That's what I thought." Apolena laughed.

Eva raised her head, letting a laugh escape. "It's time for us to get some sleep. I'm certain tomorrow will be another long day of work on the moat."

"Sleep?" Apolena stood and began dressing. "We have a long night ahead of us!"

"What are you doing?" Eva watched her movements. Had Apolena gone mad? The hour had grown late and the entire monastery slumbered. Did she intend to sneak out?

"Our plans. Tonight is the night, remember?" Apolena paused. Her eyes on Eva were expectant.

"Wait . . . what?" Eva slid off the side of the small bed. "I don't understand. What plans?"

"Stop playing at some sort of farce." Apolena waved her hand and continued to pull on her chemise.

Eva's brows furrowed. "I tell you, Apolena, I do not know what you are talking about."

Apolena put her hands on her hips and met Eva's eyes.

They squared off for a moment. Eva began to wonder if Apolena would ever tell her.

"You truly do not know?"

Eva shook her head, a sense of dread falling over her.

"I do not understand how no one has told you." Apolena crossed her arms, a brow quirked. Did she still not believe Eva?

"Perhaps *you* should tell me." Eva wanted to step toward her friend, but the sense of foreboding that filled her also paralyzed her.

Apolena continued to stare hard at Eva but, at length, let her arms fall to her side. "Tonight is the night we will expel the nuns from this monastery and burn it to the ground."

Eva was struck. Apolena could not be serious. She searched Apolena's eyes for any sign that she had spoken in jest. Perhaps she intended to punish Eva for forgetting whatever their planned ruse was. But Apolena's features betrayed nothing of the sort. Her hazel eyes remained set on Eva with such intensity that Eva did not question her veracity.

"W-Why?" Eva found her tongue with some difficulty.

"How can you ask that?" Apolena's forehead creased. "These women are not serious about their stand for Christ. They lack the zealousness He requires. It is as if they are playacting. And we will not tolerate such a farce."

Eva felt as if she had been hit between her shoulders by a boulder. But she tried to disguise it.

Apolena came around her bed and stood next to Eva, laying a

hand on her shoulder. "Can't you see, Eva? We have to do this." Her new friend seemed so sincere in her plea. She truly believed in what she was doing. Who was Eva to tell her she was wrong? But it still felt wrong.

All Eva could do was nod. What could she do to stop this plan? Could she warn the nuns? It wasn't as if they planned to burn the monastery down with the nuns inside. They intended to turn them out first. Should she stop them from burning the structure to the ground? How was she to do this?

Zdenek.

She had to find Zdenek.

Without anything further, Eva moved to where her dress and chemise lay and started the process of readying herself.

Apolena moved back to her own dress. "You will see. What we are doing is necessary. It is right."

Eva nodded but bit her lip. She twisted toward the wall so Apolena could not see the errant tear that escaped.

They finished dressing in silence. Then Apolena indicated they should make their way out of the room.

Eva's insides turned. She had to find a way to get free of Apolena, to sneak out and get to Zdenek.

Apolena led the way out the door and down the hall. They were met by some of the other Taborite women in the hallway near the stairs. A simple nod was the only greeting.

The women pointed at themselves and in different directions, perhaps indicating who should go where. Thankfully, Eva was to go down the staircase.

Apolena whispered that she would meet up with another group of Taborite women there.

Eva parted company with the party, praying she could make it down the stairs before any others intercepted her.

Down one level, she spotted no one. She continued to descend the last set of stairs until she was at the door to the exterior.

Taking one last look behind her, she let out a soundless breath.

No one followed her. She lifted the latch with care and opened the door just enough for her slender form to slip through.

Once in the open air, she ran for the northern end of the city. The men were camped on an island in that vicinity. It took several minutes to reach them, and her breathing was ragged, coming in gasps when she neared.

But her way was barred by centuries guarding the path. And they appeared none too happy for the disturbance.

"What can we do for you?" One of the men rose, his frame silhouetted in the moonlight. He was massive.

"*Dobry vecer,*" she greeted them, trying to control her breathing. "I must speak with my husband. It's urgent."

The guard glanced at the other, still seated, examining his sword. He shrugged, seeming bored as he spun his weapon, allowing the metal to catch the moonlight. "As long as you don't disturb any of the other sleeping soldiers."

"Of course." She had no intention of upsetting anyone.

"You may pass." The glowering guard grumbled. He moved out of the way so she could walk between them.

As much as she wanted to run, she thought better of it and took quick, lengthened steps onto the small island. Once in the camp, she realized how difficult her task would be. Some of the men had erected makeshift tents, some were sleeping in the open air. Would Zdenek be in a tent? Would she have to look inside each one? Examine every occupant? There were over 9,000 men camped here!

But Zdenek had a horse. Not every man did. That would narrow her search . . . some. She closed her eyes and tried to picture his horse. Eva had always been good with horses. A dark brown mare with a black mane and tail. Yes! That was it.

Picking her way through camp, she gazed at the horses, looking to find the ones matching that description. It proved to be more work than she anticipated, but it did help keep her from having to check every single man.

Several dark brown horses into her exploration, she spotted a familiar figure lying nearby on the ground. The dark hair and beard reminded her of Zdenek's friend Radek. Was Zdenek near? As she drew closer to where the man rested, she found an empty bed mat. Had Zdenek been here?

Should she wake the man she assumed was Radek? It had always seemed he didn't care for her. But the situation had become rather urgent. Much time had already passed. Too much time. She needed to find Zdenek now.

Pushing her trepidations to the side, she leaned over the figure and placed a hand on his shoulder.

He jerked to the ready, pushing her back, hand on the hilt of his sword.

Eva stumbled away, hands rising to defend herself.

The man's eyes were on her. "What are you doing here?" His voice was harsh, accusation thinly veiled.

"Please. Are you Radek? I'm looking for Zdenek. It's urgent."

The bearded man looked at the empty bed mat. "I don't know where he is," he grumbled. "And you shouldn't be here."

Eva swallowed past a lump forming in her throat. "I need help."

Another figure, a blond man, moved toward them. "Radek? What is the matter?"

Radek's eyes met hers, glaring. Then he looked at the other man. He opened his mouth to speak, and Eva prepared herself for another harsh rebuke.

"Eva?" Another voice, this one from behind her.

She spun toward the sound and came face-to-face with Zdenek. "Zdenek!"

"What are you doing here?" His soft eyes were confused. But there was something underneath that. Anger?

Eva stepped toward him. "I . . . we can talk later, but right now I need your help." Would he help her? She had nothing left but to trust him.

His eyes darkened for a moment and then softened as she reached for his hand, their fingers grazing. "Tell me."

She let out a breath. "The Taborite women are preparing to burn down the monastery. We have to stop them."

Zdenek's eyes widened and he glanced at the blond man. "Why would they do this?"

Eva's eyes filled with moisture. "They think the nuns aren't truly committed to Christ. That they aren't zealous enough." She took his hand. "Come, we must go!"

The blond man stepped closer. "We will follow."

Zdenek exchanged another look with the man and nodded toward Eva. He did not release her hand as she led him from the camp, his blond friend trailing behind.

Once they were on the streets of Prague, she beaconed them to hurry. The smell of burning ash and smoldering wood filled Eva's nostrils long before they arrived. And the tendrils of black smoke were visible from a distance. Still she trudged on.

"Eva!" Zdenek shouted and tugged at her.

But she continued to pull him onward. There had to be something they could do. It couldn't be too late. Not after everything she had done.

They rounded the last corner and the structure came into full view, alight with flame and ember.

Zdenek halted and pulled her back into his arms.

The blond man continued to move on toward the monastery.

Eva stared at the building she had been in maybe an hour ago and could not stop the tears.

Huddled in a mass beside the monastery were the nuns. They comforted one another and wailed. That's where Zdenek's friend went. Perhaps to ensure their safety.

Eva cried for them, too. For the injustice, for their loss, and for her inability to do anything to change their fate.

How long had it been? Days? Weeks? Karin did not know. One day passed into the other as the emptiness of her room and bed kept her restless each day and into every night. Wasn't she stronger than this? Pavel had believed her to be.

Gazing at her journal, she was mocked by the empty pages staring back. She had sat for nearly an hour and yet no thoughts worth writing came. Not even the view of the countryside out the nearby window could divert her.

Pages turned behind her and she shifted so she could look at Pavel's parents seated farther away by the fireplace. Though there was nothing burning in the hearth, the chair closest to it allowed Alex to have his back to the window, giving him more adequate reading light. Marketa worked her needle and thread not far away. She hummed. A bit loudly. But it did not seem to disturb her husband.

So Karin watched her new parents at leisure. They had gone to great lengths to make her comfortable. But it wasn't the same without Pavel. She doubted anywhere would be.

Her heart ached for him, for his arms. And to know all would be well. As it was, she worried. Would he be safe? Would his injury lead him to become compromised in battle?

She sniffled as a tear escaped. Reaching up, she caught it before it made a trail down her face. But she found the baron's eyes on her.

Offering him a small smile, she hoped to reassure him.

He nodded and returned to his book.

She spun in her seat and lifted the writing tool once again. It would be best if she could get her feelings out on paper. Then she might have some relief.

No sooner had she made an ink stroke on the clean parchment than the door flew open.

A manservant rushed in, followed by a man dressed for battle.

"My lord, our lands are under attack!" The manservant appeared flushed and harried.

Karin's eyes were on Alex.

He rose as the soldier stepped past the manservant.

"My lord," the soldier interjected, not waiting to be announced properly. "I am charged with taking you and your family to safety at once."

"Yes, of course." Alex waved at Karin and Marketa.

Karin stood on shaky legs and stepped toward the soldier.

As the three converged where the soldier stood, Alex spoke to the man, "We must get the women to a safe place, but I will stay and fight."

The soldier's eyes were hard on Alex. But as he studied the baron, his gaze softened. "As you wish, my lord. Your sword will be a great asset."

Karin watched Alex's features as they settled into a proud mask. When she glanced at Marketa, however, the woman was biting her lip. Did she want to speak out against it? If so, her restraint was admirable. For she uttered not a sound but took Alex's hand as the soldier led them to the stables.

The manservant split off from the group. Was he not to go with them? What would become of the servants?

Before long, Karin sat in a saddle, prepared to go. She had not one possession with her. Marketa lingered in a moment of farewell with Alex. Karin averted her eyes, focusing on the horse beneath her. The light tan of its hair was soft under her hand and the black of its mane felt coarse in her fingers. Though the horse stirred under her, she trusted he had sure feet and good speed.

Marketa came up beside her, already in a saddle. But Karin saw moisture in her eyes. This was a lot to take in at once.

The manservant appeared with Alex's battle garments and sword. He began fitting his master for war.

A loud voice disturbed her thoughts as the soldier cut off her view of Alex, walking his horse into her sightline. "Come, ladies, we must away."

Karin nodded at the man who she supposed she should trust and urged her horse into a trot. The clomping of hooves behind assured her Marketa followed.

As they came around the front of the estate, more soldiers surrounded them. Unnerved, Karin almost pulled back on her reins. Were they friend or foe? Was this some kind of elaborate trap?

A glance around told her that resistance would indeed be a futile effort. So, she peered at Marketa's paled face and held on as they pushed their horses into the night.

Zdenek's thoughts were absorbed. Eva was here. She had defied his better judgment and come with the Taborite army. What was she thinking?

And now, because of the Taborite women, there was a great upheaval in the Hussite community. Perhaps not all was the fault of the women. There had been underlying unrest since the Taborites came to Prague. The Hussites in the golden city just weren't as extreme in their beliefs. And the people of Prague led a more extravagant lifestyle, which the Taborites found to be rather . . . ungodly.

Zdenek still wasn't sure what was godly. Who was God? What was truth? So, he wasn't sure he should judge what was ungodly.

A meeting had been called. And here he was, seated in a rather large room, glancing about at the various representatives from the Old and New Towns of Prague as well as University Masters and representatives of the city's allies.

As he watched on, the meeting was called to order and great discussion ensued. Zdenek always had a difficult time following these sorts of things. But a glance to his side at Radek and Pavel told him that his friends tracked the meeting just fine.

This did not bother Zdenek. It allowed his mind to wander where it longed to be—on Eva. When she came to him the other evening, he had wondered if she was a product of some fantasy. After his discussion with Pavel, he had needed a moment to think. He could never have imagined that when he returned, he would find Eva facing off with Radek.

But when she spun toward him, his heart had stopped. Though out of breath and bedraggled, she was striking. And in that moment, he pondered how he ever left her behind. But it had been for her own safety. Once he realized she was truly there, he became concerned about her presence. And a bit angry.

Though when she reached for him, pleading for his help, how could he refuse? All the while, he thought it best to let the Taborite women handle their own problems the way they saw fit. But how could he refuse *her* anything?

Then they were too late. He had nothing left to do but hold her. And he did until there were no more tears. By then other soldiers had come to the aid of their wives, the Taborite women. They took them into their camp and that was the end of it.

Until the Praguers started pointing fingers. The civil unrest increased. Now here they were.

Zdenek forced his attention back to the speakers. As he began to put together the happenings of the council, he gathered that they had just elected new city councils for both towns.

"There will be a full scale purge of all who remain in the city but are unwilling to accept communion in both kinds," one of the new council members said.

"Yes, there are too many German Catholics who remain among us as traitors," another council member spoke up.

"How shall we accomplish this?" One man raised his voice.

The man who had suggested the purge thought for a moment. "We shall go door-to-door and insist everyone sign a pledge to the cause of the Chalice. Whoever refuses shall be expelled from the city."

Radek grunted.

Zdenek glanced at him. Did he disagree? It had not escaped Zdenek that Radek had been having some . . . hesitations. Still, he did not ask his friend about it.

The new council members went on to discuss and refine the fourth article of the stated Four Articles.

Zdenek tried to maintain his attention, as he knew this was important to the cause.

Radek crossed his arms and leaned his head back as if to doze. Was he no longer interested?

Then Commander Zizka stepped forward. "The military command structure needs to be reviewed."

Zdenek leaned forward, and he sensed Radek raise his head as well.

Was Zizka stepping down? Or was he vying for more power? The military units in Prague were under different commanders. They didn't operate as one. Perhaps that was what he wanted to change.

There was debate on the matter, during which Zdenek thought he saw even Zizka appear bored. Eventually, they elected twelve captains and named Zizka captain-general of Prague. Everyone seemed pleased.

Zizka gave a report about the recent goings-on in Tabor. There were skirmishes. Ulrich of Rozmberk had taken advantage of Zizka's absence.

Pavel tensed beside him.

And Zdenek knew. His friend had left just before these things transpired. It haunted Pavel that he was not there to defend his wife, his parents, and their estate. He did not have to say as much for Zdenek to sense it to be true.

But, between the contingency sent from Prague and the small army left in Tabor, they had been able to defeat Rozmberk.

Zizka noted, with shoulders that seemed weighed down and an intensity in his gaze, that Rozmberk had taken several priests as prisoner. It was known that he sentenced them to be imprisoned and starved. And if Zizka had the chance, he would make Rozmberk pay.

Much of the remainder of the meeting was lost on Zdenek. There was nothing for it. His mind was elsewhere. As the monastery burned, sad as they had been, he and Eva had connected in a meaningful way. Yet his anger was not quelled. She had defied him. Now she was in danger.

And there was nothing he could do to prevent the crusade that was coming. None of them could. It was only a matter of time until the Royalist army arrived in full force. Prague, the prized capital of their lands, the crowned jewel of Bohemia, would be the focus of the entire conflict. It would all come down to this one city. And she was here. In the midst of it.

The wind blew past Lenka as she stood atop her balcony high above the rolled out landscape that seemed to move in waves. She always marveled at it—how it changed from day to night. When washed with the light of the sun it fairly glowed, springing forth with life. But as darkness fell, it took on more ominous movements. It teemed with shadows and glimpses of wild, untamed things.

These things sought her out this night. Just as the wind itself pierced through her, it searched out her very soul. Clasping her hands to her heart, she attempted to keep at least that one piece to herself. For she would not betray the hidden things there to the madness of the shifting wind. Nor, it would seem, to the probing of her husband.

She wondered anew why she had defended her secret-keeping. Why had she chosen distance over reconciliation? The cold wind beating against her howled its judgment upon her, but it could no more press guilt on her than she did so herself. For she was lost.

Had her dealings with Karin been right? Her heart spoke in the affirmative, though everything around her denied her succor. What was she to believe?

Should she stand her ground and await Petr's change of heart? Or admit her wrongdoing and beg forgiveness for a grievance she wasn't certain she had committed? Or was she?

At length, she drew her body away from the torment of the wind and inside the hall. Only then did she realize she heaved great breaths from her fight against herself. Her eyes took in the limited light in the hall as the moonlight crept in through occasional openings within the safety of her home. Had none of the servants thought to light candles for their mistress?

Her heart pounded as she stepped carefully into the darkness. Sure she could find her way to her room no matter the circumstance, she preceded, her footfalls slow as she made her way in the direction of the stairs.

Once up the stairs and to her room, she breathed a deep sigh. There would be no more of it tonight. No more war, no more struggle. Only her and her bed. She would ponder on what would become of Petr in the morning.

Her door had been opened and a candle lit within. So Sharka had not forgotten her. Pushing the door to widen the opening, she stepped into the room.

And her breath caught.

A figure sat, silhouetted by the lone flame.

She scrambled backward, hitting the door, slamming it shut. There was no escape.

The figure shifted, sitting straighter and raising its head toward her. "Lenka?"

The voice, soft in its delivery, concern belayed in its tone, was familiar. As he stood, she could discern his features. Petr.

Her whole body slumped. She wished to chastise him for the fright he had given her but could not find the words.

He stepped toward her, now only an arm's length away. "Lenka, are you well?"

She nodded, her hand still over her heart, reassured by its pounding that she had not, in fact, died of fright.

"I have been here for near an hour. What has kept you?" There was no accusation in his voice. Only concern.

Part of her wanted to respond in harsh tones, biting at him for his earlier behavior. But she found she could not. "I was enjoying the night air."

As the flame now sat behind him, she could not see his features. His nod was all she made out.

He sighed deeply. "I could not rest."

She licked her lips, but did not move.

Petr let out a long breath and took another step toward her. "I cannot sleep when there is strife between us."

Though she could not see his face, she felt his eyes upon her.

"What would you say, wife?"

She took several breaths before she spoke. "I know not what to say, my lord. I fear I cannot discern in my own heart whether to spurn my behavior or defend it."

Her words were met with a long stretch of silence. When he did speak, his voice was much softer. "I cannot blame you for the whole of it. Nor can I absolve it."

"Then what would you have me do?" She swallowed, placing her hands against the door behind her and lowering her head in submission.

Gentle fingers on her chin raised her face once again. "I would have you be true to yourself. And I would love you for it."

Lenka could not hold back the tears that stung her eyes.

His arms surrounded her. Caught in the shelter of his embrace, she allowed the tears to come. In the emotion of the moment, his lips found hers. And all was well.

Marketa awoke from a restless sleep, itching. Slumbering on the ground did not suit her. Was it some bug? Or the grass? She reached for her leg and scratched through her skirts. How many nights had she endured such offense to her comfort? How many more must she yet?

The warmth on her back indicated the fire burned though she

had not opened her eyes. And there were voices. Were the men still awake? She strained to hear. Only two, perhaps three, distinct voices were discernable. But their words were difficult to make out.

"What say you?" one man spoke a bit harshly, raising his voice to a level that made it easier to hear. Was his speech slurred?

"I don't like it one bit," another chimed in.

"Just look at them. So helpless. Like lambs." Was it the first voice? Or a third?

"And here we are . . . like watching children. When we could be fighting," the voice grated. Angry. At she and Karin? Marketa held her breath and stilled her scratching.

" . . . nothing to show for it . . . "

The words came in snatches. Were the men lowering their voices?

"Perhaps . . . we could . . . or . . . "

There was a menacing quality to the voice. Did they plot ill upon her and Karin? Marketa's eyes widened. She bit her lip to keep it shut.

Karin slept on, a short distance away. What should she do—wait for the men to seek sleep? Or would one remain alert for watch? Perhaps she should rouse Karin. But how to do so without raising suspicion?

No, it was up to her. But how? And could she? A couple of things were certain: she could not overcome more than one soldier, and she had to find the courage to do this.

Refocusing on the men across the campsite, she strained once more to hear their voices. Minutes passed into an hour as she waited for them to subside. They finally did. Quieting her breath, she counted several more minutes away to ensure the other men were indeed asleep.

Now. It has to be now.

Rolling slowly onto her back, she gazed across the span of the camp and noted that the site was devoid of movement. Four of the soldiers were on the ground, sleeping. One slumped against a tree near the fire. Had he also fallen asleep? Perhaps from too much drink? Could she be so fortunate?

Sitting up, she narrowed her eyes and studied his form.

Nothing.

A noise nearby caused her heart to stop.

Jerking her head around she realized it was the snorting of the horses as they shifted. Marketa forced her breaths in and out evenly. Then she reached for Karin.

"Can I help you with something, my lady?" a loud voice said.

Turning, she lost her breath again. The man stood behind her. Was it her imagination or did he have a sneer on his face?

She forced her hand to loosen its grip on the fabric over her heart. Then it was all she could do to make words come forth. "I . . . need to . . ." *How was one to say it when the words wouldn't come?*

The man's face relaxed and an eyebrow quirked. "You need your friend for that?"

"I . . . do not know these woods."

"Afraid of the dark?" A crooked smile crossed his features.

Marketa twisted away as her face warmed. She could not lie. And she feared her eyes would betray her plans. Would she have the courage to do what she must? Her gaze cut to Karin. She had to.

"On your feet. I'll take you." The man sighed, as if it was the last thing he wanted to do.

Rising, Marketa did her best to avoid looking at the man. That would only make everything more difficult.

He held an arm out in the direction of the densest part of the forest. Did he expect her to go first?

She picked up her skirt and made her way into the darkness. The sounds in the thick undergrowth unnerved her. But this man would protect her. And her heart dropped. How could she do this thing? Even if she could find a way? There was no way . . . it was not in her.

After they had walked a short way, Marketa paused. "I think this will do."

All she could discern was his form silhouetted against the moon-light. It seemed that he nodded.

She stepped off to the side.

"Just remember, my lady, if you need help, I'm a soldier, not a chambermaid." And he laughed.

His grating voice reminded Marketa of the things said earlier. Images of Karin being harmed or dishonored by these men flashed through her mind. This would not happen. Not while she could do something about it.

Bending down, she searched the ground. It took some moments, but she came across a good-sized branch. It would take all her might and all her nerve. But it was their best chance.

Drawing it close to her body, she circled around the tree. Where had the soldier gone?

"Looking for me?" The voice came from behind her.

She froze. How did he know? Had she been so obvious?

"Drop it."

She couldn't, could she? This was the only chance they had. It was now or never. Closing her eyes, she swung.

And fell when the force of her swing did not connect.

Had he ducked?

Marketa grabbed at her shoulder. Pain tore through her body and she fell.

A booted foot nudged her onto her back, and she looked up at the moonlight-rimmed form of the soldier.

"Now you've made me angry. I . . ."

A loud crack sounded through the night air and the man dropped to his knees. Another smack and his body thudded to the ground beside her.

The form standing over hers wielding a large branch was defi-nitely feminine.

Pavel repositioned his hands on the wooden beam, wincing as a wood shaving punctured his skin.

"Something amiss?" Zdenek grunted, leaning down and taking on most of the plank's weight.

"Nothing." Pavel refocused his attention on their work and ignored the stinging sensation in his hand.

Together, he and Zdenek maneuvered the beam into place and relinquished it to the growing pile, which was beginning to resemble a wall as the wooden fort took shape.

Pavel took a moment to scan the area. A large portion of Prague was visible from atop Vitkov Hill. Surely he could see for miles. But what he saw did not put him at ease. For there, in the distance, he could just make out the edge of Sigismund's camp. Thousands, even tens of thousands, of soldiers lay in wait, prepared to strike.

It gave him pause, and he sent up a silent prayer. His hope was not built upon the reasoning of man. God had proven He could deliver the Hussite army against overwhelming odds before. Pavel had seen it. And he had faith that God would do it again. Why shouldn't He?

Zdenek's heavy breathing nearby alerted Pavel that his friend had come up behind him.

"Intimidating, no?"

Pavel drew in a breath. "Not from where I stand." He caught Zdenek's eyes.

Confusion was written on his friend's face.

Raising his arms, Pavel indicated the men, women, and children bustling about them, busy preparing the hilltop for the battle that was sure to come. "We are strong of heart and spirit. God will prove us the victors."

Zdenek offered Pavel a blank stare, but said nothing.

"And General Zizka is prepared. He has thought out every possibility. Surely you must agree that Vitkov Hill is what it comes down to."

Wiping his brow, Zdenek nodded. "Yes, I believe so."

"Then we are fortifying the right places." Pavel stepped to his friend and placed a hand on his shoulder. "You shall see. All will be well."

"And we, my friend, had better get back to work." Zdenek's brow rose.

Pavel nodded.

They made their way down the hill, stepping around those who were digging the moat and dirt wall, which would be reinforced with rocks before it was completed. As they continued toward the southern slope, they passed the old watchtower. This building, once useful for guarding the vineyards on this side of the hill, would become part of their plans as well.

Zizka would place thirty men in each of the two forts. In the event of a surprise attack, they would be able to hold off enemy soldiers until reinforcements arrived from the main city. The landscape had changed in these last days. Trees and houses that impaired sightlines had been removed. They were preparing for the inevitable.

Prague was nestled in the bend of the Vltava River, running along the west and north sides of the city. Across the river to the west was the Hradcany, held by the Royalist army, which also allowed them to hold all roads to Prague's north and west. To the south, Prague was hemmed in by the Vysehrad, also under Royalist control. Giving them the southern routes as well.

Vitkov Hill remained the last avenue the Hussites had in and out of Prague. If they lost it, they would be choked off and would lose the great city. They might as well surrender if that were to happen. The events of the next few days would determine the course of the future of their country. It was that important.

Not long after their preparations neared completion, they saw the tents and soldiers appearing across the Spitalske Pole, the plain to the north of Vitkov Hill. Pavel was certain that, while these Royalist soldiers had been promised forgiveness of their sins and escape from purgatory for their service, many were simply mercenaries. And they wanted nothing more than their share in the plunder that lay within the city. This is where the lines were drawn. The Hussites did not fight for blood or money, but for freedom, for God, for country.

The Royalists had numbers, and they would not show mercy. No, any Czech caught would meet certain death, Hussite or not. These soldiers were intent on killing every man, woman, and child within Prague's walls. And so, for Pavel, it was up to him, his men, and those that fought with him to ensure their safety and the safety of every Hussite living in Bohemia. For he was certain these mercenaries would not stop here.

Sounds of rushing water were ever present. But it did little to assuage Stepan's overheated condition—he couldn't remember a summer so hot. He had already stripped down as far as he dared. The other men in camp were likewise dressed down. Still, his clothing clung to his body, soaked with sweat. It seemed the stream served merely to taunt him.

Stepan came to camp two days ago and was appalled at what he saw. The Royalist army was massive, at least 80,000 strong. Little hope remained for the Hussites. They must know that. As surely as he could see Prague beyond the Vlatava River, they must have eyes to see this army. Would they raise a white flag? Would it matter? Many of these soldiers were bloodthirsty and would not be dissuaded.

They bid their time, waiting for the Emperor to give the signal that would bring an end to the Hussite movement once and for all. Stepan did not mourn the coming end of these heretics. Yet he could not deny the sick feeling that settled in his stomach at the thought of the slaughter he would be party to.

He turned his attention back to his sword. As he ran the whetstone against the edge of the blade, he found comfort in the scrape of the metal. His sword had not failed him. And as God was his witness, it would not.

Movement to his right startled him, and he shifted his sword in that direction without thinking. His eyes followed, only then discovering who had come upon him.

"Calm yourself." Dominik held his hands up. "A bit skittish, are we?"

Stepan pulled his blade back and continued sharpening it, shrugging. "It is best not to sneak up on a man with a sword."

"Perhaps so." Dominik took a seat next to Stepan, pulling at the front of his tunic to fan himself. He glanced around and leaned in toward Stepan. "How do you find camp?"

Stepan shrugged again. "Hot."

"Dreadfully so." Dominik then lowered his voice. "I meant the Germans, the Bulgarians . . ."

Meeting his gaze out of the corner of his eye, Stepan gave him a hard look. "We are a stronger army together."

"But do you not consider what it means to have Germans in our lands? Perhaps obliterating Prague? What do they care of our grand city? Or perhaps occupying Prague? What of that? Maybe they won't stay there. Perhaps they will not be satisfied but will spread. Even to our estates."

Stepan refocused on his blade. "You concern yourself unnecessarily."

"Do I?"

Though he wanted to believe Dominik's words were nonsensical, Stepan could not deny they had taken root in his mind. His hands slowed their work, and he shifted to face his friend again. "What would you propose?"

"There are many of us who believe it should be Czechs alone who handle this Hussite issue. That would eliminate the concern of these foreigners destroying our lands or taking what they want for themselves."

"But Sigismund has already recruited these men and promised them the spoils. And forgiveness from their sins. What of that?"

"He must be convinced to release them."

Stepan stopped his work altogether. "And just how do you imagine to do that?"

Dominik lowered his voice even more. "Do you not remember what I spoke of earlier? There is a faction that intends to offer Sigismund the crown of Bohemia."

"Aye. I remember. But you forget yourself. It is not that simple. The country is not unified, they will not be behind him."

"Who truly holds the power in Bohemia if not the nobility? I think he will accept it if offered." Dominik's face became serious.

Stepan thought on that prospect for a moment. Which side would it serve him best to be on? It was becoming a political game. And he did not wish to be caught on the wrong end of anyone's sword.

Karin flung the branch to the ground as she shook. What had she done?

"Karin? What are you . . . ?" Marketa's voice faded into oblivion as Karin wrestled with what must be done. They must act. Now. If they were to escape.

"No time for that." Karin bent down and took Marketa's hands, pulling her to her feet. "We must go."

Marketa nodded.

Karin gripped Marketa's hand and led her through the darkness toward the distant firelight. As they approached, they slowed.

What were they going to do? How to get out of there without waking the soldiers? How long would the other soldier remain unconscious? Would he be all right?

Karin paused.

Marketa bumped into her.

Reaching for the sturdy trunk of a nearby tree, Karin attempted to maintain her balance.

One of the soldiers stirred.

Karin froze.

He shifted onto his back and commenced his snoring.

She pivoted, gripped Marketa's hand, and with the other, pressed toward the ground twice. Would the baroness understand that Karin wanted her to stay where she was?

As Karin moved off, Marketa remained.

Stepping toward the group of horses, to the far right of the dwindling fire, Karin ensured careful footfalls. As she neared the animals, she placed a gentle hand to the backside of the closest horse—a gray mare. Flinching initially under Karin's touch, the horse stilled as Karin spoke soothing words in soft tones. Then Karin moved forward, careful to keep her hand on the horse's side. Spooking the horse would create unnecessary challenges.

Touching the horse's mane, she rubbed the animal's neck as she drew closer. Moments later, Karin was nuzzling the horse's nose. The dark brown horse next to the mare became interested. Karin lifted a hand to touch its soft muzzle as well.

A horse not far away in the cluster became agitated.

Would it wake the soldiers? Could Karin hide here among the horses? Would her and Marketa's absence be noted?

Thankfully, the horse quieted and no other sounds could be heard. Karin waited several moments more to ensure no one awoke.

As the minutes passed and no one moved, she let out a breath.

Taking the reins of the two horses, she urged them forward while she worked at the knots of the ropes securing them to the tree. When at last they were free, she walked them to where she had left Marketa.

To her relief, she found the baroness still settled by the same tree.

Karin extended a hand toward her mother-in-law.

Marketa's hand was trembling when it made contact.

Giving it a slight squeeze, Karin hoped to reassure the baroness.

But could she? They were not safe yet. Still, there was naught their worry could do but create risk.

Karin passed the reins of the gentle gray mare to Marketa and led them, on foot, deeper into the forest. As much as she ached to mount and gallop into the night, it would be safer for them to create distance between themselves and the camp before doing so.

The minutes passed into an hour or more before Karin paused. Had the soldiers awakened to find them gone? Was it safe for them to take flight upon the horses? The sun had already begun to light the horizon. If not now, when?

Nodding to Marketa, Karin gripped the saddle and pulled herself up.

It was not long before Marketa sat atop the gray mare.

Once Karin assured herself that her mother-in-law had control of the horse, she dug her heels into the animal underneath her and they took off.

If they pushed the horses, they would arrive at the Krejik estate before nightfall.

The sun rose high in the sky. Zdenek fought a wave of tiredness as it threatened to overtake him. Sleep had been difficult to come by, situated in a fort on Vitkov Hill. Each man and woman was ever on alert though it might be his or her time for rest. The sounds of the enemy army taunting them throughout the day haunted him at night.

"Ha, ha! Hus, Hus! Heretic, heretic!" They would chant.

All day long it would go on. At night they would stop for sake of their own rest, but their voices never seemed to leave him.

It was not the words they spoke that bothered him, but the force of their voices together. It told of how strong their army was. A glance at the horizon could inform anyone of the general size of the camp. There were far too many tents for his liking. But when the men stood together and shouted, it was if the walls of Jericho would crumble again. They were, indeed, a force to be reckoned with. If their goal was to intimidate, they had succeeded.

Zdenek did not have Pavel's faith. How could he when facing such odds? The best they could hope for was a quick and painless end. But he would not run. He would stand and fight with these men and women he had come to know. And he would do all he could to protect Eva.

Chancing a glance across the tight space within the confines of the fort, he met her eyes and quickly turned away. Nothing had been settled between them though she had done everything she could to explain herself. But how could he help this tightness in his chest when he thought about how she had lied to him? She had taken her life in her own hands and rejoined the misfit band of Hussites to come here and, what, die? And for what? What had she gained?

He let his head hang. There it was—the painful constriction around his heart. But was that all of it? Or was there part of him that ached for something more? For a chance to marry, have a family? Yes, there was this too. And in the dimness of the enclosed space, he met her eyes again.

In that moment, when their eyes locked, he saw hers glisten. Had she regrets as well? He longed to close the small distance between them and pull her into his arms, whispering that somehow, someway they would be together. The urge overwhelmed him, and he shifted to stand when the soldier next to him put a hand out to stop him.

"Shhh . . ." the man called into the din of voices.

All became silent.

Zdenek's heart thundered in his ears, but even so he heard it— the soft thundering of horses' hooves on the hillside.

This was it.

Bodies scrambled in the tight enclosure, preparing weapons and vying for the best view out of the makeshift windows.

Zdenek stood his ground though bumped and shoved from varying angles.

There was no mistaking the Royalist colors topping the slope and coming toward them.

"At the ready, men!" a voice shouted.

As they watched, the Royalist soldiers crossed the moat and took the watchtower without much effort. They were helpless but to stand at the ready.

Zdenek wished for better weaponry. Why had they been left with merely stones and lances?

"How will we defend ourselves?" one of the younger men worried.

"Take courage, lad. We have God on our side. What more do we need?" a gruff voice replied.

Zdenek shifted to look at the cowering young man. He couldn't have been more than nineteen years old. Had he seen battle? Moving to where the young man crouched by the earthen wall, Zdenek became aware that he had emptied the contents of his stomach nearby.

"Take heart. We are in this together." Zdenek placed a hand on the man's shoulder.

Wide brown eyes stared up at him, untrusting.

"We have nothing left to do but fight. For our country, for our lives." Zdenek walked to the pile of stones and grabbed one. He returned to the shaking young man and handed it to him. "Your life is worth everything. If anyone tries to take it from you, do your best to aim this at his face or chest."

The man did not stop trembling but nodded at Zdenek, taking the rock in uneasy hands.

Zdenek paced back to his place of vigil by the opening and fought every instinct within him. There was a big part of him that wanted to run, to save himself. But he would not. He reached for a lance and nodded at the men to his right who stood at the ready.

The Royalists were almost in range. And they would not show mercy.

His eyes sought out Eva. She stood with her friend from the

monastery. They were prepared with stones as well. As he watched her, Eva's face inclined toward his. Her mouth was set, but her eyes betrayed her fear. How he longed to tuck her under his arm and keep her safe there. But he could no more provide that assurance to her than he could to the young man behind them still clinging to the back wall.

"Ready, steady . . ." one man said with a voice much more calm than it should have been.

And Zdenek watched as the Royalist soldiers made their approach. He let out a loud cry as he hurled his lance, not even following its trajectory as he spun to grab for a stone.

The Royalists were only mildly deterred by the defensive maneuvers of the men and women in the forts. It would only be a matter of time. And they all knew it. But they fought ever more fiercely as the cavalrymen gained ground toward the forts.

All of a sudden a loud scream pierced the air.

Zdenek could not help but glance in the direction of the noise.

Apolena, Eva's friend, grabbed for the last lance at their disposal. "Let us show them our courage! Let them feel our conviction!" she cried.

A few of the men roared their agreement, and the small band moved to squeeze out of what little protection the fort offered.

"No," Eva screamed, rushing after her friend.

Zdenek's legs moved underneath him more quickly than he thought possible, and he intercepted Eva before she stepped outside.

"Apolena," Eva called. "Come back!"

Zdenek held her still. "You can't go after her. She is already dead."

Eva cried then, sobs shaking her body.

Torn between consoling Eva and returning to the desperate fight, Zdenek spun her to look at him. "Eva, we can't. Too much is at stake. We must keep fighting."

Eva stilled her body and nodded, pulling back from his arms.

Then, grabbing yet another stone, she made for the opening with fresh determination.

Zdenek followed her. And he wished he hadn't pushed her so soon. For they were at the window-like openings in time to watch as Apolena and the few men who followed her came around the fort to face their enemy.

"No true Christian must ever retreat from Antichrist!" Apolena shouted. Then she charged forward, lance in hand, into the thick of the cavalry.

Zdenek closed his eyes against the reality of such senseless deaths. And prayed Eva did the same.

For it would only be a matter of moments before they joined them.

CHAPTER 13
WAR

Pavel moved about the streets of Prague. How much longer would it be? How much longer would the Royalist army taunt them? He would much rather engage the enemy and be finished with the whole thing. Waiting was difficult.

And now it was Zdenek's turn in the fort. Pavel prayed for his safety and trusted God would watch over him. All the same, he did not like being separated from his friend. It also made Radek tense. Quite tense. The man had become overly agitated these last few days. All the more so since Zdenek's shift in the fort began.

"*Prominte prosime!*" a voice behind him shouted.

He knew that voice. Turning, his eyes confirmed it was Radek. His friend pushed through the somewhat crowded street. Something was amiss. Radek's eyes were wild and his movements hurried.

Pavel stepped forward to intercept him. "Tell me, friend? What has you so disturbed?"

Radek's harried eyes met Pavel's. Fear had settled there. "They have come. The Royalists are attacking Vitkov Hill."

Pavel wasted not one more moment. He moved in the direction from which Radek had come—the direction of the Hussite soldiers' camp. His pulse quickened, but he fought down the wave of apprehension with a prayer for strength.

Moments later, he arrived back at the camp with Radek in tow.

General Zizka barked orders at his men, mobilizing the soldiers and militia.

They obeyed without question as they had been trained to.

Pavel did not stop until he reached his horse. Mounting easily, he urged the animal to Zizka's position. He only hoped Radek would follow suit.

As he listened, Pavel discerned Zizka's intent for the Hussite army to march up the southern slope of the hill to join the fight, while he and his small band of guards and comrades would go ahead by horseback to intervene for those in the forts.

Zizka gave his final command and looked to the men closing in around him—his bodyguards and longtime comrades.

"General, may I go with you?" Pavel pulled his horse alongside Zizka's.

Zizka's eye fell on Pavel. His gaze was stony and cold. But then softened. Did he recognize that it was Pavel's friend in the fort this day?

The general nodded and refocused on his men, firing off a few short instructions. Then he rallied them around himself and raced toward Vitkov Hill.

They climbed the gentler southern slope. As they neared the top, Pavel spotted the Royalist cavalry attacking the bulwark. The narrowness of the ridge prevented the enemy army from making a broad attack or flanking the forts. If not, the Hussites would surely have found a massacred and defeated stronghold. As it was, the forts held, if only barely.

Zizka, with a loud cry, plunged into the fight. There was such might in him that Pavel doubted anyone would be able to stop him.

If this man had the courage to drive into the fray, then what was to keep Pavel from doing the same? God was with him. Ducking his body, Pavel gripped his sword tighter and pushed his steed into a vulnerable space in the flank of the cavalry.

And there was great fight in them. Amongst the clashing of swords and cries of the wounded, Pavel knew that Zizka's men inflicted great damage. But the Royalist's numbers were too great.

In the few breath's space Pavel was granted, he watched the scene before him. The small contingency Zizka led was nearly overcome. How would they prevail?

By God's might! They must. They would. But Pavel's mind told him that his faith could not save them from imminent defeat without miraculous intervention.

Oh, God! Send Your mighty hand to sweep away our enemy!

In the chaos, Pavel sought out Radek. Their eyes met. Radek's were hollow and his face weary, dismayed. Pavel felt it in his own spirit, too. But he would not go down easily. No, he would fight until the bitter end.

The tensions in Tabor ran high. But the battle had been theirs. Rozmberk was defeated. And Alex had proven useful after all. He and his men defended his manor and lands against Rozmberk's men.

But now the house fell quiet. How long would it be before Marketa and Karin were returned? His inquiries after them led to precious few answers. He was assured they had been taken to safety. And that word was sent to their protectors it was safe for them to return.

Still, the silent days stretched.

Alex busied himself helping those in Tabor that were in need of assistance. Some had been left without anything. And in the absence of the priests, there were many needs to be seen to. His estate, though situated a fair ride from the main city, was perhaps the closest barony to the collection of Hussites.

He admired their desire to not be governed by the nobility as he admired their fervor after God, but he was unsure he could see the sense in it. These people had needs. And they needed an earthly lord to see to them.

Still, they insisted they could collectively see to each other.

And so, day after day, he sent provisions as necessary and rode into the town to see to the people.

But after some time, his concern after his wife and daughter-in-law had so greatly grieved him that he had maintained constant vigil for these last four days together, neither setting foot off the estate nor eating much, so great was his burden.

Perched high in the watchtower, he kept his eyes to the horizon. Would it be today? Would word come today?

He refused to become overly concerned after their fate. No good could come from that. Once one allowed his mind to wander into that territory, it would not end. Faith and hope were one's best companions in these situations.

Yet as the days passed and word of the crusade in Prague reached Tabor, he could not help but entertain the possibility that he might not see Marketa or Karin again.

Closing his eyes, he allowed that prospect to sink in and then dismissed it. For he was not a man of dismay. He was a man of faith.

Gazing back to the horizon, he spied movement. Two figures appeared on the farthest hilltop. And faith once again proved the victor.

Pavel wearied as his sword clashed again and again. The spark in him began to dampen. Was there no end to the Royalist cavalrymen? He glanced at Zizka as the man's sword plunged without relent. And he marveled once again at the warrior who led this group of misfits. But it would be no matter in the end. They had fought a good fight, valiantly, for their God. But, pending a miracle, they would succumb to their enemy.

Shouts and singing voices surrounded them, a thunderous sound. Pavel was stunned into inaction. Had it come from the forts? No, the voices were too many. The Royalists? No, they seemed equally confused. Pavel scanned the area and saw the source—the Hussite soldiers and militia had come!

Led by a priest, they shouted battle cries and sang hymns as they came from the left. The hill's slope had prevented them from being seen until they were almost to the crest, but their voices carried into the heat of the battle.

The enemy soldier beside Pavel covered his ears and cried out as if in pain. As Pavel watched, the man's eyes widened and he pulled on the reins of his horse as if to back away from the approaching force of men.

But it wasn't just this soldier. A great number of the Royalist soldiers reacted in kind. The men backed away until they neared the edge of the northern slope and its steep drop-off. Why would they react in such a way? Were they so afraid of the approaching Hussites?

The Royalists still outnumbered them. What did they fear, then?

Pavel continued to stare in disbelief as a large number of the cavalry, with some help from the Hussite army, were forced off the side of Vitkov Hill.

Just like that, hundreds of cavalrymen were dead.

What had bewitched the Royalist cavalry, Radek did not know. But they reacted strangely to the sounds of the Hussite army as they sang and shouted. Was it due to the enemy army's lack of familiarity with one another? They were a collection of various armies. Was it the unfamiliar ground on which they fought? Was it the lack of a battle plan and their inability to make adjustments? Or perhaps they were superstitious and feared the chanting of these men?

Or could it be that the hand of God truly was with the Hussites and had struck some unearthly fear and confusion into the hearts of the Royalist cavalrymen?

Radek narrowed his eyes, watching as the men inexplicably fell off the steep northern slope to their death, and could not discern a reasonable answer. And so he sat in his saddle, sword drawn, not knowing what to do. Many of the Hussite cavalrymen and soldiers moved to assist the enemy in their folly as they journeyed toward the treacherous edge.

Either way, all eyes were on them. This might be Radek's best opportunity to execute his plan. A plan that had been laid out long before. A plan he had been unable to carry out while Zdenek and Pavel's well-being were uncertain. But they were safe now.

A part of him wished he could see his friends once more. What would that yield but more questions he couldn't answer?

Radek pulled his horse's reins, directing the animal toward the southern slope. But something gave him pause. Turning his head, he saw that Zdenek had stepped out of the fort and into the open.

Their eyes met.

Did Zdenek know?

The horse shifted underneath him, but Radek held Zdenek's eyes.

His friend raised a hand to bid Radek come.

Radek shook his head.

Zdenek's brows furrowed.

The girl, Eva, came from the safety of the fort to stand by Zdenek, and Radek's resolve strengthened.

He jerked the reins and kicked at his horse's flank. The animal leaped into action, carrying him down the slope and toward the Royalist camp. Working off his outer clothing containing any hint of his connection with the Hussites, he made sure his defection was complete.

The Hussite army continued to engage the enemy.

Metal scraped on metal behind Pavel. A sword being unsheathed? He whirled around, his own sword at the ready.

Steel clanged and his weapon blocked a deathblow from the attacking soldier. When he met the man's eyes, his heart stopped.

It was Stepan.

The brown eyes that were once so familiar now glowered at him with anger and hatred. As they lit with recognition, the weight of Stepan's sword lifted and the weapon withdrew.

Pavel stared in disbelief at his once-friend. Though Stepan had struck with an upper hand, it was Stepan's life that was in grave danger. He fought to keep from being pushed off the ledge.

Still, Stepan did not plead for his life. His eyes remained cold. But something more flashed behind their hard surface. Regret?

Pavel did not speak, but lowered his sword and shifted his horse out of the way, gifting Stepan a route of escape.

Stepan's eyes widened for just a moment. He glanced around himself and then pushed his horse through the narrow opening.

Pavel did not watch him go. He dropped his head and let out a breath, wanting to release the emotions coursing through him.

The Hussites did not let up with the retreat of the Royalist army. They took up a great chase, pushing the remainder of the enemy across Spitalske Field to Vlatava River. There, Royalist soldiers foolishly tried to swim across the river in full armor only to drown.

Pavel wondered if Stepan was among them. A part of him, however, prayed Stepan was among the number that made it across and back to their camp. Hopefully never to be seen again.

A shiver shook Karin though her flesh was quite heated from the summer's warmth. She leaned forward from her relaxed position on the chaise lounge and rubbed her arms. What had brought on the shaking of her body that lifted her from sleep?

Thinking back on the images from her dream, she conjured a

visage of Pavel. She did so ache for him. If only it were his hands that soothed her! But it was not. Even then, he was many miles away in battle.

Her heart was heavy at this thought. *Lord, be with him.* This prayer had become a familiar chant, almost reflexive. Still, it calmed her to pray and she continued to do so.

Resting back on the chaise, she gazed out the window at the moonlit sky. How had she drifted to sleep in the lounger? Had no one come to prepare her for bed?

Shouts in the hall drew her attention. They came nearer. She clambered to her feet, striding across the room toward the door, but it burst open before she was midway there.

"The stables are on fire!" Nicol screamed. Her face flushed. She trembled from head to toe.

Karin jerked back, the blood draining from her face. Fire? Here? She and Marketa had just settled back into the estate after the Rozmberk scare, and now they were to be plagued thusly? How massive was the fire and how far had it spread? What measures were being taken to put it out?

Nicol waved Karin to the door. "Please, my lady, we must away at once!"

Lifting her skirt, Karin tarried no longer. She followed Nicol through the door and into the hall.

"Where is your master?" she demanded as they two raced to the stairs.

Nicol did not respond.

Karin turned Nicol to face her at the landing.

Her maidservant shook with fear and there were tears in her eyes.

Setting a hand upon her shoulder, Karin offered what support she could. "Nicol, I must know where the baron has gone. Will you take me to him?"

"I do not know, my lady. But I think he is at the stables, seeing after what can be done to fight the horrid fire."

Karin's eyes widened. Yet did she expect anything different? "And what of the baroness?"

"Sharka has gone to retrieve her. We are under strict orders to see you to safety in Tabor."

Karin nodded. They would be safe there. But would Marketa go without Alex? Should they? Or should they stay and attempt to assist in the fight to save the manor?

"You must see to the baroness. I am going to the stables."

"My lady, you must know I cannot. I would be horsewhipped if I let you . . ."

Karin's eyes flashed. "I assure you that will not happen."

Nicol stumbled. Was Karin's gaze so intense?

"Make haste!" Karin raised her voice. "Get the baroness to safety. Or I shall see you whipped."

"Aye, my lady. As you wish." Nicol scrambled to right herself and moved back up the stairs.

Karin stepped down and coughed, her eyes began to sting. The air in the house took on a different quality. The fire must be spreading! She wagered it best to exit through the servants' hall and out of the estate in that direction. Then circle back around to the stables.

Once she stepped outside, she saw the black cloud that choked the left side of the grounds. More smoke than she had imagined. The fire had claimed much. As she rounded the corner and the stables became visible, her heart sank. They were a loss.

The men now worked to contain a blaze sweeping the eastern wing of the Krejik's home. Surely they attempted the impossible.

Karin sank to her knees, paralyzed by what was before her. Who had done this thing—targeted them in such a malicious way? Had this foe intended to burn them alive in their beds? As much as she wished to aid in the fight against the angry flames, she could not make her limbs move. So she settled further into her seated stance and prayed.

As the last of the Royalist soldiers disappeared from view, a great shout went up from among the Hussites. Zdenek and Eva descended Vitkov Hill and joined the others in Spitalske Field.

The fighting had come to an end. Against all odds, the forts held. Contrary to what should have been, the Hussite cavalry held out for reinforcements. And when it should not have happened, the Royalist soldiers spooked and fell to their own deaths.

If there had not been enough evidence of an Almighty God watching out for the Hussite army before, there was now.

Zdenek needed no more proof. His heart turned, and as the group, led by the priests, broke out in a hymn of praise and thanksgiving, Zdenek lifted his eyes heavenward and said his own prayer of gratitude.

Yet his heart ached. What had become of Radek? He did not want to acknowledge what he knew to be true. His friend had left the Hussite army. Scanning the encampment across Vlatava River, he knew.

Radek had struggled all along with their decision to join the Hussites. The manner in which they had been swept into this movement had never set right with him. Now a choice had been made.

Zdenek searched for Pavel. There would be little hope of finding him amongst the crowd. He would have to seek him out later.

A tug on his arm drew his attention to his right side. Dark eyes gazed up at him—Eva. He drank in the sight of her. Had it only been minutes ago he thought they would be lost? Now the future seemed bright.

Without a word, he reached forth with long fingers to graze her jaw and drew her to himself, his lips coming down on hers. Whether or not there would be obstacles in their way, he was determined she would be his bride.

As they parted, he noticed her eyes had slid closed. He touched her chin with a crooked finger. They opened.

He swallowed, taking in every minute part of her features. "Eva, I love you. Say you will stay by my side forever."

Her eyes widened. "Aye, Zdenek, for I am hopelessly lost to you"

His lips met hers again as the singing around them grew. The Hussite army continued to praise God until dawn touched the sky.

Karin cried as she prayed. Where was Pavel? She needed him. He should be here. To comfort her, to be with his parents. His parents! Where were Alex and Marketa? Had they made it out safely?

Pavel gazed across Spitalske Field at the celebrating Hussites, his brethren. A victory well deserved. Would he now be able to return to Karin? He prayed so. It was time to finally begin their life together.

This, however, was before any of them realized it was but the first crusade against the Hussites.

Keep reading for a preview of the next book in The Lady of Bohemia Series!

Thank you, dear reader, for reading along with me! If you enjoyed this story, I would sincerely appreciate if you would submit a review. It would mean so much to me!

To read more about these characters, follow along with The Lady of Bohemia Series. Find it at:
https://saraturnquist.com/lady-bornekova-series/

AUTHOR'S NOTE

Here I am...continuing in this writing journey. My, it is a wild ride! I have learned so much in these few short years since *The Lady Bornekova* book came out...and I've seen a few more books reach reader hands. It thrills me to know that people are enjoying my creative work!

It was so much fun to come back to these characters. They are each, to a certain extent, crafted after people I have known. So, there is a little piece of me that enjoys spending time with these "old friends" become new - a mixture of these familiar personalities with my own imagination. One of the things I love about the writing life!

Historical work comes with its joys and challenges - research being one of them. For the longest time, I struggled to find good sources that were in English. But I stumbled upon an amazing book - *Warrior of God: Jan Zizka and the Hussite Revolution* by Victor Verney. This accounting of the details surrounding Zizka and the Hussite side of the wars has been, well, a godsend!

There is so much fact woven into the fiction in this book. The Battle of Vitkov Hill, perhaps the most fantastical occurrence, is the hardest to imagine, but absolutely based on fact. Historians do not have a good explanation for why the Royalist army began going over the steep slope of the hill to their deaths. Or why they seemed to go mad at the sound of the praises of the approaching Hussite army on foot. They outmatched and out-weaponed the Hussites. By all rights, they should have won. But they didn't. Make of that what you will.

A SNEAK PEEK
THE LADY AND HER CHAMPION

Pavel Krejick closed his eyes. Karin's face was before him. How long would it be before they were together? He and his wife—separated by this war—would they ever know what it was to live together?

That should not be such a far-fetched hope.

The Hussites had prevailed. Once things were settled in Prague, he could return to Tabor. Then he and Karin would begin their life.

Leaning back, Pavel allowed the sting of the recent loss of their child to wash over him. Had he truly grieved? Or would he yet be swept away by it? What of Karin? How did she fare?

A hand landed on his shoulder.

He jerked to attention, eyes wide, reaching for his sword's hilt.

A young man crouched beside him. How had he come upon Pavel without notice?

"Excuse me, my lord." The young man's eyes were clear. "General Zizka sends for you."

Zizka? What might he want?

Pavel nodded and rose. Whatever the general needed, it would be important.

The short walk through camp to Zizka's tent seemed longer than it could have possibly been.

Though the hour was late and nearly all the men had long since surrendered to sleep, Zizka worked still over a table, poring over maps lit by candles. The flame flickered across his features, casting shadows and drawing attention to different angles in alternating patterns. His stern expression became all the more severe.

Pavel halted a few steps short of the simple desk.

Moments passed before Zizka's gaze diverted toward him. Was the man so focused? Surely he must have realized he had company. But Pavel did not find offense in it—he had long since accepted that the good of the majority was more important than his needs. He could wait for Zizka to finish whatever strategic planning he had engaged in.

Once his eye fell on Pavel, Zizka set his tools to the side and stepped around the table, moving toward the man who was several years his junior.

"Pavel," he started, his voice low and his words measured. "Thank you for coming."

"Of course, General."

Zizka stopped a couple arms' lengths short of Pavel. He nodded at the other men around them. They moved several paces away.

Pavel worked to keep his features neutral. What could this mean? What manner of news did Zizka have? Or was there some task he wished Pavel to perform? Some delicate or dangerous matter? Did Pavel have more fight in him?

The man's steely gaze leveled on Pavel once more. It seemed to bore into him. Certainly it saw more than Pavel wanted it to.

"There is news. From Tabor."

Karin! Was she unsafe? His heart raced and his chest tightened. He had great difficulty moving air. Forcing a breath in and then pushing it out, he worked to calm his body. This was no time to fall apart.

"Your parents—the Baron and Baroness—their home has burned to the ground."

Now it was impossible to take air in. Nothing would move. Then his breaths came in and out rapidly. He had no ability to control them. Nor a care to try. His vision became hazy.

No. Not now. Not like this.

Once again forcing rhythm to his breathing, he brought stability to his body. And clarity to his mind.

"And what of my parents? My...wife? Are they..." He drew in a deep breath. He would stand. He would maintain his hold on himself. "Do they live?"

Zizka's mouth, now a thin line, hardened. "We have word from the Baroness Krejikova. She is well and in Tabor."

"The others?"

The larger man's head dipped. "Nothing."

The ground opened up and Pavel's stomach fell through it.

Zizka lay a large hand on Pavel's shoulder. "That means only that there was not news at the time the messenger was dispatched. Nothing is certain."

Pavel nodded, swallowing hard. He wished to speak, but his emotions were too close to the surface. Surely they would spill out.

Zizka's brow rose.

"May I..." A lump in Pavel's throat caught his words and cut off his request. He drew in a breath and pressed on. "General, may I take my leave to return to Tabor?"

"God be with you." The man squeezed Pavel's arm and the one good eye caught Pavel's gaze. What was that in his regard? Sadness? Regret?

It would be of little gain to attempt to decipher Zizka's emotions when Pavel's own rushed and tumbled through him, cluttering his mind and heart.

And only one thing was clear: he had to get to Karin.

To read more, find *The Lady and Her Champion* here:

https://saraturnquist.com/the-lady-and-her-champion/

Read the rest of THE LADY OF BOHEMIA SERIES!

The Lady Bornekova (Book 1)

The red-headed Karin is strong-willed and determined, she tries to keep her true nature a secret to avoid being deemed a traitor by those loyal to the king.

Karin and her father butt heads over her duty to her family and the Czech Crown. However, her heart soon becomes entangled though her father intends to wed her to another.

The turmoil inside Karin deepens and reflects the turmoil of her homeland, on the brink of the Hussite Wars.

The Lady & the Hussites (Book 2)

Karin and Pavel have found their way safely to his parents home, but things are not as well as they seem. There are secrets between them. A wall goes up. And then Pavel is called into battle.

Radek and Zdenek find themselves pulled into the conflict despite their best efforts to remain neutral, while Stepan finds himself ready for bloodshed.

With tensions mounting within their circle and throughout their country, what will become of Pavel and Karin? Can they find their way back to each other?

The Lady & Her Champion (Book 3)

She needs someone to fight for her. He needs to be rescued.

Karin and Pavel have become separated by war and the destruction of his family's home. When Pavel hears of Karin's predicament, he rushes to his beloved. But what will he find?

Will the pull to remain by her side be stronger than the tug to return to the front lines?

While the Hussites maintain a tenuous hold on their lands, will internal conflict prove their undoing?

The Lady & Her Secret (Book 4)

She seeks the forbidden. He struggles to find peace.

Karin and Pavel are at last reunited. But her desire to take on a task long prohibited has Pavel worried for her safety and that of his new family. She strives to keep her work a secret while he faces his own fight—one of a warrior weary of battle.

While the Hussites wrestle with internal conflict, will the enemy take advantage of their vulnerability...and overtake them?

The Lady & Her Mission (Book 5)

COMING SOON

Acknowledgments

There are so many people to thank when it comes to putting a book together and sending it out into the world. It's hard to remember everyone who touched the manuscript in a significant way and influenced me along the creative process to see this work into your hands. But I will try.

My beta readers - Stacy Schoenwetter, Christina Horton, and Hillary Harvey - are invaluable to me and I couldn't do it without their input.

The editors that give of their talents and efforts to sharpen my work and make it that much more presentable :-)

Cora Graphics...another amazing cover! You impress me every time.

VerBull Photography, I am amazed by your talent as well...how you catch my good side so consistently, I'll never know.

My writing mentor, Hannah R. Conway, you have taught me so much and our shenanigans have brough me so much laughter. I really appreciate all of it.

The critique group of my heart, Clarksville Christian Writers, your encouragement and feedback have been so helpful. Thank you for listening to me week after week.

To my family and friends...you keep me going.

ABOUT THE AUTHOR

Sara is a coffee lovin', word slinging, Historical Romance author whose super power is converting caffeine into novels. She loves those odd little tidbits of history that are stranger than fiction. That's what inspires her. Well, that and a good love story.

But of all the love stories she knows, hers is her favorite. She lives happily with her own Prince Charming and their gaggle of minions. Three to be exact. They sure know how to distract a writer! But, alas, the stories must be written, even if it must happen in the wee hours of the morning.

Sara is an avid reader and enjoys reading and writing clean Historical Romance when she's not traveling.

Please follow along with her journey through her newsletter at:
http://saraturnquist.com/list

Happy Reading!

facebook.com/AuthorSaraRTurnquist

instagram.com/sararturnquist

x.com/sararturnquist

youtube.com/@SaraRTurnquist

pinterest.com/sararturnquist

ALSO BY SARA R. TURNQUIST

CONVENIENT RISK SERIES

A Convenient Risk

An Inconvenient Christmas

A Less Convenient Path

A Convenient Escape

An Inconvenient Acquaintance

These Golden Years

A Less Convenient Arrangement

Ranch Hands Collection (ebook only)

CRIPPLE CREEK SERIES

Hope in Cripple Creek

Christmas in Cripple Creek

Faith in Cripple Creek

Love in Cripple Creek

- Prequels -

Leaving Waverly

Leaving Stoneybrook

RAILWAY ROMANCE SERIES

Laura, The Tycoon's Daughter

ACROSS THE YEARS SERIES

Among the Pages

Between the Lines

STANDALONE NOVELS

The General's Wife

Trail of Fears

Off to War

www.ingramcontent.com/pod-product-compliance
Lightning Source LLC
Chambersburg PA
CBHW061802190726
48289CB00007B/2044